Chapter One

Nancy, the director of Whistling Pines Senior Residence, swept into my office, interrupting the contemplation of our weekly movie schedule. "Something's come up and I need you to sit in on the Two Harbors Chamber of Commerce meeting."

I pointed at my half-completed list of movies. "Can't Wendy do it? She's the assistant director. I'm the recreation director."

"I can't find Wendy, and the meeting starts in fifteen minutes."

I set aside my pen and paper. "Where's the meeting?"

"At Judy's Café."

"Is there anything controversial that I should be prepared to handle?"

Nancy rolled her eyes. "It's winter in Minnesota. The tourists are gone, and the only agenda item is finding volunteers to plan the Chamber Christmas party."

I stood and reached for my jacket. It hung on the coat rack behind the door of my office, which happened to be a former broom closet. "Do I get a free cup of coffee?"

Nancy smiled. "You'll get coffee *and* a Danish."

* * *

Judy's was half full. I was searching for a seat near someone I knew when I spotted a hand waving in the back. Kerry Stone, the new police chief, was sitting alone in the farthest corner with his back to the wall.

I waded through the room, nodding at the Chamber members as I passed. "Hi Kerry, what's up?"

"It's amazingly quiet this time of year. This morning I responded to a complaint from Junior Johnson. The blue spruce in his front yard was cut down during the night, probably by someone who thought it would make a nice Christmas tree. Other than that, the town has been dead, at least from a police standpoint."

"That's good, right?"

"It's good, but boring."

Meg Cochran, the Chamber president stood, and the conversations ended. "I know the only agenda item is the Christmas party, but something came up this morning." Meg reached for a pair of reading glasses dangling from the decorative chain around her neck and looked down at a sheet of paper. "I got an email from Ellen Vang, the producer of *World Eats*. Jonathan Edwards is coming to Two Harbors to shoot a live

Whistling Bake Off

Whistling Pines book 6

Dean L. Hovey

Print ISBNs
Amazon Print 978-0-2286-2092-1
B&N Print 978-0-2286-2093-8
LSI Print 978-0-2286-2094-5

Dedication

To Jeri and Lee Westfall

Acknowledgement

While struggling to find a plot for the next Whistling Pines book, I fired off a plea for help to my trusted experts, Julie (my wife), Natalie Lund, Fran Brozo, Brian Johnson, Mike Westfall, and Deanna Wilson. Natalie suggested a Whistling Pines cookbook fundraiser and the other ideas started flying. Brian, Deanna, and Julie helped form random thoughts into a cohesive plot and kept me from writing myself into a corner. In addition to their crazy ideas, I solicited their favorite ethnic/regional recipe ideas. Brian sent me pages of recipe ideas (not the entire recipes). Mike sent me his favorite family recipes. Within a week the six of them had me swimming in recipes, interesting characters, and plot twists. Without their ideas, suggestions, and support, I'd still be staring at a blank page.

Thanks to Anne Flagge, Jeff Telker, and Natalie Lund for proofreading.

Thanks also to Jude Pittman and the people at BWL Publishing for their guidance and support.

* * *

"We have two seasons up here on the North Shore—Winter and August." -anonymous

Christmas episode of Jonathan's syndicated cooking show, and she asked us to assist with the planning and broadcast."

Someone coughed and uttered "lutefisk." A ripple of laughter passed through the crowd.

Blanche Emerson set coffee and Danish pastries in front of Kerry and me. She leaned close. "I heard they're going to use the Norwegian Lutheran Church for the show."

Meg waited for the laughter to subside. Removing her glasses she continued, "The producer will be here to look at possible locations including the VFW, and the Swedish and Norwegian Lutheran Churches. We'll also discuss ethnic foods for Mr. Edwards to showcase during the show. He wants to prepare favorite recipes with local cooks." Meg paused. "I'd like a couple volunteers to meet with Ellen."

I suddenly felt like I was at an auction. The room fell silent, no one daring to twitch or scratch their nose, fearing any motion would be taken as a sign of volunteering. I was startled when Kerry cleared his throat. "Peter and I can do that."

My head snapped around so fast I nearly had whiplash. I went from terror, to shock, to anger in a fraction of a second. Kerry, whose face was badly burned in Iraq, was smiling with the unscarred side of his face.

Meg smiled and nodded. "Thank you, Chief Stone. The producer will meet with us at the VFW."

I pushed my plate aside and leaned across the table. "Why did you do that?" I whispered.

Kerry shrugged. "I'm bored, and I didn't want to do this alone."

"I'm not bored. I've got a five-month-old baby at home and I'm getting by on four to five hours of sleep a night."

Kerry continued to smile. "I'm not doing this alone and you're the only other person I know well enough to drag along."

"This is not funny. I'm busy."

Meg continued speaking and the meeting wrapped up before I'd finished berating Kerry.

"Eat your Danish, Peter."

Simmering, I bit into the cream cheese Danish. Crumbs fell onto the table as I began to eat the wonderful creamy pastry.

Kerry was sipping coffee when Meg joined us. "Thanks for volunteering, Chief. I don't expect this to take a lot of time. We'll meet with the producer and agree on the location. Meanwhile, I'm not sure how to find people to prepare ethnic foods. Do you have any suggestions?"

I ate the Danish and sipped my coffee, signalling my intention to not speak. Kerry quickly exploited the flaw in that strategy. "I'm sure there are dozens of wonderful cooks at Whistling Pines, many with great ethnic recipes to showcase."

I snorted my coffee, choked and wiped my face with the paper napkin Meg handed me. "Are you okay, Peter?"

With coffee tickling my throat, I nodded, coughing.

"Talk to Nancy and decide how best to narrow the field of cooks to six or eight. I left a message with the Lake County Fair food competition coordinator to see if any of the baking contest winners are interested in being on TV. We'll let the producer choose which foods and cooks they want to use in the show." Meg swept away while I was still choking, ignoring my hand signals to stop.

Kerry handed me another napkin. "There's coffee on your shirt."

I dabbed at the dark stains. "That was underhanded."

Kerry smiled and stood. "I have to be devious sometimes. I've learned that's often the best way to get unwilling volunteers."

"Is that what they taught you in the Army?"

Kerry pulled on his coat. "Nope. I came up with that all on my own."

"What if I can't get any volunteer cooks?"

"I think your problem will be narrowing the field of volunteers."

* * *

I drove back to Whistling Pines, while stewing over Kerry's underhanded shenanigans. I stalked into Nancy's office to complain, but her computer was off, and her coat was gone. I walked to the nursing office, hoping to find Jenny so I could vent.

Jenny was on the phone. She gestured for me to sit in her guest chair. As she hung up the phone, she raised an eyebrow. "What's the matter, husband?"

"Kerry volunteered me to help set up a cooking show."

"What are you talking about?"

I took a deep breath and let it out slowly. "Nancy sent me to the Chamber of Commerce meeting where they announced that some television cooking show plans to broadcast their Christmas episode from Two Harbors. Meg Cochran asked for volunteers. Kerry raised his hand, then told her he and I would do it."

"What television cooking show?"

"That's not the point," I said, throwing up my hands. "I didn't want to volunteer."

"Yet, here you are, the co-sponsor of the event. What cooking show is coming?"

"I don't know. I've never watched a cooking show."

"Settle down. If you don't know the name of the show, can you at least remember the name of the host?"

"No. Wait. It's someone who used to live in Two Harbors."

Jenny put her hand on my arm. "It's not Jonathan Edwards, is it?"

"It might be."

Jenny's eyes lit up. "Peter, he's an international celebrity. His show is broadcast in like a hundred countries."

"The show's producer is coming, and we're supposed to find local people who'll cook their holiday favorites with him. Kerry suggested I find some residents who have ethnic Christmas recipes they could prepare during the broadcast."

Jenny held her hand over her mouth. "OMG. Do you have any idea how much chaos this is going to create? Everyone will want to be on the show. How are you going to narrow the field?"

"Me? How am *I* going to narrow the field?"

Jenny stood. "You're the one who volunteered."

"I didn't volunteer. Kerry suckered me into this project."

Jenny was headed out the office door. "Come on. We need to talk to Nancy."

Nancy was hanging her coat up when we trooped into her office. She glanced at us and said, "Is the Chamber feeding us chicken and Jell-O salads again for the Christmas dinner?"

When I didn't answer quickly enough, Jenny jumped in. "The Two Harbors Chamber of Commerce is hosting Jonathan

Edwards' *World Eats* Christmas show. Peter volunteered to help find cooks to be featured on the broadcast."

Nancy gestured for us to sit in her guest chairs. "Tell me more, Peter."

"First of all, I did not volunteer. Kerry Stone said he and I would help coordinate with the show's producers. Secondly, the show is looking for people to demonstrate their favorite holiday recipes and Kerry suggested I recruit from Whistling Pines."

"That sounds fabulous!" Nancy exclaimed. "I'm sure we'll have many interested people. How are you going to choose between them?"

Wendy, the assistant director who is never around when I need her but always around when I don't want her, stuck her head in the office. "I heard Peter is setting up a cooking competition. The dining room is buzzing."

I looked at Jenny, who shrugged. "I haven't told anyone."

Nancy leaned back. "Do it, Peter. Wendy can help you organize the competition."

Wendy's eyes sparkled. "All we need to do is post a sign-up sheet. I'm sure some of the residents would volunteer to be judges."

I felt the room closing in on me. "I'd rather not..."

Smiling, Nancy leaned forward. "Oh, Peter. This is a wonderful community outreach program. We can't pass up this opportunity to connect with the townspeople and possibly even get national exposure. I'm so pleased you volunteered."

"But I didn't…"

Jenny put her hand on my arm before I could finish the sentence. "You're right, Nancy. This is a great opportunity, and it will really help our residents get into the holiday spirit."

I drew a breath, knowing I'd lost the argument.

Chapter Two

I was making popcorn for the afternoon movie when Mary Gilbert walked into the community room.

"Hi, Mary. The movie won't start for ten minutes."

She nodded. "I heard you volunteered to help with the Jonathan Edwards television show."

"I was dragged into it. I didn't volunteer."

"I was his piano teacher."

I stepped back and started the popcorn. "I didn't realize he was musical."

"Back then, he was Donny Koloski, and he had a band. He played the organ with three guys who added guitar, bass, and drums. The group was 'Donny and the Dream Makers.' I heard they worked in Las Vegas for a while, then the band broke up and Donny moved to California."

"When did he become Jonathan Edwards?"

"I'm not sure. Years later, I was watching a home shopping show and he was the host talking up the value of air fryers. I did a double take and realized it was Donny, but his co-host was addressing him as Jonathan. The next thing I knew; he had his own television show and was traveling the world to sample unusual foods."

Kathy Christensen walked into the room. Having overheard us, she joined the conversation. "I was his mother's hairdresser, so I kept up with his career. Donny has had a few rough spots, but he's a survivor and always comes back stronger and on top." Kathy was petite and looked a decade younger than her age which she said was due to her Danish genes. Her red hair was always carefully done.

The room was starting to fill, and Kathy nodded toward the residents. "I suppose all sorts of rumors about his past are going to come out."

Mary shook her head. "Not from me."

I smiled. "Is that because you don't know any stories about him, or because you won't spread them?"

"Yes," Mary said, turning away and joining Karla Telker in the front row. Karla was a relatively new resident, a former teacher who always dressed nattily and carried herself with confidence. She was known for her memory of former students and her tact.

I looked at Kathy. "Donny's mother was a client and friend. I won't be the source of any rumors."

"But you heard all the rumors because everyone talked to you."

Kathy nodded. "And I listened intently but didn't dish anything I heard."

"That seems like a prudent way to keep customers."

Kathy raised her eyebrows. "Everyone here is either related, has friends, or has enemies. If you start telling stories about anyone, positive or negative, you lose customers."

I handed out bags of popcorn as the chairs filled. The residents had requested more comedies for the weekly movies, so I'd chosen *Calendar Girls,* the British comedy about a group of aging women who'd chosen to make a calendar for their annual flower club fundraiser. They'd decided to use nude photos of the members, with strategically placed flowers, to maintain a PG rating. I dimmed the lights and started the movie. Sitting in the back row, I mulled over Kathy and Mary's remarks.

The movie was as popular among Whistling Pines residents as it had been at the theater and several people mentioned how much they'd enjoyed the show as they departed the activity room.

Karla stopped next to me. "Mary and I were talking about Donny Koloski. I taught him in kindergarten, and again in fourth grade. He was a…bit of a troublemaker. He was smart but liked to stir things up when he felt the mood was too quiet, like during a test. I knew most of his teachers over his school years. We all remember the best, the worst, and the most annoying students. Donny was in one or more of those categories every school year."

"I've heard that about many Hollywood people. They're extreme extroverts who tend to be troublesome."

Karla leaned close. "He was as much trouble outside of school as he was in school."

"What do you mean?"

"Smoking. Drinking. Fast cars. Girls with reputations. He was into them all."

Hulda Packer, a source of irritation and twisted rumors, ran over my toes with her walker. "I think we should do a fundraiser."

"What should we use the funds for, Hulda?"

She waved her hand dismissively. "Two Harbors is always looking for money to fund something. Maybe the hockey club needs new bats."

"I think they're called hockey sticks, not bats."

"Whatever. You find a worthy cause and I'll talk to the ladies about a fundraiser."

Howard Johnson, the self-appointed mayor of Whistling Pines, was the last person out the door. "So Peter, what do you think the ladies will dream up for a fundraiser?"

"The buddy poppies always sell well on Memorial Day."

Howard's grin made me uneasy. "Do you think Hulda would choose daisies or petunias for her calendar concealment?"

I gasped. "No! That won't happen."

Howard raised his eyebrows. "Wasn't Hulda the person who pushed for the Buccaneer Days naturist cruise?"

My mind flashed to the sight of more than a dozen Whistling Pines residents joining the twenty members of the Twin Ports Nudist Club, in robes and beach coverups as the naturist tour boat pulled away from the dock the previous summer. "That was a sight I wish I could unsee."

Howard nodded. "I didn't see it. Still, I can't put the thought of wrinkled skin and sagging tattoos out of my mind."

"What sagging tattoos?"

Howard's eyes lit up. "You didn't hear?" He turned and walked away.

Chapter Three

Day 2

Being the recreation director of a senior living facility isn't usually glamorous or exciting. The solitude is part of what attracted me to the job, allowing me to recover from my Iraq PTSD in a low stress environment. Each day I drive to Whistling Pines, greet the people in the lobby, boot up the computer in my office, then walk to the dining room for a cup of coffee. No big deal.

People think I'm slacking or goofing off in the dining room, walking from table to table and drinking coffee. I'm actually gauging the mood of the residents. There's no better way to casually greet them and talk than by sitting with them and drinking coffee. The dining room is where rumors abound and are shared. I can squelch most rumors at breakfast by listening, pointing out the rumor's fallacy, then steering conversations to new topics.

"Peter!" A female voice called out from the back of the dining room. Kathy waved and beckoned me to her table. I sat in the open chair with Kathy, Karla and Mary.

"Nice to see you ladies. What can I do for you today?"

"Peter, we're concerned about the fundraising calendar."

I sipped my coffee while framing my response. "There were some jokes about making a calendar after yesterday's movie. There's not going to be a calendar."

Karla leaned forward. "Hulda Packer is talking about finding a photographer and using the profits to buy prayer candles for the Baptist church."

I tried to hide my smile. "Hulda's confused. There's no photographer and Baptists don't light prayer candles."

Mary looked around to see if anyone was listening. "Hulda's calendar idea isn't getting much traction, and that's a good thing. On the other hand, I think we should start a fundraiser. The Two Harbors City Band is still raising money to pay off the loan on the bandshell. We could help."

"How would we raise money?"

Karla watched Bingle, the maintenance man, decorating a Christmas tree in a corner of the dining room. "It'd be fun to do something seasonal, like sharing a collection of Christmas cookie recipes."

Mary's eyes lit up. "It needs to be more than cookie recipes. I think we could make a collection of Christmas recipes, things like rotmos, lefse, and lutefisk."

"What is rotmos?" Karla asked.

"Rotmos is rutabaga and potatoes, mashed with butter and cream. We always had rotmos with potatiskorv— Swedish sausage on Christmas Eve."

Kathy shook her head. "Our family had lutefisk and mashed potatoes with butter gravy. I don't think anyone wants those recipes." She paused. "Oh, let's be honest, even *I* don't want those recipes."

Karla grimaced at the mention of lutefisk. "My father was German, and not a fan of lutefisk, but we had a smorgasbord of Christmas cookies. Mom would start baking after Thanksgiving and we'd deliver platters of cookies to the nursing home and all our neighbors."

I stood and smiled. "I think a cookbook is a wonderful fundraising idea and I like the idea of ethnic recipes. Would you ladies talk it up? See if someone would be willing to pull it all together."

Kathy's eyes lit up. "I think it would be fun. I've got a great rhubarb torte recipe."

Karla, a former teacher, leaned back looking at her tablemates. "The three of us could do this. Peter, if you'd post a notice asking people to submit recipes, we could sort them and arrange them in a book."

I walked away, feeling good about diverting the calendar plan into a cookbook project and finding people to take it on. My solitude was interrupted by a call from the back of the dining room. Wendy sat at a table with a crossword puzzle spread in front of her. I was tempted to pretend I hadn't heard her, but her retribution for such slights had been more painful than responding to her.

I pulled out a chair across from her. "What's up?"

"The theme of the crossword is root vegetables, and not being a cook, I'm not making headway. I need a five-letter word for Brit rutabaga. It appears the fourth letter is a D."

"Swede."

Wendy glared at me. "I'm serious."

"So am I. The British troops stationed next to us in Iraq called rutabagas Swedes."

Wendy penciled in the letters. "Why do they call them Swedes?"

"I suppose they were introduced from Sweden."

I started to get up, but Wendy waved me back. "Okay, the next one is a four-letter word. The clue is beet genus."

"B E T A."

"Like the Latin letter."

I smiled. "Actually, beta is the second letter of the Greek alphabet."

Wendy didn't like to be contradicted and glared at me over her glasses. "I'm sure it's Latin."

"It's jokingly referred to as Latin for 'still doesn't work.' As in the alpha version of the software didn't work and the beta version means it still doesn't work."

Wendy flicked her wrist, not conceding my point, but moving on. "Okay, smarty pants, how about a three-letter word for N.Z. yam."

"O C A, as in ocarina."

Wendy filled in the letters. "I heard we're doing a fundraiser for the hockey team."

"No, I was just discussing a cookbook for the band shell fundraiser. Karla said she'd pull it together with Kathy and Mary."

Wendy's grin gave me goosebumps. "The calendar is happening."

"There is no calendar. I just spoke with Karla, Mary, and Kathy. They're putting together a Christmas cookbook."

Wendy twirled her pencil. "We'll see."

* * *

The recipe announcement was printing when I felt a presence behind me.

"Did you hear that Frankie Valli and the Four Seasons wrote a cookbook? They called it *Wok Like a Man*."

I turned as Brian Johnson sat in my guest chair. "What happened to the tuba and pirate jokes?"

"I've changed in honor of the upcoming culinary visit."

"That wasn't any better than a tuba joke."

Brian's eyes sparkled. "The clock wrote a cookbook. *It's About Thyme.*"

I smiled. "That's better."

"You know, it wouldn't kill you to laugh."

Tempted to comment on the quality of Brian's jokes, I bit my tongue. "Did you have something special on your mind?"

"Meg's calling around town, trying to find people who have award-winning recipes."

"I heard she planned to contact the person who coordinates the county fair food competition."

"Meg called my wife. Mary Beth's pickled beets won the county fair pickle competition for ten consecutive years. The eleventh year they asked her not to enter."

"Is she going on the show?"

Brian shook his head. "Pickles don't work well for a one-hour show. They have to age in the brine for weeks before they're done. Besides, her recipe is a secret. She hasn't even given our kids the recipe."

"She won't share it with her children?"

"Nope. Some recipes from Oscar's Lunch were also secret. Oscar wouldn't even give the full recipes to his part-time cooks. He'd mix the seasonings up before the staff came in and let them finish the dishes with his pre-prepared spice mixes."

"Where's Oscar's Lunch?"

"The Blackwoods Restaurant took over that location when Oscar closed."

"That was before my time."

"He served pies while the owner of Betty's Pies was still taking home economics classes. His sour cream raisin pie was a huge hit and one of his biggest secrets. Nobody made that pie like Oscar." I must've grimaced because Brian went on. "I think raisins are a dying thing, like dates and prunes. Dried and candied fruits are a thing of the past."

"My mom used to make fruitcake until she shipped one to me in Iraq. I sent an email and told her the Marines were using it as a doorstop. As it turned out, she didn't like fruitcake either. She made it because she thought I liked it."

"A lot of ethnic foods are going to die out in a generation or two." Brian stood up and wrinkled his nose. "Like anything made from liver or other internal cattle organs."

With the printed recipe request in hand, I was about to step out of my office when the phone rang. Recognizing the THPD caller ID as the Two Harbors Police Department, I said, "Hi Kerry."

"How did you know it was me?"

"The caller ID says THPD. That's you, right?"

"That's the police department, not necessarily me. It could've been the dispatcher or one of my officers."

"You're the only person who calls me from the police department. What do you want?"

"Have you lined up some cooks for the television show?"

"Actually, I'm using subterfuge to get them."

"Huh?"

"We're assembling a Whistling Pines cookbook as a fundraiser. I'm going to screen the recipes and talk to the most likely participants."

"How are you going to screen the recipes?"

"By throwing out the ones I don't like."

"You can't do that. There might be some real delicacies that aren't to your taste but could be very popular with the TV audience."

"You mean, things like head cheese, lutefisk, and oyster stew?"

Kerry paused so long I thought he might've been called away from the phone. "Okay, point taken. But just because they're weird doesn't mean the show doesn't want them. I talked to the dispatcher, and she says Jonathan travels all over the world sampling interesting local delicacies. She mentioned him eating live baby octopus in Korea and tree snails in the Amazon."

"I thought tree snails were poisonous?"

Kerry sighed. "You know damned well it's tree *frogs* that are poisonous. Get serious."

"Too bad there isn't thick enough ice on the lakes for fishing. Maybe someone could whip up a batch of eelpout soup."

"Um, not being local, I don't know what that is, but eelpout sounds…disgusting."

"For some reason, eelpout fish only bite during the winter. The fishermen pulled them out of the hole and the fish wrap themselves around the guy's hands and arms."

"Like an octopus?"

"More like an eel."

"And people catch them on purpose?"

"I think they're caught when people are fishing for other species, although the town of Walker, Minnesota, has an eelpout festival. I think it's more of an excuse to drink than an actual attempt to catch and eat eelpout, but having never been there, I shouldn't comment."

"Meg called and the producer will be here in two days. You need to start sorting recipes quickly or we're going to be in trouble."

"Listen, Kerry. I didn't volunteer for this and I'm only doing it because you twisted my arm. Cut me some slack. I'm working on it, and I'll have something for the producer." I took a breath. "So, what locations are they considering?"

"We're going to look at the kitchens for both the Swedish and Norwegian Lutheran Churches, and the VFW. The Sons of Norway president heard about this and he's promoting the Norwegian Lutheran Church because it was founded by Norwegians." Kerry paused, "He's asked me to attend tonight's meeting because he expects some dissention when the Swedish members hear about his call. Depending on who shows up, Swedes versus Norwegians and how much aquavit they've consumed before the meeting, he thinks there may be some raised voices."

"You're joking."

"Only about the Swedish members drinking aquavit before the meeting."

"The Sons of Norway accept Swedish members?"

"I guess they'll take anyone who claims Scandinavian heritage, which includes most of the Two Harbors population. Do you want to fill in for me?"

"Kerry, I've got a baby at home. I hope to get a couple of hours of sleep at some point tonight. Jenny and I have been taking shifts feeding Amelia, and neither of us is getting much rest."

"I thought you named the baby Amy?"

"We named her Amelia but we're calling her Amy. She howls more like an Amelia than an Amy."

Kerry chuckled. "Fine. I've got the Sons of Norway duty and you handle the baby. But, seriously, get some cooks and recipes lined up for the producer."

Chapter Four

I posted the recipe request on the bulletin board and mentioned the fundraising cookbook idea to the few people sitting in the entryway and by the mailboxes. I was surprised by the positive responses I got. At least three women left to make copies of their favorite recipes.

Bitsy Olson's face lit up when I mentioned the television show. "I've seen Jonathan Edwards. He went to Sweden and they ate a traditional meal with fermented herring. You know, that's not available in the U.S. The government won't allow surströmming to be imported because it's got live cultures in the fermenting cans."

I waited for the punchline, then realized she was serious. "Does fermented herring taste like pickled herring?"

Bitsy thought for a moment. "I don't really know. It's something my parents spoke about as a Christmas treat, so I assumed it was like pickled herring. That television segment was so funny. When they opened the can it hissed, and Jonathan pretended he was gagging."

"Are you sure he was pretending?"

"Oh, yes. It couldn't be any worse than Limburger cheese."

Bitsy hustled to the elevators and I contemplated food with odor so strong it would make the star of a food show gag. My thoughts were interrupted by Jenny.

"Will you talk to Kerry about our neighbor's rock band practices? They keep waking Amy."

I clenched my eyes. Two young men had moved into the rental house next door. The aroma of marijuana smoke had drifted out the door when I'd gone over to introduce myself. The resident's body language made it clear my visit was an intrusion.

"I don't think the city has a noise ordinance."

"Okay. Will you go over and talk to them about keeping the volume down after ten o'clock?"

I hated confrontation and was now faced with the prospect of an immediate argument with my wife or a later uncomfortable discussion with our new neighbors. Like all procrastinators, I chose the deferred confrontation. "Sure."

Jeri Westfall rushed out of the elevator holding a note card. Spotting me she asked, "Where's Karla. I have a recipe for her."

"The last time I saw her, she was in the dining room."

"This is so exciting. I might be on television!"

She walked into the dining room waving her recipe card and hailing Karla.

Howard Johnson sidled up to me. "I think you've created a gold mine and a manure pile all in one swift move."

"How so?"

"The residents are very excited about the prospect of having their recipes included in a Whistling Pines cookbook, so you've lifted morale in this somewhat dreary time of the year. On the other hand, each contributor thinks her recipe will win a spot on the television show."

I froze, lacking a response. "Can you help manage expectations?"

Howard smiled. "Peter, I'm not inserting myself into this."

"I need someone to sort and prioritize the entries."

"Peter, find someone outside the facility to do the sort."

"Who would you suggest?"

"I think the best judge would either be someone who's universally hated, or someone the residents wouldn't dare challenge."

"Give me examples."

Howard thought for a second, then his eyes lit up. "Your friend, Brian would be a good choice. Everyone jokes about tuba players, and he sheds insults like water off a duck's back."

I chuckled at the thought of suggesting the role to Brian. "Give me an example of someone who's above criticism."

Howard pondered that, then his expression changed to something approaching a smile. "I don't think anyone would criticize the new Lutheran minister. He's a polished professional and more than half the residents are Lutherans."

"Why would he be willing to take on something like this?"

"He's new in town and is still in that honeymoon stage. He's trying to connect with people, and everyone thinks he can walk on water."

I nodded. "He won't know he's stepping in a cowpie."

Howard put his hand on my arm. "Exactly!"

I walked back to my office and called Brian's house. His wife answered. "Hi, this is Peter from Whistling Pines. Is Brian around?"

Mary Beth laughed. "He's been practicing in the basement tubararium for hours."

"The what?"

"Brian calls his practice area the tubararium. Please tell me you've got something for him to do."

"Nothing immediate, but something longer term."

"Hang on."

I heard muffled tuba music. When Brian paused for a breath Mary Beth called his name and Brian came up the stairs. "Peter's on the phone."

"What's up Doc?" Brian asked with a chuckle, having repeated the phrase made famous by Bugs Bunny. He'd started calling me Doc years ago when he learned I'd been a Navy corpsman treating wounded Marines. Over the years I've tried to discourage people from using that nickname. I knew Brian was impervious to my admonitions to not call me Doc.

"I've got a job for you."

"My calendar is filling up. Who's the band and when's the gig?"

"What's your calendar look like tomorrow?"

"I've got a meeting of the watershed district board at ten. I'm open after that."

"Perfect! Whistling Pines residents are submitting recipes for a cookbook, and I need someone impartial to help distill the submissions down to a few of the best. We'll bring those to the television producer."

"I'll skip lunch so I can sample the entries."

"Um, we're just looking at recipes, not actually sampling them."

"What? There's no actual food involved?"

"There'll be all the coffee you can drink, and I'll have the cooks set aside a cinnamon roll for you."

I heard Brian talking with his wife, then he came back. "Mary Beth says she'd be happy to get me out of the house. What time should I be there?"

"Come at one. We'll meet in the dining room." I had another thought. "Brian, do you know the new minister?"

"Sure, we met Reverend Olafson at the welcoming reception."

"I need a second judge and his name came up. Do you have his phone number?"

"Hang on, I'm sure it's on the church bulletin." I heard Brian and his wife talking, then he came back and gave me the number. "He's the pastor at the Swedish Lutheran Church. You might want to contact Reverend Norgaard, at the Norwegian Lutheran Church, too."

"I think we only need two judges."

Brian sighed. "It'd be best if you invited both of them. Otherwise, someone will accuse you of being biased against the Norwegian entries. Come to think of it, you might want to invite Father Brennan, from the Catholic Church, so you can cover even more ethnic groups. He's got Germans and Slovenians in his congregation."

"That's way too many people. I'll call Reverend Olafson. The two of you will be enough."

Brian paused. "Well, I'm Swedish and so is Olafson. But we do represent some diversity. His heritage is Smaland, in central Sweden. My family is Olandic, on the Baltic."

"I think that's splitting hairs."

Brian laughed. "Those are fighting words for some Swedes."

"Just come at one and I'll deal with the ethnic battles, okay?"

"Say, Doc, why did you pick me? I'm not a culinary expert."

"Your name came up because you're so good at handling all the kidding you get about being a tuba player. The person who suggested you said you deal with tuba insults as if they were water off a duck's back."

Brian laughed. "Oh great! I'll paint a bullseye on my back."

"Thanks. I really appreciate your willingness to do this."

"You may have to play the piccolo for a couple concerts as payback."

"I can deal with that."

I called the Swedish Lutheran Church and the woman who answered put me on hold. "This is Pastor Olafson, how can I help you?"

"I'm Peter Rogers, the recreation director at Whistling Pines Senior

Residence. We're accumulating recipes for a cookbook and need to choose a few that will be submitted for the cooking show that's going to be broadcast from Two Harbors. I was wondering if you're available tomorrow afternoon to help us with prioritization of the recipes."

Olafson's voice sounded mature, and he laughed. "We've been contacted by Meg, at the Chamber of Commerce, about the use of our kitchen for the filming. This show is creating quite a stir. The Lutheran Women of Tomorrow are planning to welcome the producer. Tell me more about your prioritization."

"Our residents are submitting their favorite recipes for a cookbook. We're going to review the submissions, then choose a few for the producer to consider."

"I'm not much of a cook, Peter. I think you might be better off with one of my parishioners."

"I don't need a great cook. I need someone who likes to eat and can be objective. Your name came up because you're new in town and wouldn't be seen as biased."

I heard paper flipping. "I can move my meeting with the choir director. That opens up my afternoon. Give me directions to Whistling Pines."

"Thank you."

"Your people are going to be up against stiff competition. The church secretary told me that Reggie Sandberg will be making the sour cream raisin pie recipe from Oscar's Lunch."

"I don't know Reggie."

"She was Oscar's baker and inherited all his recipes when the restaurant closed. I've been told that Oscar's sour cream raisin pie is heavenly."

"I'm not much of a raisin fan, so it wouldn't be a hit with me."

Olafson chuckled. "I wouldn't choose that over blueberry, but people tell me the crust melts in your mouth and the sour cream complements the sweetness of the raisins perfectly. I guess Reggie has held that recipe pretty close to her chest since Oscar gave it to her."

"Well, let's hope there's something submitted here that will challenge Reggie's pie."

I hung up and sensed someone behind me. Howard Johnson was standing in my doorway, smiling. "You've got two judges?"

"Both people you suggested will be here tomorrow for a prioritization of recipes."

Howard nodded. "Did I hear that Reggie Sandberg is making pie for the competition?"

"That's what the Lutheran pastor said."

"That's going to cause quite a stir. Oscar's recipes are well-kept secrets. I'm surprised Reggie's willing to give any of them away."

"I'm not sure she's giving away the recipe. I think she'll just whip up a pie for the show and Jonathan Edwards will sample it."

Howard shook his head. "The producers post all recipes on their website. I assume that's part of the deal when you're on the show."

"All of our recipes will be published in a cookbook, so that won't be an issue. I'm not sure the county fair winners or the restaurant chefs will be as willing to part with their recipes."

I thought about the beet pickle recipe Brian said his wife wouldn't share. *Are there really recipes so secret the owners won't share them?*

I shut down my computer and grabbed my coat. On the way out I saw Karla and Kathy sitting at a dining room table with piles of recipe cards and three women standing nearby talking to them. I set my coat on a chair and walked to the gaggle of ladies.

"It looks like you're getting a good response to the recipe request, Karla."

She placed a recipe card on top of a pile and looked up. "It's incredible. I had no idea we'd have so many responses this quickly."

Mary came in with a handful of rubber bands. She sat in a chair next to Kathy, who was studying the recipe in her hand. "Peter, can you believe this response?" She picked up a stack of a dozen recipe cards and secured a rubber band around them. "These are just the side dishes."

Kathy put the recipe she'd been reading on top of a pile. "This is the dessert stack. The ones in front of Karla are entrées, and the other piles are breads, cookies, and Jell-O salads."

"You have Jell-O salads in a category of their own?"

"We started putting them in with the side dishes, but there are so many we decided to make Jell-O a separate category."

Failing to grasp the diversity of gelatin salad options, I said, "Give me an example."

Kathy picked up that stack and started reading off the titles. "The first one is orange Jell-O with shredded carrots. The next is lime Jell-O with mandarin oranges, followed by orange with mandarin oranges. Then there's cherry with canned fruit salad…"

I raised my hand to stop the recitation. "I get the idea."

"But you stopped me before I got to the Bavarian orange Jell-O with powdered cloves and sweetened sauerkraut."

At a loss for words I exclaimed, "Wow!"

"I know! I copied that one and I'm sending it to my daughter in Harris. I'm going to bring it to Anna's house for Christmas, but I'm not sure if I should put whipped cream or mayonnaise on top."

Karla looked up and stuck out the tip of her tongue before mouthing *mayonnaise?*

Nodding, I said, "I think I'd put the topping on the side and let people make their own choice."

"Oh Peter, what a great suggestion!"

Karla rolled her eyes.

"We need to winnow these down to a few that we'll present to the television producer. We'll let her decide which they'll put on the air."

Karla leaned back. "I'm planning to include the submitted recipes in the Whistling Pines cookbook. I wouldn't have a clue how to choose a few recipes, especially when there's such a variety across six categories."

"I've found two impartial judges who can do the sort for us."

Karla breathed a sigh of relief. "Who did you rope into it?"

I understood the unsaid, *what fools would be willing to do this.* "I recruited the new Lutheran pastor, Reverend Olafson, and Brian Johnson from the city band."

"A minister and a tuba player?" Mary asked.

"They're unbiased and willing. Those were my two filters."

Karla's smile said she understood what I'd done. "What time will they be here?"

"I told them we'd do the sorting at one o'clock tomorrow."

"Super! We may have a few more recipes come in after that, but it appears most of the residents will have their cards to me after breakfast. Mary, Kathy, and I can have them sorted before your judges arrive."

"Perfect!"

* * *

Jeremy was sitting at the dining room table doing homework. Next to him were a half glass of milk and remnants of a peanut butter sandwich. He was now a fifth grader, with more difficult homework and an appetite that matched his recent growth spurt.

He looked up when he heard me walk in. "What's for supper?"

"Liver sandwiches."

"Yuk! No, what's *really* for supper?"

"I was going to brown the hamburger and make goulash."

"Cool. Use the spiral pasta instead of the elbows. The sauce sticks to that kind better."

After changing clothes, I browned the hamburger, added tomatoes, paprika, and diced onions, then set the burner on simmer. Remembering my promise to speak with the neighbors, I put on my coat and trudged across the grass, now brown and crunchy for the winter. I felt a song's bass thumping before I got to the steps.

I pressed the doorbell, which brought a barking dog to the other side of the door. After a few seconds, the inner door opened, and a dog flung himself at the storm door. The young man who answered the door looked shaggy, with a few days' growth of scraggly beard, a tattered flannel shirt over a dirty t-shirt, and low-slung jeans.

"We don't want any of whatever you're selling."

He was about to close the door when I blurted out, "I'm your neighbor. Do you have a second?"

The door stopped mid-swing and he stared at me. "What?"

"We've got a baby and your music has been waking her up."

His look of disgust was disturbing. "We're in the house with the doors and windows closed. I don't see how that's a problem for you."

"I understand, and I respect your right to do what you want. But could you quit or turn it down after ten o'clock?"

The guy shook his head. "Buy her some earplugs." He was about to close the door when Kerry's police car stopped in front of our house and he got out. The guy looked at Kerry, then at me. "You called the cops on us?"

"Like I said, you can do what you want, but you're keeping the baby awake. Please turn the music down tonight."

Kerry saw my animated discussion and walked over. "Is there a problem?"

"Their music has been keeping Amy awake."

Kerry looked at the teen behind the door and put on his game face. "There's a noise ordinance. You have to turn your music down at ten and you can't mow the grass before eight in the morning. Understand?"

The kid looked disgusted. He closed the door without answering.

"Is there a noise ordinance?" I asked as we walked to our house.

"I don't know, but it sounds reasonable."

I held the door for Kerry, then rushed into the kitchen to stir the goulash. "Is this a social call?"

Kerry let out a sigh and leaned on the doorframe between the kitchen and dining room. He checked to make sure Jeremy was occupied, then said, "I wish it was. There's been a murder."

"What? Who?"

"We just found Reggie Sandberg dead in her house."

I froze. "I just spoke with the Lutheran minister about her. What happened?"

"I'm not sure. It appears she interrupted a burglary. Her house had been ransacked."

"She was going to provide a pie recipe for the cooking show."

Kerry nodded. "I'd heard that. Whoever broke into her house spread recipes all over her kitchen and living room."

"Someone broke in to steal recipes?" I asked, as I set a pot of water on the stove and took down the box of rotini.

"I don't know what they stole, Peter. Her wallet was open, and the burglars took her cash and credit cards, but they left without taking her wedding ring or watch. On the surface, this has the look of teenagers taking the cash, then trashing the house. But something isn't right. Reggie was stabbed with a kitchen knife in her living room."

"A knife from her own kitchen?"

Kerry nodded. "The killer stuffed her mouth with recipe cards."

"That sounds like an east-coast mob hit, trying to leave a message about giving away secrets." I paused, realizing what I'd just said. "Did you see any pie recipes?"

Kerry shrugged. "There are hundreds and hundreds of papers, letters, bills, and recipes strewn around the first floor of her house. The house looks like a paper bomb went off; it's impossible to know what's missing."

"She was going to make sour cream raisin pie for the cooking show. Is that recipe missing?"

"Like I said, there are hundreds of recipes strewn around among the other papers. I haven't looked at any of them. I don't know what should be there, so I don't know what's missing."

"She was a cook at Oscar's Lunch, and I heard Oscar gave her all his recipes when he closed."

"I don't know Oscar's recipes from her favorite Christmas cookie recipes. There are recipe cards everywhere." Kerry paused. "Can you look through them and determine what's missing?"

"Me? Oscar's closed before I moved to Two Harbors. You need to find an old-timer who knows Oscar's menu."

"I saw one of Oscar's menus in the mess. You could use that to determine what's missing."

I put up my hands. "I'm up to my eyeballs with the cookbook and my other job duties." The pasta water started to boil, so I poured in the rotini and set the timer.

"Peter, you're the one person I know who will be discreet."

My arguments were struck down one by one until we heard the crunch of Jenny's tires in the driveway. The back door opened, and Jenny walked in holding Amy in a baby carrier. She nodded at Kerry. "I saw your car outside."

"Hi Jenny. I was trying to talk Peter into helping me with an investigation."

Jenny seemed unsurprised by the comment. "I heard there was a stabbing in town."

"It might be linked to the upcoming cooking show."

Jenny slipped off her coat and scooped Amy out of the carrier. "Someone was killed over the cooking show?"

"That's what I'm trying to determine."

The timer sounded and I took the pot of pasta off the stove and poured the contents into a colander that I placed under running cold water. "I'm trying to stay out of it."

Jenny watched me pour the drained pasta into the tomato mixture. "Go with Kerry. I'll deal with supper and the kids."

Kerry smiled, his face lopsided due to his burns. He knew I'd lost the argument. "Grab your coat."

"Supper's ready. Have some goulash with us, and then I'll go to the crime scene with you."

Kerry hesitated, obviously more interested in moving the investigation ahead than eating supper with the Rogers family. "What the hell. She's not going to be any less dead in an hour."

Jeremy scooted into the kitchen at precisely the wrong moment. He looked at Kerry. "Did you just swear, Chief Stone?"

Kerry's eyes darted to Jenny and he shook his head. "I'm sorry. It was a slip of the tongue."

Jeremy looked at me to see if I had accepted the apology. "He's forgiven…this time. Set the table for four. Chief Stone is having goulash with us."

As he took plates out of the cupboard, Jeremy casually asked. "Who's not going to be less dead?"

Kerry stared at the ceiling, having been busted for swearing and for revealing information about an investigation. Undoubtedly, that information would sweep through the school like a wildfire. He knew better than to lie to a ten-year-old so came out with an edited version of the truth. "A woman died today and I'm investigating it."

Jeremy walked past with plates. "What did she die of? It's pretty cold out. Did she freeze to death?"

"There's a doctor in Duluth who'll tell me for sure."

Jeremy nodded and walked into the dining room. "What are we drinking with supper? Can I have root beer? You usually let me have root beer when we have company."

Jenny was about to say no, but I cut her off. "Chief Stone, would you like a root beer with your goulash?"

"That'd be good. I can't remember the last time I had root beer with supper."

Jeremy walked past us and tromped down the basement stairs sounding like a herd of elephants. "Really?" Kerry said. "You're feeding me root beer?"

Jenny walked past carrying Amy who was still asleep. "You're only getting root beer because you're a guest. If you were family, you'd be drinking milk."

I put my hand on Kerry's shoulder and steered him toward the dining room. "Too bad you're on duty or you could have a real beer."

"Yeah, this job has really cut into my drinking." He watched Jenny unwrap Amy, who started to stretch as her blankets were peeled back. "I hardly remember Jacob that age. I was deployed half the time he was growing up."

Jenny had a fork halfway to her mouth when Amy started to cry. "How does she know every time I'm going to eat?"

Jeremy was shoveling goulash into his mouth like he was afraid someone was going to steal the plate before he finished. "She can smell the food, Mom. Maybe you should give her some goulash. She might like it."

Jenny took a bite and picked up the infant while she chewed. "Amy's too little to eat goulash."

Jeremy looked troubled. "Why can't she have real food?"

"Babies' tummies' aren't ready for real food until they're older. Don't worry, in a couple years she'll be eating just as much as you."

Jeremy finished before the rest of us and quickly pushed his chair back. "May I be excused?"

"Sure, but you'll have to do the dishes alone. I'm going out with Chief Stone."

Jeremy stopped and stared at us. "Is this about the dead person?"

I nodded, expecting a discussion. Jeremy got out of his chair and walked to the living room.

Jenny started to get up, but Kerry waved her down. "If you have to feed Amy, I'll go into the kitchen. Finish your supper."

Jenny put her hand on Kerry's arm. "Thanks for being a gentleman, but if you don't mind, I'll put a blanket over my shoulder and all four of us can eat."

Kerry looked away while Jenny arranged Amy and herself. "It's safe now, Kerry. I won't flash you."

We finished supper, cleared the table, and I walked to Kerry's car. "What exactly do you expect from me?"

"I want you to stand back and take in the scene. Tell me what you see and what concerns you."

"I assume the body has been removed."

"She's gone, but the rest of the scene is intact. The Bureau of Criminal Apprehension is sending a team to process the evidence, so we can't touch any of the paper strewn around the floor. There's something about the house that seems off. I just can't put my finger on it."

* * *

Reggie's house was in a residential area that had been built after World War II. The houses were all one-story ramblers, nearly cookie cutter designs, thrown up to accommodate the returning vets and their families. Minnesota's Iron Range was still booming, so there were plenty of jobs and the town of Two Harbors was prosperous. The design and prices now fit the budgets of senior citizens and young people just starting out.

Reggie Sandberg's house was unremarkable except for the crime scene tape strung between the trees in the front yard. Like the rest of town, Sandberg's house had brown grass poking through a thin layer of snow. Dead shrubs and flowers hinted at Reggie's green thumb. It all looked bleak in the stark light of Kerry's headlights when they flashed across the front of the house as he pulled into her driveway.

"Who found her?" I asked as we walked to the rear steps.

"Her neighbor, Carol Hobbs, noticed that the back door was ajar. Carol called and when Reggie didn't answer, she walked over to close the door. Noticing the mess, she called out before walking in to check on Reggie."

"I don't suppose she saw a car parked in the driveway or someone strange walking down the sidewalk."

"None of the above. She'd gone grocery shopping and was carrying in bags when she noticed the door ajar. Most of the neighbors were working and none of the others saw anything."

Kerry handed me purple nitrile gloves and we put them on before he flipped on the kitchen lights. We stood just inside the back door, taking in the scene. As expected, there was paper all over the floor. Mixing bowls, spices, and canisters were set out on the counters along with milk and egg cartons. The smell of cinnamon and vanilla were masked by the sickly-sweet metallic smell of blood.

"Reggie was whipping up something," I said.

"I turned off the oven when I was here earlier."

"Aside from the mess on the floor, everything is neat and clean. The African violet on the table is watered and there's not a single speck of dust on the windowsills."

"Does anything seem out of place?"

I shook my head. "Not really. The kitchen appliances are here. The cupboards are closed. There are clean dishes in the drying rack next to the sink. Am I missing something?"

"Why spread paper all over the place to make a mess? If you were a vandal and wanted to really mess things up, wouldn't you dump the flour and sugar on the floor?

Maybe open the cupboards and smash dishes?"

"You think this looks contrived."

"Don't you? That's why I wanted your opinion. This seems too carefully staged."

I thought for a moment. "There would be fingerprints and footprints if the flour and sugar were spilled."

"You get a gold star. What else?"

I studied the kitchen again. "Reggie had been baking. She's got ingredients, mixing bowls, and measuring cups. I assume the recipe she was preparing is somewhere in the mess on the floor." I looked at the counter where the mixing bowls were arranged, then at the floor. "There's no recipe box. There are recipe cards all over the floor, but there's no box for them."

Kerry flipped off the lights. "Who would steal a recipe box, Peter?"

"Aren't we going to look in the living room?" I asked.

"We're going to walk around to the front door rather than tracking through all the paper."

Kerry opened the front door and we stepped inside. There was paper strewn everywhere. But again, everything was orderly and clean. "What do you see here?"

My eyes were drawn to the puddle of dried blood on the carpet. "She didn't interrupt a burglary. There weren't any papers under the body. The papers were scattered after her death."

"Anything else strike you as odd?"

"Her sewing machine is open and she was in the midst of a project. None of the fabric pieces were disturbed and her sewing basket is upright and full."

"This wasn't done by vandals. Someone tried to make it look like the house had been vandalized, but whoever did this had no idea how vandals mess up a house. The person or people who were in here grabbed mail, emptied a file cabinet, threw recipe cards, but didn't overturn a table or even disturb her sewing project."

Kerry turned off the lights and locked the door. Both buried deep in thought, we drove back to my house. I struggled to process the information I was mulling. "Why didn't you take your young cops to this scene?"

"I did. They didn't catch any of the anomalies you mentioned. I tried to lead them through my thought process, but they didn't get it. That's why I wanted you to look at the house, to make sure I wasn't out in left field."

"So, someone broke in, killed her, threw papers and recipes all over, took her cash and credit cards and left."

"Right."

"Someone staged the house to make it look like a botched robbery and vandalism. But the robber didn't know how vandals would trash a house and wasn't a real burglar because he left her watch and diamond ring."

Kerry parked in front of my house where we could feel the pulsating bass from the neighbor's band. "If there are fingerprints, I think they won't be in the FBI automated fingerprint identification system. AFIS only has criminals, military personnel, and others who were fingerprinted for government security clearances. I think whoever did this got his or her CSI information from television shows and has no previous criminal record."

"That narrows the field."

"It hardly narrows the field at all, and it makes this person much harder to identify." Kerry looked at the neighbor's house. "Do they play every night?"

"Every night since they moved in last week."

"And when does it quit?"

"They play until two or three in the morning. I think they're practicing for a gig."

Kerry shook his head. "They'll be deaf before their performance."

"They'll have hearing aids by the time they're forty."

"I'll have a word with them. You get some sleep."

Jeremy was watching reruns of old sitcoms and Amy was asleep in her playpen. Jenny was curled up under a quilt and asleep on the couch. Even in the living room,

I could feel the bass playing next door. I tapped Jeremy on the shoulder and gestured for him to follow me upstairs. "Brush your teeth and get ready for bed."

He stopped me at the top of the stairs. "Did you and Chief Stone see a dead person?"

The music stopped abruptly. Kerry was speaking with the neighbors.

"We didn't see a dead body. We just looked at a house where there'd been a crime."

I tucked Jeremy in bed and went downstairs. I considered waking Jenny and sending her to bed, then decided her uninterrupted sleep was more important than moving her. I was loading the dinner dishes into the cupboard when there was a gentle knock on the back door. It opened before I could get to it.

Kerry stepped into the kitchen. "I think your neighbors will be more respectful of your peace and quiet. I told them if I could hear their bass past the property line, they were all going to be ticketed."

"Thanks," I said, then asked. "Will this result in my car being egged?"

"I've already dealt with that. I told them if they retaliated against any of the neighbors, they'd each get a ticket before they drove out of the neighborhood."

"That would be harassment."

"That's leverage. They've got beat up old cars with broken taillights and cracked windshields. I'd have every right to issue tickets requiring them to be repaired. Then, they'd have to deliver the proof of repair to the police station or get a summons to appear in court."

"That's devious."

Kerry shrugged. "It's a way of dealing with the problem. Get some sleep; you look tired."

Chapter Five

Day 3

I let Jenny sleep and dressed in the bathroom. After rousting Jeremy from bed, I made a pot of coffee and put bread in the toaster. Jeremy wandered into the kitchen and poured himself a bowl of cereal.

"What's happening at school today?"

Jeremy shrugged. "It's the same every day, Dad."

"When does your Christmas break start?"

"I don't know. Mom marked it on the calendar."

"Are you having a holiday pageant this year?"

"I dunno."

"Have you been practicing songs or anything?"

"Some."

"Is there anything interesting in your life?"

"Nope."

"How do you feel about having a baby sister?"

He succinctly summarized his view of a young sister. "She's a pain. She cries all the time and poops in her diapers."

I made sure he had lunch tickets, his homework was complete, and he'd stowed it in his bag. He knew when to catch the bus, so I left him eating cereal and went out to scrape frost off my windshield.

The neighboring house was quiet and dark. There were five old cars in the driveway and on the street, which made me wonder about the sleeping arrangements in the two-bedroom house. It wasn't my problem, but I liked the landlord who'd treated me fairly. He'd been sad when I'd moved out and told me he appreciated a polite, tidy renter. I assumed his new tenants were neither polite nor tidy.

* * *

The Whistling Pines dining room was full of residents eating breakfast when I arrived. I greeted a few people and retreated to my office to hang up my coat and boot up my computer. I was logging on when I sensed someone behind me. I turned and found Hulda Packer standing in my doorway, leaning on her walker.

"Peter, you need to get onboard with this calendar project."

"There is no calendar project. We're doing a fundraising cookbook."

Hulda's attempt to give me the stink-eye looked more like she'd had a stroke. "We'd rather have you with us, but if you're not willing to participate, we'll go on without you."

"Who else thinks there'll be a calendar?"

"Well, if you're not buying in, there's no need to reveal the rest of our group."

With that, Hulda turned and left. I turned to the computer and created an announcement, advising that the fundraising calendar was cancelled. I typed a second message announcing that outside judges would be reviewing the recipes submitted for the Whistling Pines cookbook with the winners being considered for the upcoming television show. I printed a copy of each announcement and posted them on our bulletin board. With that accomplished, I took my coffee mug to the dining room and drew coffee from the urn.

The crowd in the dining room was thinning, the early risers already gone. Many of the remaining tables were occupied by people sipping coffee and socializing. Karla waved at me from near the center of the room.

I found Karla, Kathy, and Mary seated at a table covered with recipe cards.

"It looks like we got an outstanding response," I said as I sat in the fourth chair.

Kathy waved the card she was holding. "The response has been incredible and there are so many recipes that sound wonderful, like this lemon curd ice cream cake with graham cracker crust. Just reading it makes my mouth water."

Mary smiled. "I think it's funny that half the recipes are desserts."

"I don't know what the show's producers are looking for. I've heard Jonathan does a lot of appetizers and entrées. Does he include many desserts?"

Karla paused, holding a card in her hand. "I think he likes to feature dishes that come with a story. For example, Hjelmer Rasmussen submitted a recipe for pickled herring, explaining the three methods of preparing the fish. The recipe varies depending on whether the herring is salted, or fresh, and whether you use cutlets of large Baltic herring or smaller whole herring."

"I'm not a big fan of raw fish," I said.

Mary laughed and waved a recipe card. "You'd prefer sylta? This recipe starts by boiling a whole pig's head to make the gelatin that holds head cheese together."

I put up my hand. "I'll skip that one, too."

Marlene Horvath rushed up with a recipe card. "Do you have a poteka recipe yet?"

Karla accepted the recipe card. "I don't remember seeing poteka. Is that a dessert?"

Marlene nodded. "It's a Slovenian nut roll made from sweetened dough spread with ground walnuts or hazelnuts. My family's recipe uses walnuts and butter."

Reading the recipe, Karla nodded. "This sounds really good."

"It's a recipe I taught my children. Now I'm teaching it to my grandchildren when they visit." Marlene paused. "I've been teaching them how to make pasties, too. Has anyone submitted a pasty recipe yet?"

Kathy put her hand on a small pile. "These are the pasty recipes. I've got Polish pasties, Scottish meat pies, Czech pasties, Cornish two-crust pasties, and more."

Marlene's eyes narrowed. "They don't ruin it by putting rutabaga in them, do they?"

Mary laughed. "Some have rutabaga. Some don't. Some use only cubed beef and other recipes use ground veal and pork. The only things they all have in common is onions and a pie crust wrapper."

Marlene wrinkled her nose. "Who'd put ground meat in a pasty?"

Kathy pulled out a recipe and read it. "This recipe uses mutton."

Marlene rolled her eyes. "Mutton? What butcher would have mutton in his store? I had a neighbor who made mutton stew and my husband claimed he could smell it cooking before he left the mine!"

Kathy smiled as Marlene stalked off. "Everyone has an opinion."

Mary broke into laughter. "And each of them thinks their recipe is the only correct way to prepare the dish. Ronalda Harju gave us a pasty recipe and pointed out that it should only be served with tomato sauce or ketchup."

I put up a finger. "I really like gravy on my pasties."

Mary nodded. "Ronalda said only Protestants and heathens serve pasties with gravy. I'm not sure she discriminates between the two denominations."

"Yeah, I heard that when I asked for gravy with my pasty at the VFW."

Karla looked at me and smiled. "So, which are you?"

"Protestant, with a gravy preference."

"Your judges will be here at one o'clock?" Karla asked.

"Yes. I'll bring them here, to the dining room."

Kathy leaned back. "What are your plans for crowd control?"

I froze. "Crowd control?"

"There are some pretty strong feelings."

"You're kidding? People feel strongly about recipes?"

Kathy picked up a pile of recipes. "These are the pasty recipes, and each person thinks their recipe is the only proper mixture. Didn't you just listen to Marlene?"

Mary nodded. "I hope your judges understand what they're getting into." When I shook my head she added, "They're like lambs being led to the slaughter."

"Oh, it won't be that bad."

"The tuba player and minister are both Swedes. Can they be unbiased?"

"Their surnames are Swedish, but they're generations away from their Swedish forefathers. I'm sure they'll be open-minded and objective."

Karla looked around to see who might be listening. "I don't think their ethnicity matters. I suspect there will be people who feel bias because their recipes weren't chosen."

"You three can help with the sort. That'll help with any perception of bias."

Kathy raised her eyebrows. "Peter, our parents were Swedish, Norwegian, and Danish. There are people who've already told us we're biased because we're all Scandinavian."

"But you're not excluding any recipes from the cookbook, are you?"

Mary laughed. "Of course not. We don't want to be lynched!"

I walked away feeling like I'd stepped in a cow pie. The discomfort only increased when Nancy, the director, cornered me near the aviary in the atrium. "Peter, do you have a second?"

We moved to a back corner, away from prying ears. "Are you and Jenny getting any sleep?"

"Last night was better. The new neighbors didn't blast music at us until the wee hours of the morning. Amy only woke up when she needed to be fed."

Nancy smiled, not her corporate smile, but a warm human smile. She put her hand on my arm. "I worry about you two. There's a lot on your plates."

"Thank you. We appreciate you allowing us some flexibility in our hours so we can deal with daycare and school things."

"I've been there, so I realize how challenging it is to balance home and work. You two are covering what needs to be done here. That's all I can ask of you." She paused and looked down. "I heard the police chief took you to the murder scene."

I paused, unsure how to answer without revealing too much about the case. "Yes."

"Do you think…is there any reason to believe it's tied to anything that's going on here, at Whistling Pines?"

"I'd be very surprised if there was any direct link to anyone or anything here."

Nancy nodded. "I understand that several of the residents knew the woman who was killed. A couple people have spoken with me about transportation to the funeral."

"Two Harbors is a small town, so I'm not surprised some of our residents knew or were related to the deceased."

"How are we doing on the cookbook?"

"Karla, Mary, and Kathy have collected an impressive number of recipes."

Nancy raised her eyebrows. "But?"

"Karla's organized and takes charge. I think it's under control, and together they'll create a nice product."

"I heard some arguing in the dining room this morning."

I took a breath. "There's some controversy over what's correct."

Nancy cocked her head. "Correct?"

"Whether you put rutabaga in a pasty and whether the meat should be cubed or ground."

Nancy closed her eyes. "You're serious?"

"There seems to be some variation depending on your ethnicity. They told me the only thing everyone agrees on is the crust. Oh, and that everyone puts onions in them."

"How are they going to deal with that?"

"They're planning to include all the recipes and the readers can choose the variant that suits them."

"Good plan. I like going right down the middle of the road."

Nancy was about to leave but I stopped her. "I have two people coming in to sort the recipes this afternoon. The television cooking show wants a short list of local recipes to consider for their live broadcast."

"You don't want me to be a judge…"

"No, I've got a Lutheran pastor and Brian Johnson from the city band coming. I thought it'd be better if someone outside the facility did the judging rather than having one of the staff members incur the wrath of someone who feels slighted because her recipe wasn't chosen for the television producer."

"That's a decision worthy of Solomon." Nancy turned away, then hesitated. "What's going on with the fundraising calendar?"

"I've done all I can to kill the idea."

"You didn't think we could support two fundraisers at the same time?"

"It's more an issue of the photo content of the calendar. Hulda was motivated by this week's movie, *Calendar Girls,* and she thought we should do something similar."

Nancy's mouth opened, but she froze. "Um, that's the movie about the British garden club who posed nude behind flower arrangements. Right?"

I nodded.

Nancy looked around us. "Who here would be willing to pose for something like that?"

"I tried to squelch the idea before recruitment began. But Hulda has been huddled with Wendy and they may be conspiring on something."

Nancy put a finger to her lips. "I'll speak to Wendy."

I was passing the dining room enroute to my office when I heard raised voices. Liz Potter was standing in front of Karla's table with her arms in the air. "You CAN NOT include a recipe that uses a cake mix and a box of pudding!"

I couldn't hear Karla's response. Kathy looked at me with pleading eyes, so I rushed over. "What's the problem, Liz?"

"Violet Lundberg submitted a pudding cake recipe. It's just dumping two off-the-shelf mixes together, adding milk, then baking it. I mean, what kind of recipe is that? I think our cookbook should be things made from scratch, not some…store-bought mixes that you dump together. Any grade school child can do that."

Karla put her hand up. "Like I said, we're only sorting the recipes into categories, not weeding out the ones we don't like."

"Well, I think the cookbook should involve real cooking!"

Struggling to find some way to de-escalate the situation, I reached into my limited knowledge of cooking. "Kathy, aren't there other recipes that use shortcuts like canned soup, self-rising flour, or other ready-made ingredients?"

The women started flipping through recipe cards. Kathy held up a card. "Here's a green bean casserole with cream of mushroom soup and canned onion rings."

Mary pulled out a card. "Here's a sloppy joe recipe with canned tomato soup and ketchup."

Within seconds there were five recipe cards set aside, all using some form of semi-prepared ingredients from the store. I looked at Liz. "Do you think we should pull these out?"

"Well, no. No one's going to make a green bean casserole and make their own mushroom soup."

Karla clasped her hands. "It's not our job to throw out recipes. We're putting all of them in, and the people who buy the cookbooks can decide which recipes they want to make. There could be mothers who would be delighted to have their young daughters make a pudding cake."

Kathy, who often held her opinions until she had something profound to say, spoke up. "Liz, not everyone is a master chef. We need to put in easy and difficult recipes so there are things that appeal to everyone."

Liz's fire was dying. She was still unhappy, but she was back from the brink of an outright battle. "Fine. If you're going to do that, maybe you should make a section of beginner recipes for children."

I chuckled. "Or bachelors."

Looking at my smile, Liz eased down further. "Or busy mothers."

Karla looked relieved. "I think that's a great suggestion, Liz."

Nodding, Liz walked away. Mary put her hand on my arm. "Thank you. I thought Liz was going to start tearing up recipe cards."

Kathy shook her head. "It's my fault. Liz handed me a recipe for pudding cake, and I said we could put it right next to a similar, three-ingredient recipe."

"It's not your fault, Kathy," Karla said. "There are people with strong opinions about food preparation. I suspect there will be fireworks this afternoon when Peter's judges start sorting recipes for the television show."

Running my hands over my head, I took a deep breath. "Maybe I won't come back from lunch."

Mary laughed. "That was my plan. The problem is, I'm going to eat here. I'm trapped."

* * *

The banana and peanut butter sandwich I'd made for Jeremy's lunch was dry and gooey. I'd assembled it before he'd declared it was a hot lunch day, so I brought the brown bag from home and ate in my office. I was munching sandwich cookies and reading an email when someone cleared their throat behind me.

Greta Sorenson stood in my doorway; her arms crossed. As always, she wore a dress, usually blue, a tribute to her Swedish heritage. "Peter, you need a fika."

I froze, reviewing Swedish foods in my head. Coming up blank, I said, "What's a fika? Is it an entrée or dessert?"

Greta sighed. "It's a rest break. Swedes know it's important to slow down and take a breath—to take a fika."

"I agree. It's just hard to find the time for a fika."

Greta shook her head. "This afternoon is hardly going to be a fika. You know people will be crazy about the recipes."

"I've sensed that this morning. We had quite a discussion about using recipes with pre-packaged ingredients."

"It'll get worse. You haven't discussed rice pudding yet."

"Rice pudding?" I tried to envision how pudding could be a point of controversy.

"There's stirred rice pudding, which is the proper way to prepare it. Then, there's a baked custard with rice that some people call rice pudding."

"I take it that rice custard isn't *real Swedish* rice pudding?"

"Of course not! It's not a pudding. Have you ever had chocolate pudding that's the consistency of custard? No! It's not pudding."

"Easy, Greta. I see your point, but we agreed to include all submitted recipes in the cookbook."

"Fine. Put it in, but don't call it rice *pudding*." Greta stepped back but hesitated. "And there's still the issue of raisins."

"Um, raisins are an issue?"

"Peter, please try to keep up. Of course, raisins are an issue. Norwegians don't put raisins in their rice pudding. Real rice pudding has raisins." She shuddered as a thought passed. "I've even read that some Norwegians have put sour cherries in, or on their rice pudding. That's terribly wrong."

"Should they use lingonberries?"

"Uff da, Peter." Greta rolled her eyes. "Not on rice pudding."

"Okay, so it has to be stirred, no cherries, with raisins."

Greta nodded. "Please make sure that's dealt with." She paused. "After your fika."

Chapter Six

I was standing at the front door shortly before one o'clock. There were a few people around the mailboxes and a group of women were playing bridge near the aviary. I was focused on the parking lot, awaiting the arrival of the judges when Wendy startled me.

"You know you're going to get chewed up and spit out this afternoon."

"Over the cookbook?"

Wendy sidled up next to me. "You've opened a can of worms. You thought a calendar was going to be controversial, but you have no idea how passionate people are about their recipes."

"Greta Sorenson clued me in on the impending rice pudding conversation."

"Rice pudding is only the tip of the iceberg. There are many more recipe disputes on your horizon."

Two cars pulled into the driveway and parked in guest spots. "I suppose our judges will have to deal with that. I plan to stay out of it."

"Get real, Peter. There's no way you can be out of the target area when the shit hits the fan."

Brian and Pastor Olafson got out of their cars and shook hands. I nodded toward them. "Who can get mad at a minister and a tuba player?"

Wendy turned so she was facing me. "Everyone." Then she was gone.

Brian was gesturing as the two judges walked to the front door. They stopped under the portico while Brian finished whatever he was saying. Pastor Olafson broke into laughter and slapped Brian on the back.

I held the door for them as they walked in. Olafson was still chuckling and Brian was beaming. "Pastor Olafson knows how to appreciate a good joke when he hears one, unlike other people…"

The minister put out his hand. "I assume you're Peter Rogers. I'm Ron Olafson." Under his parka the minister wore a blue shirt with a clerical collar. His hair was gray, carefully combed, and his blue eyes sparkled.

"It's nice to meet you, Pastor."

"Please call me Ron." He patted Brian's arm. "Our friend, the tuba player, has quite a repertoire of jokes. He cracks me up every time I see him."

Brian's eyes were wide, anticipating an invitation to tell the joke he'd just shared with the minister. I nodded.

"What do you call a fake noodle? An impasta."

Brian beamed and the pastor laughed again. I stifled a groan. "We're gathering in the dining room."

I took Brian and Ron's coats and led them to the table where my ladies were sitting with stacks of recipe cards. I made the introductions and got chairs for our guests.

Karla passed her right hand over the stacks of cards. "We've sorted the recipes into several categories, and I thought we'd read through them one at a time. I plan to read the titles in a first pass, then we can get into them more deeply after we complete the first elimination round."

Raising my hand, I added, "We plan to include *all* the recipes in a fundraising cookbook. Right now, we're trying to identify a few especially appealing recipes to be considered by the producers of the cooking show. The people who contributed the chosen recipes will be invited to prepare them on a live television broadcast and tell the story behind the recipe."

Ron nodded. "Ahh, so we're not just trying to find appealing recipes. We want to find things that can be prepared in front of an audience and that might have a backstory."

Kathy nodded. "Pastor Olafson, you stated that very well. Peter's explanation was rather lengthy and ambiguous."

Reaching for the closest stack of recipes, Karla grinned at me, knowing I was biting my tongue. "These are entrées. Mary will read through the titles. If any strike you, let me know and I'll set it aside for further consideration."

Mary tapped the cards into a neat pile and started reading titles. Brian or Ron asked for a clarification of a title or foreign word a few times, but the team breezed through the entrées, choosing only Irish Stew with Guinness to be passed on to the television people.

Kathy picked up another stack. "These are all variations of pasties."

Looking at the rather large stack of the Iron Range staple meat pies, usually made from a single crust folded over the filling, Brian cocked his head. "I like pasties. I'm amazed there are more than a dozen variations here."

A small group had gathered around us, some seated, others standing and looking over their shoulders. May Clark leaned forward. "Several ethnic groups have adapted Cornish meat pies, then claimed them as their own. I'm not sure why you're…honoring them by even considering the imposters."

Ron Olafson smiled and put up his hand, calming the emotions starting to boil. "I'd like to hear all of the variations. I know the Chinese invented pasta noodles, but the

Italians have added some enhancements I find very appealing."

Karla glanced at me, her smile flickering at the pastor's quick smothering of the ethnic uprising. Kathy quickly flipped through the recipes, mentioning the key variations differentiating the recipes. "This is made with ground veal and lamb. Verna Mattson's recipe has rutabaga, pork, and potatoes. May Clark's Cornish pasty recipe is the only one that uses two crusts, like a pie. Here's a Polish hand pie with sauerkraut and mushrooms."

Several people tried to stop Kathy's reading of the recipes, interjecting criticisms or comments. Each time the pastor smiled, raised his hand, and asked the crowd to let all the recipes be read before there was discussion.

After the last pasty recipe was read, Brian surprised me by deftly defusing the situation. "There's no way to choose one recipe out of all these great options. My mouth is watering just listening to all these tasty variations. Kathy, can I have copies of all the pasty recipes, please. I'll bring them home and we'll try them out on my kids when they come up for Christmas. I think they'll love all of them."

Karla stood up, cutting off several people who were trying to protest. "Let's take a break. I'll show our guests where the bathrooms are, and we'll all get a cup of coffee before we resume." She smiled and leaned close to Mary. "Don't let anyone touch the recipes. I'll bring you a can of Coke when we come back."

I smiled and nodded my approval.

Kerry was standing next to the dining room door. He nodded for me to follow him, and we walked outside into the cold. "I heard back from the Bureau of Criminal Apprehension."

"Could you tell me what the BCA had to say while we sit in your warm car?"

Starting the engine, Kerry took a deep breath. "You know, solving crimes was easier in Iraq."

"Why?"

"People don't wear winter gloves to a Baghdad crime scene. There wasn't a fingerprint inside the house that didn't belong to the homeowner."

"No fingerprints, no DNA, and no clues to follow?"

Kerry's sly smile told me he had a card up his sleeve. "The killer wore leather gloves and left bloody glove prints on the knife."

"Like I said, no clues."

"One of the things crime shows haven't picked up on is the unique patterns in leather. A piece of leather is almost as distinctive as a human fingerprint and the prints from three, four, or five glove fingers, each with a unique pattern in the leather, are

75

nearly as good as a DNA match and better than a single fingerprint."

"I sense a 'but' coming."

"Since I can't put a glove print into the FBI automated fingerprint identification system, I need to find a bloody glove to match with the prints."

I chuckled. "Call the LA police to see if they still have the bloody gloves from the O.J. Simpson trial."

"Not funny, Peter."

"Sorry. I'm still a little short on sleep."

Kerry's unscarred eyebrow rose. "Were your neighbors quiet last night?"

"No blaring music and they didn't egg my car in retaliation." Karla was waving from the front door. "Looks like we're ready to resume the recipe judging."

"How's it going?"

"There've been some tense moments, but Pastor Olafson and Brian Johnson have defused them well."

"I don't need to send an officer for crowd control?"

I opened the door and climbed out. "Not yet, but you're welcome to hang around."

"I'll pass, but feel free to dial 911 if a riot breaks out."

Squatting down, I looked Kerry in the eye. "I suspect there may be some hurt feelings, but no physical assaults unless someone rams me with a walker."

Kerry waved as he pulled out of his parking spot. Karla met me as I hustled in the door, shivering. "I thought you were bailing on us."

"No, just talking with the chief. Are we ready to start again?"

Karla scanned the area. "I was going to go through the rice pudding recipes, but I've been warned about potential raisin arguments."

"Yeah, I heard about raisins and stirred versus baked pudding. Apparently, purists consider a baked pudding a custard."

"Who told you that?"

"Greta Sorenson stopped off to see me while I was eating lunch."

"Ha! That was your first mistake—not leaving the building to eat."

"I love your twenty-twenty hindsight." I drew a breath and looked at the crowd gathering around the judging tables. "Is there something less controversial we can use to ease into the judging without immediately throwing gas on the fire?"

"I think Jell-O salads are pretty safe."

Taking Karla's elbow, I steered her into the dining room. "Jell-O it is."

Olga Solberg was whispering in Kathy's ear when we walked in. Karla sat down and reached for the Jell-O recipes, but Kathy looked upset.

I leaned over to her. "What's wrong?"

"Olga wants us to push her sylta recipe when we get to the appetizers. I don't think Jonathan Edwards would boil a pig's head on live television."

"I'm sure live TV isn't prepared for a boiled pig's head. I'll point that out if sylta doesn't die on its own."

"Thank you," Kathy mouthed.

"Okay," Karla said, flipping through the dozen Jell-O recipes. "We've got several with canned fruit, a couple with shredded carrots, and one with…"

Karla froze and the color drained from her face. She held out a recipe card to Kathy and Mary, and they huddled in conversation.

"There's no name on this recipe so we're not sure who submitted it."

"What is it?" someone asked from the surrounding crowd.

"Um, it's fish aspic."

Pastor Olafson shot a look at me that said I'd pulled him into previously unknown waters. Even he was struggling to offer a polite comment. "Um, that's interesting."

Karla was speechless, so she handed the card to Mary who reached for her reading glasses. "Well, it's a Polish Christmas recipe called Ryba Galacerie. It's gelatin dissolved in garlicky fish broth with hard boiled eggs, cooked carrots, and pieces of fish. It's supposed to be sprinkled with vinegar before serving."

The crowd gasped or groaned, and Brian shook his head. "I don't think we own enough vinegar for me to eat that."

Pastor Olafson was holding his fist to his mouth. I wasn't sure if he was laughing and hiding his smile, or if he was gagging. He composed himself and sat back. "I've been told that Mr. Edwards likes to feature exotic dishes. I think we should put the fish Jell-O into the pile to pass along."

Karla looked skeptical but took the recipe card from Mary and set it aside. "We've got two more interesting recipes in this category. Here's one called Wisconsin lime Jell-O with marinated turkey gizzards and cottage cheese, and another called German orange Jell-O with powdered cloves and sweetened sauerkraut."

Brian perked up. "My wife makes a version of the Wisconsin salad and it's really good."

Kathy turned to me, and whispered, "Who'd put pickled turkey gizzards or sauerkraut in Jell-O? I think I just threw up in my mouth. Please get me a fresh cup of coffee."

Pastor Olafson overheard Kathy and couldn't restrain his laughter. I took Kathy's coffee cup and went to the urn while the judges and cookbook team discussed passing more gelatin recipes on to the television people. By the time I'd returned, the consensus was to forward only one recipe from each category.

Picking up another stack of recipe cards, Karla cleared her throat. "I've already had some input on the rice pudding recipes. I'd like the crowd to withhold your comments, so you don't bias our judges."

That brought a murmur from the spectators as Karla flipped through the recipes. "These fall into two broad categories: half are stirred puddings; half are baked puddings. It's been explained to me that the stirred recipes have a creamy texture, and the baked recipes are more like a firm custard."

Raising a finger, Brian made a valiant attempt to defuse the dissention among the people watching. "I'm three-quarters Norwegian and one-quarter Swede. One grandmother made the stirred recipe and the other baked her pudding. While they were different, I love both recipes."

Pastor Olafson saw the wisdom in Brian's statement and added, "My wife makes a baked recipe without raisins, but I really prefer my grandmother's stirred recipe with raisins, then sprinkled with cinnamon."

Karla pulled a recipe card from the stack. "Of all the rice pudding recipes, this one has the most interesting twist. It's a Christmas recipe for a stirred pudding that calls for the cook to drop a blanched almond into the mixture before the stirring is complete. The pudding is divided into custard cups, then each cup is sprinkled with cinnamon. The children each choose their cup, then the adults pick theirs. The person who gets the almond is blessed with a year of good luck."

The crowd was surprisingly quiet, whispering among themselves about the twist with the almond. Pastor Olafson broke the ice. "I really like the recipe with the almond and whoever submitted it should be recognized."

"This recipe was submitted by Jodi McCallie. It's from her grandma Esther Peterson."

Standing to the side, Jodi blushed as people congratulated her.

The pastor went on, "Because there are so many rice pudding recipes, and Jonathan Edwards focuses on more exotic foods, I think we should move on to the next category."

Karla quickly set the rice pudding recipes aside and paged through another stack. "These are breads. I'm amazed by the variety and number of ethnic groups represented by this group. There are five wonderful white bread and dinner roll recipes. Then there's Finnish pulla, Slovenian poteka, Polish babka, Danish julekage, Norwegian julekake, and Italian panettone. All sound wonderful and I'd like to try every one of them."

Drawing a deep breath, Pastor Olafson leaned back. "I agree with Karla. These recipes make my mouth water. But I don't think there's anything exotic enough in the bread recipes to attract the attention of the television producer."

Brian nodded. "It looks like there's only one stack left."

"I think this is the category everyone's been awaiting," Karla said, picking up the last stack. "These are desserts and cakes."

A voice from behind me asked, "Are any of these made with sauerkraut?" The question brought a chuckle from the crowd.

Flipping through the recipes quickly, Karla replied. "Here's sauerkraut cake with chocolate cream cheese frosting."

Kathy turned to me and held out her cup. "Quick, I need more coffee."

Mary had overheard Kathy's request and started laughing. The crowd soon joined her.

The laughter died as I rushed Kathy's coffee refill to the table. She looked up at me. "I'm not a sauerkraut fan, and the thought of it in cake…well, it's not appealing."

Desserts were obviously a hot topic, and nearly a third of the submissions were some variety of cake, bar, cookie, or crumble. The flavors varied from chocolate cakes to cherry tortes, with apricots, dates, nuts, and coconut in between. Discussion among the cookbook team and judges was intense, but polite. The standard recipes, like devil's food and chocolate cakes were quickly set aside, as were tollhouse cookies and 'better than sex' cake, although that title alone generated laughs and discussion.

Holding three cards, Karla quieted the crowd. "We're down to three recipes: Elsie Pasch submitted her recipe for giant salted espresso chocolate cookies. Jeri Westfall's recipe is Czech black magic cake. Mary submitted her ultimate gooey brownies."

Brian's head was shaking. "They all sound mouth watering. Please read each recipe, Karla."

Reading the recipes did little to differentiate them. The pastor leaned back. "I watched Jonathan Edwards revel in the telling of the derivation of a recipe he was preparing. Are the three ladies here? Could each of you tell the story behind your recipe?"

Elsie stepped forward. She was a large woman who looked like she really enjoyed food. It made me instinctively trust her ability to choose recipes. "I'm afraid there's not much story to the espresso chocolate cookie recipe. It was the top recipe of the year on a food magazine poll. I made the cookies, and they were a hit with my family. I've made them four or five times and people always rave about them."

Karla looked around the crowd. "Is Jeri Westfall here?"

Jeri was a petite woman with an engaging smile. She stepped forward. "My mother was in the hospital after my youngest sister was born and shared a room with a Czech woman. They were both in the room for several weeks and became close friends. After they recuperated, Mrs. Zingula invited our family over for dinner. She served us black magic cake for dessert. It was like white candy melted on top of a moist chocolate cake. My mother asked for the recipe, but Mrs. Zingula hesitated. The recipe had been created by her father for his bakery in Brno, and it was one of the few possessions her family had when they fled at the end of World War II. Then Mrs. Zingula cried, declared us her American family, and gave my mother the recipe."

Pastor Olafson's eyes were misty. "That's incredible, Mrs. Westfall." He hesitated. "Let's hear about the gooey brownies."

Mary, still sitting at the table, smiled. "There's not much story. I got the recipe out of the Mahtowa Covenant Church cookbook."

Karla smiled. "I think we have a winner with the black magic cake."

Jeri looked both pleased and embarrassed as people congratulated her. Our judges stood as Karla, Kathy, and Mary gathered the recipes. Brian nodded to a back corner of the dining room. Olafson, Brian, and I separated from the crowd and moved to the quiet corner with big windows overlooking Lake Superior. A lone ore boat moved across the water.

Ron Olafson put out his hand. "That wasn't so bad, was it Peter?"

The grin on Brian's face was cherubic, like always. "That was kind of fun."

"I can't thank you two enough for your willingness to take this on. You each defused some tense moments. I'm afraid the crowd would've been ugly if you hadn't spread oil on the waters."

Brian's eyes lit up. "What did the drop of oil say to the water?"

The pastor smiled. "I don't know."

"I can't mix with you guys."

I grimaced, but the pastor laughed.

Brian beamed. "I've got to run unless you need me for something else, Doc?"

Pastor Olafson looked confused. "Your nickname is Doc, Peter?"

Jumping in before I could explain, Brian blurted out, "Peter was a Navy corpsman in Iraq. He dragged a bunch of wounded Marines to safety and saved their lives."

I froze as my mind flashed back to the battlefield, IEDs exploding and the smell of burning gunpowder in the air. I felt a hand on my arm and looked down at Pastor Olafson's hand.

"Are you okay, Peter?"

"I'm fine. Just a momentary flashback."

The three of us shook hands and Brian left. I was about to excuse myself when the pastor stopped me. "I was a chaplain deployed with an Army unit during the first Iraq war. If you ever need someone to talk to…"

"Most of my demons are under control," I replied.

Olafson searched my eyes for a moment, then nodded. "I might benefit from a group therapy session as much as you. Please call."

"Have you met Kerry Stone, the police chief?" I asked.

"I don't recall his name, but I'm still struggling to remember the names of my deacons."

"He was badly burned in an IED explosion. I'll try to get the three of us together for coffee sometime."

"I have a coffee pot in my parish office, and we can close the door."

"Thanks, Pastor. I'll mention it to Kerry."

* * *

I returned to the dining room where Karla, Kathy, and Mary were flipping through recipe cards. "I need copies of the recipes you chose to share with the television people. We're meeting with the producer tomorrow."

Picking up a short stack of cards, Karla got up. "Let's use the copier in Nancy's office."

"There's a copier behind the reception desk," I said as Karla led me out of the dining room.

"Let's see if Nancy is in."

My mind raced, trying to remember some transgression from the judging. Unable to come up with anything, I braced myself for the worst. Nancy was reading an email on her computer. I closed the door after we stepped in.

Nancy gestured for us to sit in her guest chairs. "Hi, Karla. What can I do for you?"

"You should give Peter a gold star. The judges he chose were perfect. Between Pastor Olafson and Brian Johnson, we got through all the recipes without a major row or controversy."

Nancy smiled at me, her eyes twinkling. "Thanks for sharing that, Karla. I don't tell Peter how valuable and appreciated he is nearly enough. It means even more as an unsolicited comment from you."

"These are the recipes the judges chose for the television show." Karla handed Nancy the recipe cards. "Peter needs a copy of them for tomorrow's meeting with the cooking show producer."

Nancy accepted the cards and read through them before making copies. "These sound wonderful. I'm making extra copies for myself."

Karla looked uneasy. "I'm concerned that the death Peter and the police chief are investigating is tied to the upcoming television show. I wonder if we should warn the producer."

Handing the recipe cards to Karla, then giving me the copies, Nancy sat down. "What's your concern?"

"The whole town is simmering and I'm afraid the situation is going to boil over," Karla said. "The woman who was murdered cooked for Oscar's Lunch, taking all the recipes when the café closed. Oscar's family is arguing they were stolen. Reggie Sandberg always said Oscar gave them to her."

With raised eyebrows, Nancy looked at me. "I don't see a dispute over the ownership of recipes as a murder motive. Peter, what has the police chief told you?"

"I'm not at liberty to discuss Kerry's investigation. But, I can confirm that the victim's house was strewn with paper, including hundreds of recipe cards, and the recipe box is missing."

"Oscar was a widower who raised three children, two sons and a daughter.," Karla said. "I taught all of them when they were in school. Oscar's daughter is married and lives out of state. Both his sons live here in town. Ken is a real estate agent who was smart and level-headed. Joe was a poor student who enlisted after a couple run-ins with the local police. I heard he was deployed to Iraq. He was wounded and hasn't been able to work since his discharge. I've tried to speak to him a few times but he's distant and doesn't talk except to answer questions."

I wrinkled my nose. "If Joe is suffering from PTSD, he's more likely to hurt himself than someone else."

Karla nodded. "I witnessed a confrontation between Ken and Reggie Sandberg in the grocery store. He was agitated and demanded that she turn over the recipes. She said he'd had his chance to manage the café and passed it up. Oscar gave her the recipes because none of his children were interested in running the business."

Nancy leaned back. "Ken sold our house. I think if he'd wanted the recipes, he would've taken Reggie to court. He wouldn't have killed her."

Smiling, Karla stood. "I don't disagree. I don't think anyone would kill another person to steal a recipe, but not everyone is rational. Someone killed Reggie when she was about to reveal one of Oscar's secret recipes. That could make someone very angry."

"Thank you for sharing," Nancy said as she escorted us to the door. "I'm sure Peter will pass the information along to his friend, the police chief."

We walked out of Nancy's office and Karla put her hand on my arm. "Please don't mention my name when you pass this along."

"Chief Stone is very discreet."

I got another cup of coffee, planning to go back to my office and think about all that had happened. That plan ended when Wendy called my name from a back corner of the dining room.

"What's up?" I asked, pulling up a chair to the table where Wendy and Hulda were sitting.

The crossword puzzle was pushed aside, replaced by a pile of calendars. "What do you think about this style of calendar?" Wendy opened the first page of a calendar and passed it to me.

The picture featured a naked young woman milking a cow. The cow and her arms were strategically placed to cover her naked breasts. I slid the calendar back. "Why are you showing me this?"

"We're trying to decide on the style of photos we should use in the fundraising calendar.

Hulda opened another calendar and handed it to me." How about this 'Boots and Dudes' calendar?"

The shirtless cowboy in the picture glistened with sweat as he carried a saddle.

Thankfully, he was wearing jeans. I passed it back. "I haven't seen many cowboys in Two Harbors."

Hulda rolled her eyes. "Peter, we're not going to use cowboy pictures, I was trying to illustrate the style of photos we planned to use."

"There will be no calendar. We're doing a cookbook fundraiser."

I got up, but Wendy wasn't through. "You're obviously not on board with the calendar. You do the cookbook. Hulda and I will handle the calendar."

I raised my hands in surrender. "Whatever."

Safe in my office, I leaned back with my feet up, sipping coffee. I closed my eyes, trying to banish the vision of hunky, sweaty cowboys from my mind.

"Excuse me, are you Peter Rogers?"

I sat up, slopping coffee on my shirt and pants.

"Sorry, I didn't mean to startle you."

The woman standing in my doorway was twenty years too young to be a resident. She was attractive without makeup and had a touch of gray in her blonde hair. Wearing a flannel shirt and jeans, a woman who wasn't out to impress anyone, but was serious about life.

I dabbed at the coffee stains with a couple tissues. "Yes, I'm Peter. You caught me in a moment of deep contemplation."

"I'm Nola Saarvala. I think I've seen you around town."

I gestured for her to sit in my guest chair while I searched my memory. "I'm fairly new to Two Harbors. I don't think we've met."

"You don't recognize me out of uniform. I'm the assistant produce manager at the grocery store. I'm always wearing a hairnet and green apron."

"I think you want to talk to the cook if you're here about vegetables."

Nola leaned forward, resting her elbows on her knees. "Actually, I was told that you're the person I need to speak to. I'm going to open a Norwegian-themed restaurant. I just signed a lease on a building north of town and we're in the process of remodeling it."

"You chose a Norwegian theme? I'm not sure what that means."

"I plan to serve lutefisk year 'round, and there will be a lot of salmon and other fish on the menu. I'm working with one of the commercial fishermen and he's going to supply fresh herring and lake trout. His family is Norwegian, and he's given me a couple fish recipes. I'll also be serving pickled herring prepared in house."

"If you serve something other than pickled herring and lutefisk, I'll bring my wife to your restaurant when we have a date night."

"I plan to serve a lot of other dishes, which is why I'm here."

"I don't understand."

"I heard you're assembling an ethnic cookbook with a broad variety of recipes. I've been scouring the internet for ideas, but I think my local customers would prefer recipes from local cooks."

I smiled. "Norwegian comfort food. Recipes the local people grew up eating."

"Exactly!"

"Three of the residents have been gathering recipes. They've organized them into categories, and I think they're trying to find a printer to publish the cookbook."

Nola looked disappointed. "When will it be available?"

"I'm not sure. We'd like to have it done before Christmas, so people can give them as presents, but I don't know if that's possible."

"I'm planning my grand opening in a few days. Is there any way I can get the recipes now?"

"Um, not really. They've got stacks of recipe cards, but I'm sure they're days or weeks away from the finished product."

Nola reached into her back pocket and pulled out a folded stack of currency wrapped around her driver's license and a debit card. "I'd be happy to pay for a cookbook in advance if I could get copies of the recipes. How much are they going to cost?" She peeled off two twenty-dollar bills and held them out to me.

"I'm sorry. I can't sell you the recipes without talking to Karla Telker, the person who's coordinating the cookbook project."

"Can we talk to her now?"

I pulled up a list of residents and dialed Karla's phone. I put the call on speaker when she answered.

"Hi, Karla. I've got a lady in my office who'd like to buy a copy of the cookbook recipes."

"I spoke with a printer in Duluth and they're going to publish the cookbook next week, but I need to enter all the recipes into a computer file first. I've just started, so there won't be cookbooks I can sell for at least a few more days."

"Hi, Karla. This is Nola Saarvala. I'm opening a new restaurant in a few days and I'm planning to feature regional and ethnic recipes. I'd like to buy a copy of all the recipes now so I can include some of them on my menu."

"All I've got are loose recipe cards and I can't sell them to you. I'm sorry. You'll have to wait until the cookbook is published."

"That's too late. I'll gladly pay for a cookbook now if I can get a copy of the recipes."

"Peter, is there a way you can copy them?"

"There's a copier in the lobby, but it would take an hour and we usually charge five cents a page for copies."

Nola thought for a moment. "If you could scan them, I'll print them off my computer."

I waited for Karla to respond. "Peter, can you scan the recipe cards?"

"My printer has a scanner. If you bring the recipes down, I can scan them and email the file to Nola."

"I'll be down in five minutes."

I ended the call. "I'm not sure what Karla plans to charge for the cookbooks."

Nola held out the twenty-dollar bills. "Will forty dollars cover it?"

"You and Karla can negotiate the price."

Nola told me about her plans for the restaurant and the Norwegian fisherman while we waited for Karla. I smiled, but wondered how a menu of comfort food, heavy on herring, cod, and lake trout, would prosper in Two Harbors.

Karla swept into my office carrying her stacks of recipe cards. Nola jumped up to introduce herself, then cocked her head. "Mrs. Telker? You were my sixth-grade teacher."

"Yes, Nola Saarvala, how are you? I'm sorry but I don't remember your married name."

The sparkle left Saarvala's eyes. "I'm divorced and went back to my maiden name."

"Nola Saarvala it is. Please call me Karla, I'm way past having my students address me as Mrs. Telker."

"Okay Karla, Peter said you're the person coordinating the cookbook. I'm interested in copies of the recipes you've collected."

"They're intended for a fundraising project."

Nola nodded. "I understand and I'm more than happy to pre-pay for a cookbook if I can get the recipes now."

"The recipes are sorted into categories and each group is held with a rubber band." She handed me a stack. "These are the entrées."

I set the cards on the scanner two at a time, with Karla handing them to me as fast as the scanner cycled. Nola read the recipes as they came off the scanner and bound them in their stacks.

"These are wonderful!" Nola declared as she flipped through several rice pudding recipes. "Grandma Anderson made a stirred rice pudding like this. And Grandma Saarvala made this Finnish pulla bread. I've never seen a recipe for pulla before."

The scanning process went quickly with the three of us working together and I put all the scanned documents into a single file. "Nola, give me your email address."

I sent the file to Nola as she and Karla gathered the last cards into a pile. "I hope this goes well for you."

Nola got up and hugged Karla, then jammed forty dollars into her hand. "I hope this is enough to pay for the first cookbook."

Karla looked at the cash. "I think we were going to sell the cookbooks for eighteen dollars."

Nola leaned down and hugged me in my chair. "Let me know when they're ready and I'll pick up two of them."

Nola's phone chimed and she looked at the screen. "The email is here. Hang on while I open the attachment." She ran her finger over the screen and after a few seconds she smiled. "It's here and the recipes opened. Thank you."

Karla watched Nola leave, then turned to me. "If energy is enough to make her restaurant successful, she's going to be a millionaire."

"You're comfortable selling her the recipes?"

"Why not? They're all going to be in a cookbook in a week." Karla peeked outside my door, then closed it behind her. "I remember Nola. Her grandfather was the Two Harbors blacksmith, and her father took over the business and transformed it into a machine shop. I think he made parts for broken machines all over town and on the Iron Range. Nola and her brother were mediocre students who were never engaged in their lessons. I had the impression they'd planned to go into business and felt studying history and English was a waste of time.

"Nola had an extra burden because she started to develop physically before most of her peers. That brought undue, but not unwanted, attention from the boys. I think there were high school boys trying to date her by the time she was in seventh grade. She was bullied by the other girls and called all kinds of names. She moved away as soon as she graduated, which garnered rumors about a pregnancy. The last I heard she was working at a paper mill in International Falls until it went bankrupt."

"Did Billy take over the machine shop?"

"I don't think his father was ready to let go of the reins, so Billy opened a bait shop."

"He owns the bait shop?"

Karla laughed. "Billy's bait shop lasted two fishing seasons, then closed. I heard he wasn't a businessman and spent too much time drinking with his buddies in the back room. Fishermen go to the bait store for conversation, bait, *and* information. Billy didn't have the gift of gab, any interest in charming his customers, nor a head for figures. I heard he owed thousands of dollars in unpaid sales and income tax when he closed shop."

"Is he still around town?"

"Again, this is second-hand information, but I think he went to Las Vegas to make his fortune as a professional poker player."

"I think only mathematical geniuses do well at that. They don't drink, can count cards, and can calculate odds in their heads. An average guy, especially one who likes to drink, doesn't last long on the pro poker circuit."

"I don't know about that. I haven't heard anything about Billy in years."

"Is the machine shop still open?"

"The Saarvalas divorced twenty years ago and the shop closed shortly after that. I suspect Mrs. Saarvala got half the business, but her husband closed the shop rather than sending her half the profits every month. He passed away a couple years ago."

"I wonder where Nola is getting the money to open a restaurant?"

"I wonder if her Mom is putting up the money?"

I shook my head. "Maybe she got a Small Business Association loan."

Karla gathered her pile of recipes. "She's had a couple different failed businesses over the last decade. I doubt any bank in town would loan her the money. And I doubt Two Harbors can support another restaurant."

"Maybe she's banking on the tourist business."

Karla paused after opening the door. "We're half a year from the four-month tourist season. If that's her business plan, I wish her luck."

Karla left, but I felt just a touch uneasy about the recipe sale. I couldn't put my finger on the issue, but it nagged at me. The thought of someone profiting off the Whistling Pines recipe collection seemed wrong.

* * *

Jeremy was nibbling on a peanut butter sandwich and working on his homework when I got home. He looked up from the crumbs and worksheet. "What's for supper?"

"You're eating a sandwich. How can you be hungry?"

He sighed. "You say that every day, Dad."

"We have leftover Yankee pot roast. I'll put it in the oven, and we'll eat when your mother and Amy get home."

"I might need another sandwich before then."

I looked at the open bread bag, peanut butter jar, and dirty knife sitting on the kitchen counter. "I'm going to change. You have to put the bread and peanut butter away before I come back downstairs."

"Dad, I'm trying to finish my math."

"Do your math and clear the counter."

"Dad…"

I missed the last of his response as I climbed the stairs.

I was slipping into my jeans when I heard the doorbell chime. I was at the top of the stairs when Jeremy yelled, "Dad, there's someone here to see you."

Our shaggy neighbor was standing nervously in the kitchen when I rounded the corner. A tear in the elbow of his old parka exposed the white insulation.

"Hi," I said.

"Um, you used to live next door, right?"

"Yes, I rented the house before you."

"Um, the sink is, um, plugged. Do you know how to fix it?"

"I can take a look at it," I said as I put on boots and took my coat off the hook behind the door. "Jeremy, I'll be back in a couple minutes."

I followed the shaggy young man across the yard. He opened the door and a large dog of indeterminate lineage lunged past him. I recoiled, unsure if he was friendly or going to bite.

"Easy, Rambo," the guy said as the dog buried his nose in my crotch. "Don't worry. He's friendly."

I petted the dog's head and his tail wagged. After sniffing my crotch for a few seconds, he looked up at me. His coat was short and brindle, like a boxer, but his face and ears looked like a Labrador. I bent down and ruffled his ears, making his tail slap against the door frame.

"The kitchen's back here," the guy said, apparently forgetting I'd lived in the house and knew where all the rooms were.

I followed him through the hallway, noting clothing strewn around the furniture. I danced around scattered shoes and boots inside the door. In the kitchen, the table and counters were covered with dirty dishes and the smell of not quite rotten food emanated from an overflowing wastebasket.

"Here's the stopped-up sink."

Chunks of food floated in several inches of water. I flipped the disposal switch, and nothing happened.

"Yeah, the disposal quit. I think that's why it's plugged up."

I opened the cabinet door under the sink and ran my finger under the bottom of the disposal until I felt the reset button. I pushed it, then stood and flipped the disposal switch. The growl of the disposal started, the water swirled, then sucked down. I turned on the water and rinsed the sink.

"What'd you do? It was like, magical."

I knelt, which caught Rambo's attention. He raced across the kitchen and knocked me over. "Easy, pal." I reached under the disposal as my shaggy neighbor bent over. "There's a red reset button on the bottom of the disposal. Just push and release it."

"Is that all that was wrong?"

"I think so."

"Thanks, man." The shaggy guy hesitated. "Um, have we been bothering you guys with the music?"

"It's been great. Thanks for keeping it down at night."

"I, ah…" he stared at the floor. "We used to practice in my folks' garage. We always had to shut down at like nine o'clock. I just figured if we were in our own rental house, we could rock all night and no one would bitch."

"You can, but we've got a baby who wakes up if your music is too loud late at night."

"You didn't have to call the cops on us."

"I didn't. The police chief is a friend, and he was visiting when I came over to talk to you." I took a step toward the door, then hesitated and put out my hand. "I'm Peter Rogers."

His handshake was like a limp fish. "Tim. My buddy is Roger."

"Who are the other folks?"

Tim shrugged. "Mostly guys we hang out with. Or girlfriends."

I walked to the door and rubbed Rambo's head. "Let me know if you need help with anything else." I noticed a guitar leaning against the television. "Are you a guitar player?"

"Yeah, Mick and me play guitar. Roger plays bass."

I picked up the guitar and played the opening riff to "Classical Gas", a piece written for solo guitar. I set the guitar back and looked at Tim, whose mouth was gaping.

"Would you like to jam with us? That was awesome."

I shook my head. "No thanks."

"Are you a professional? I mean, that was epic."

"I'm the recreation director for Whistling Pines. My wife Jenny is a nurse."

Tim followed me to the door, and I paused. "I get that you need to practice. I do it all the time. But please keep the volume down late at night."

Tim stood in the doorway as I walked out. "Do you play anything else?"

"Some piano, flute, piccolo, saxophone, and clarinet. I'm learning the accordion."

Tim was awestruck. "Wow."

Jenny pulled into the driveway, so I said goodbye to Tim and watched Jenny unbuckle Amy's infant seat. "You met our neighbor?"

"Tim's sink was clogged, so I showed him how to reset the disposal."

Jenny pulled Amy's carrier out of the car. "I wish she'd sleep as well in her crib as she does in the car."

I opened the door for her. "I'm unwilling to drive around all night so you can sleep."

Jenny smiled as she slipped off her boots. "Supper smells heavenly. What are we having?"

"Leftover pot roast."

She handed Amy's carrier to me. "I think your pot roast is better the second day. I'm going to change clothes. I'll be right back."

Jeremy put away his homework, cleaned up the crumbs, and set the table while I pulled the pot roast out of the oven and scooped it into a serving bowl. Amy was still asleep, which meant we were trading a quiet supper for a sleepless night.

Jeremy was unusually quiet. He usually gave us a running commentary of his day, but he seemed deep in thought. "What's up, Bud?"

He pushed a piece of potato around in the gravy while he thought. "Jacob said his dad likes to talk to you about the woman who was killed."

The comment caught me off guard.

Jenny saw my hesitation and answered. "I don't think his father likes to talk about the dead woman; I think Chief Stone appreciates your dad's input on things that are troubling him. There aren't many people who die in Two Harbors. This is a big deal and your dad makes a good sounding board."

"What's a sounding board?"

I swallowed a bite and replied. "A sounding board is someone you trust and can give you feedback on ideas. I use your mom as a sounding board for some of the ideas I have about work. She listens to my ideas and then tells me what she likes and doesn't like about them. I'm that sounding board for Chief Stone."

"What kind of ideas does he ask about?"

"He doesn't really have questions. He tells me what he's thinking about his investigation, and I can sometimes suggest things he hasn't considered."

"Like what?"

"I can't answer that. He tells me things in confidence."

"Secrets?"

"They're not secrets as much as things he doesn't want many people to know."

"Isn't that what a secret is?"

Jenny reveled in my discomfort and hid her smile. "Things said in confidence are more than secrets. They're the kind of things people would tell their minister because you want his thoughts and feedback, but you know he won't ever tell anyone."

Jeremy frowned. "Like what?"

I searched for an age-appropriate example. "Let's say you got mad at Jacob and broke his pencil. You might feel bad afterwards because he doesn't have another one. So, you could discuss it with Pastor Olafson and he might tell you what he thinks you should do, but he wouldn't tell anyone about your conversation."

Jeremy's look told me I'd muddied the waters. "I wouldn't break Jacob's pencil. He's my friend."

"Okay, you broke someone else's pencil, maybe a girl in your class. Then you'd see Pastor Olafson to ask for his opinion about what you should do."

"What if he said I had to do something hard?"

"That's exactly what he might say, something hard for you to do, but he'd tell you what he thought was a proper response to breaking a pencil. You'd hear what he has to say and then you'd have to decide if that was what you thought was right and if you could do it."

"Like what?"

"He might tell you to apologize and give her a new pencil to replace the broken one."

"That's probably what I'd do." Jeremy hesitated. "But if he told me to kiss her, I'd say, no."

"There you go. You've got two possible answers and you've decided which you'd be willing to accept. I do the same thing with Chief Stone. I tell him what I think, and he decides which, if any of my ideas he likes and is willing to accept."

"Don't you get mad if he doesn't like your ideas?"

"Not at all. I know he's trying to decide what to do and I'm offering suggestions he may or may not want."

"You don't do that with me. You tell me what I have to do, then you yell at me if I don't do it."

"First of all, I don't yell. I talk earnestly. Secondly, I'm not your sounding board, I'm your dad. I'm usually explaining the rules and boundaries I expect you to follow."

"Can I use you as a sounding board?"

"Sure. I'd be happy to listen to your ideas and comment on them. What would you like me to consider?"

Jeremy thought as he ate a carrot. "I want your thoughts on changing my bedtime to nine o'clock."

"I think you'd be very tired in the morning and wouldn't be able to concentrate at school."

"I'm considering your input." He paused. "I'll be able to concentrate without any problems, so I think I'll stay up until nine tonight. Is that how having a sounding board works?"

Jenny raised her eyebrows, awaiting my wise response. "As your sounding board, I think that's a poor decision, and I recommend reconsidering a nine o'clock bedtime. As your father, who makes the rules, I'll say your bedtime will remain at eight o'clock until you're in seventh grade."

"Dad! You just told me a sounding board wouldn't tell me what to do."

"I also told you I made the rules and decided what's best. Dad's rules trump a sounding board's suggestions."

Jeremy glared at me.

"Let's try a different example. I could be your sounding board about whether to play baseball or be a runner in a track meet. I'd give you my opinions about each sport and you can decide which you'd rather be in."

"That's because choosing a sport isn't a rule."

"Right. It's like I wouldn't tell Chief Stone to let people drive faster than the speed limit through town, because that would be asking him to let people break a rule. On the other hand, I might tell him to think about talking to a teacher who's not giving enough homework to her students. There are no homework rules or laws, but he might encourage her to give more homework because it would help her students."

Jeremy finished his last bite of carrot and pushed his plate back. "I don't like that example. I already have too much homework. Can I be excused?"

I excused Jeremy to leave the table and watch television. Jenny pushed her plate away and smiled. "Nicely handled, Dad."

"I never realized being a dad was such a cerebral experience."

"Just wait until you get into the 'why' circle with Amy."

"What's a 'why circle?'"

"Every time you give an answer the child asks, why?"

"Huh?"

"It's a toddler thing. When you tell them something they don't like, they ask you why, over and over."

I stacked our dirty plates. "That's something to look forward to."

Amy cried as I was clearing the glasses from the table. Jenny got up and smiled at me. "We got to eat a whole meal together."

"And now it's Amy's turn to eat."

Jeremy washed dishes and I wiped. I was putting away the last dish when the doorbell rang. I was surprised to see our neighbor, Tim, and a young woman on the doorstep. He had an acoustic guitar in his hand.

"Um, Peter, would you play that riff for Zoey? You know, the one you played this afternoon after you fixed the sink."

I waved them into the house. "Hi Zoey, I'm Peter. Nice to meet you."

Zoey was dressed in a retro dress with bangles that reminded me of my mother, who jangled everywhere she went. Zoey's hair was henna red, and her fingernail polish was black.

Jenny heard the voices in the kitchen and walked in to see who was visiting.

"Jenny, these are our neighbors Tim and Zoey."

Jenny smiled and said hi.

Zoey's eyes were fixed on Amy. "Is she the baby our music was waking up?"

"This is Amy, and her sleep patterns are irregular. We're struggling to get her to sleep through the night."

Zoey walked to Jenny and put her finger in Amy's hand. "She's so tiny. How old is she?"

"She's five months old. Would you like to hold her?"

Zoey's eyes lit up. "Can I?"

Jenny passed Amy.

"I used to babysit a boy about this age."

I took Tim's guitar and sat on a kitchen chair. I adjusted the tuning, then plucked "Classical Gas".

Tim watched me, then watched Zoey, who was bouncing Amy and cooing to her. "Isn't this epic?"

Zoey nodded but was obviously more interested in Amy than the music. I moved on to "Light my Fire", another great, challenging guitar solo. Tim watched my fingers on the frets and nodded with the beat.

Amy started getting fussy and Zoey handed her back to Jenny. "Peter, how about something a little less…"

I nodded and picked, "And I Love Her", the Beatles ballad.

Tim's eyes went between my fingers, my face, and Zoey. "Man, you know all these by heart. That's rad. Wow."

I finished the song and handed the guitar back to Tim. "Concert's over."

"Are you sure you wouldn't play a gig with us?"

"My plate is full."

Zoey looked at Jenny. "I'm really sorry we woke Amy up. It won't happen again."

"Thank you. We appreciate it and I hope we can be good neighbors, too."

Tim nodded. "Peter fixed our disposal. That was incredible."

We all said goodbye. Jenny closed the door and smiled. "Do you think we were ever that young and naïve?"

I smiled and pecked her cheek. "One of us got pregnant when she was nineteen and the other believed he'd see the world by joining the Navy. Yes, we were that naïve once."

"Would you change any of those decisions?"

"I would've skipped Iraq."

"Then you wouldn't have met me."

"I suppose I'd be teaching music to middle school kids in a little town somewhere. That might cause a different kind of PTSD." I took a breath. "I wouldn't change anything that brought us together. You know that."

Jenny handed Amy to me. "Sing her a lullaby while I get Jeremy ready for bed."

Amy and I settled in the rocking chair, a baby gift from Jenny's parents. I hummed "Brahms' Lullaby" and rocked. Amy smiled and cooed for a few minutes, then closed her eyes. The next thing I knew, Jenny was gently lifting Amy from my arms. "Wake up so you can go to bed."

The clock on the cable box showed ten o'clock. I'd been asleep for over an hour. I drew a deep breath and stood. "It's wrong to wake someone and tell them to go to bed," I whispered as we climbed the stairs.

"I could've left you in the rocking chair until the alarm went off."

"That wouldn't have been a good option. My joints get a little cranky if I sit in the same position for a long time."

With Amy in bed, I followed Jenny to the bedroom. She slipped under the covers while I changed out of my jeans and sweatshirt. "Are your joints achy from rolling around inside a Humvee flying through the air?"

"I don't know. Maybe it's just part of aging."

I pulled the covers over my shoulders and spooned into Jenny's back. I pecked her ear and closed my eyes.

"You used to get frisky after Jeremy was asleep."

"I've prioritized sleep over friskiness since Amy arrived."

Jenny laced her fingers into mine and squeezed them tight. "Imagine that, a sailor who's more interested in sleep than making love. I'll have to post that on Facebook."

"Go ahead. No one will believe it."

Chapter Seven

Day 4

A weather front came through overnight, leaving a thin dusting of snow on my windshield. Instead of the usual scraping of frost, I wiped my glove across the glass and the fluffy flakes swirled away. Amy had slept for four hours before her only feeding of the night and other than the sensation of Jenny moving, I'd slept nearly seven hours. It was the first uninterrupted sleep I'd had since Amy's birth. I felt refreshed as I drove through town, the sleep and fresh coating of snow lifted my spirits.

I hung up my coat, turned on the computer, then walked to the dining room with my coffee mug. The room was nearly full and the chatter from dozens of voices filled the air. I scanned the room, feeling good about the comfortable dining environment. That was a change from some mornings when a controversy resulted in raised, angry voices.

"Do you have a moment?" Howard Johnson asked. He nodded toward the empty open atrium near the aviary.

"Good morning, Howard."

"There aren't bags under your eyes. I take it you got some rest last night."

"Is it that noticeable?"

Howard led me to a table covered with pieces of a jigsaw puzzle. The border had been completed along with a bottom corner. "You put up a good front, but your tail has been dragging for months. You're doing your job, but some of your sparkle has been missing."

"And Jenny?"

Always diplomatic, Howard paused, then said, "It's tough being a new mom."

"Did you just want to comment on my appearance and performance?"

"No, there's the issue of the calendar."

"I thought enough cold water had been thrown on that idea to kill it."

Chuckling, Howard leaned back. "The calendar project has momentum."

"I'll talk to Nancy…"

Howard put up his hand. "Let them have their fun. It's not going to hurt anyone, and the ladies seem to be having a good time."

"Adult children and grandchildren will be mortified if a calendar shows up with naked grandmothers standing behind strategically placed flowers."

Howard stood and put his hand on my shoulder. "Just think of the poor photographer who has to arrange the flowers." He was about to step away, then paused. "Even if they get to the point of taking the photos, they're going to look through them and saner heads will prevail. In the meanwhile, let them have their fun."

As usual, Howard, the self-appointed Whistling Pines mayor, had quietly informed me of something controversial but gave me the perspective required to deal with it. In this case, his message was clear—let the excitement die out. It was not something worth my attention and worry.

I refilled my coffee and saw Karla, Mary, and Kathy at a back-corner table shuffling through papers. I threaded my way past the diners and sat in the fourth chair at their table.

"Good morning, ladies. How's the cookbook going?"

Karla had a laptop computer open and looked a bit haggard. "I've transcribed the recipes and now we're checking them for typos and mistakes."

Kathy had a printed sheet of paper in one hand and a recipe card in the other. "Karla, you transposed the half teaspoon and tablespoon amounts of salt and sugar in this cornbread recipe."

Karla paged through the computer to the recipe and studied it for a moment. "Good catch. That wouldn't have been good at all." She made the change, then looked at me. "The teaspoons and tablespoons will be the death of me."

Mary held up a recipe card. "Here's another. I can't tell if Millie wanted a teaspoon or tablespoon of ginger powder in her gingerbread recipe. The Ts are all the same size for her small measures."

Karla and Kathy both slid their chairs over and looked at the handwritten recipe. Kathy shook her head. "It has to be a tablespoon of ginger powder and a teaspoon of vanilla extract. Don't you agree?"

"It is gingerbread," Mary said, studying the recipe card. "It's got to be a tablespoon of ginger."

Karla slid back to the computer and scrolled to the gingerbread recipe. "I'm going to change it to a tablespoon. Good catch."

I stood, happy I hadn't been drafted to help. "I need copies of the three recipes we chose for consideration by the television show. We're meeting with the producer at ten this morning."

Karla jerked her head up. "Oh, I set them aside. Um, where are they?"

Mary stifled a smile. "You put them under the computer."

Rolling her eyes, Karla lifted the laptop and handed the three recipe cards to me. "I swear, if I didn't carry my driver's license, I'd forget my own name."

I leaned over the table and lowered my voice, "The three of you are some of the sharpest knives in this drawer."

Kathy smiled and shook her head. "I guess that doesn't say much about the rest of the folks."

I put my hand on her shoulder. "Think of Hulda."

Karla put up her hand. "Now Peter, I don't know that we're any sharper than Hulda. We may have a better filter between our brains and mouths, but we're probably having the same thoughts."

"You are the queen of diplomacy, Karla."

Karla shook her head. "No, Mary's the queen. I'm just a princess."

Kathy was halfway through a sip of coffee and choked. After coughing, she broke into laughter. "I don't think Karla qualifies as a princess. She used to be Snow White, but she drifted."

Karla shook her head. "I was a bit of a wild middle child, back in the day."

All three broke into laughter. Dozens of heads turned to see what was so funny.

I put up my hands. "I refuse to confirm or deny." Then I remembered Meg's comment about the producer's request for more outrageous recipes. "I'd like to bring the fish aspic recipe along."

Kathy frowned while Mary flipped through the recipe cards. "Why bring the aspic recipe? It sounds disgusting."

"I guess they like to have one unusual recipe for each show."

Mary held out a recipe card to me. "Well, this certainly fits that category."

I'd barely started reading my overnight emails when I noticed someone behind me. "Peter, do you have a moment?"

Gretchen Taft closed my door and sat in the guest chair. She was most known for the varied color of her hair. Over the years she'd gone from shades of blonde and strawberry blonde to bolder colors. This month she'd chosen a shade I'd describe as lilac.

"You look troubled."

Gretchen drew a deep breath and let it out slowly. "You're going to meet with the television people today, correct?"

"Yes, I'm bringing the recipes we've chosen to a meeting with the television show's producer."

"You know that Jonathan Edwards is originally from town, right?"

"I've heard that's why he's decided to broadcast his Christmas show from here."

"And, you know Jonathan is not his given name?"

"I've also heard that. I think a lot of Hollywood people assume stage names when they start television and movie careers."

"My daughter, Brenda, went to school with him when he was Donny Koloski. He dated Brenda's best friend, Cate Willard." Gretchen glanced at the door as if she expected someone to barge in. "Cate came to our house in tears in the spring of their senior year. She and Brenda hid upstairs for hours, until I invited Cate down to have dinner with us. After Cate went home, I asked Brenda why Cate had been crying. She said it was a secret and wouldn't discuss it until I heard that Cate's twin sister, CeeCee, was pregnant."

"Let me guess; the father was Donny."

Gretchen nodded. "Donny left town with his band before the news spread. The ladies' club said the day after he got CeeCee's news, he moved to avoid a shotgun marriage. Brenda told me the evening of crying was after Cate found out about the one-night stand between CeeCee and Donny. CeeCee's boyfriend had dumped her, and she let Donny 'console' her."

"And he consoled her right into the backseat of his car."

"Something like that. CeeCee and Cate's family was Catholic, so an abortion was out of the question. Against her parents wishes, CeeCee decided to keep the baby and her father threw her out. She moved into an apartment and worked at the feed mill." Gretchen looked at me earnestly. "She met a nice guy, like you, who married her and adopted her daughter. They had three more children and they still live here in town."

"So, Jonathan is a shit who left his girlfriend's sister with a bastard child to raise on her own. I expect that's not a unique story for the Hollywood and television crowd."

Gretchen nodded. "That's California, not Two Harbors."

"What are you saying?"

"A lot of people around here know that story and don't think much of Jonathan Edwards."

"I respect that."

"You're not getting the drift. They REALLY dislike him. I don't want you to get caught in the blowback of his appearance here."

"Do you think his life is at risk?"

"I doubt anyone would kill him, but tar and feathers aren't out of the question."

I laughed. "I don't know that anyone's been tarred and feathered since the 1700s."

Gretchen got up slowly and stopped with her hand on the doorknob. "So, what's the twenty-first century equivalent of tar and feathers?" She opened the door and walked out.

I stared at the open door considering the question. *What is the twenty-first century equivalent of tar and feathers?*

The phone jarred me back to reality. I answered without looking at the caller ID.

"Peter, we're going to meet with the producer in the VFW." Meg's voice was distinctive and authoritative.

"I thought you were going to use one of the Lutheran churches."

"The VFW is neutral ground. I didn't want to start off with a battle between the Swedish Lutheran Church and Norwegians at the Norwegian Lutheran Church.

"Thanks for letting me know. I have the time on my computer calendar but no location."

"Have you chosen some recipes?"

"We narrowed it down to three."

Meg chuckled. "Did the process involve yelling or a fistfight?"

"I enlisted Pastor Olafson and Brian Johnson as judges. There were a few pointed comments about the *correct* recipe for a few dishes, but the judges kept things under control."

"More importantly, they kept you from being the bad guy."

"That too."

"You heard about Reggie Sandberg?"

"I did."

"She was going to bring a surprise recipe to the meeting. That's obviously not going to happen anymore. I had to make a couple calls to find a replacement."

"Who'd you find?"

"Rolf Atkinson is bringing his recipe for fried herring roe in caper butter." I must've groaned out loud because Meg's hearty laugh came over the phone. "I've heard it's very tasty."

"I guess herring isn't one of my favorite foods and anything made from herring isn't going to resonate with me."

"This isn't herring, it's herring eggs."

"You're not making it any more tempting."

Meg roared with laughter. "I'll see you at ten."

* * *

The VFW parking lot was nearly empty, few vets inclined to visit in the morning. Opening at eleven, the kitchen offered one bargain-priced entrée and one sandwich. Membership requirements had been suspended to attract a bigger crowd as the World War II vets died off and the number of vets from subsequent conflicts were fewer in number.

Vern, the bartender, who years before had arranged for my Whistling Pines interview, was wiping glasses behind the bar. He'd been with the VFW since returning from Vietnam. He winked at me and nodded toward the large round table in the back corner. Meg Cochran was seated with Kerry, a woman with Asian features, and two other people I recognized but didn't know by name.

Meg nodded and I circled to the empty chair next to Kerry, who was seated so he could watch the door. "Peter has the recipes from Whistling Pines. Jackie Pearson

124

coordinates the county fair baking competition, and Elena Svoboda teaches cooking at the high school. Ellen Vang is the *World's Eats* show producer, from Los Angeles."

I shook everyone's hand, noting that Ellen was dressed in a dark blazer and ivory blouse. Aside from Kerry, who was in uniform, the rest of the people around the table were in business casual attire.

Vern brought a coffee pot and cup to the table. He poured a cup for me, then refilled the other cups. Ellen looked at him, then glanced at the bar. "I don't suppose you could pour a shot of Courvoisier into my cup."

Looking around the table, Vern asked, "Does anyone else need an eye opener?"

We all shook our heads and he retreated to the bar. Ellen pulled a leather portfolio out of her shoulder bag and opened it. "I understand you've accumulated some recipes for potential use on the show. The ground rules are these: The recipes will be posted on the show's website and the production company owns the rights to the recipes and the images of the people who appear on the show. We'll feature three recipes and cooks. Each cook has to be conversant in English, well-mannered, respectful, and photogenic. Do those rules pose a problem for any of your cooks?"

Vern delivered a lowball glass containing a half-inch of brown liquid. Ellen nodded her thanks and poured it into her coffee. She took a swallow, closed her eyes, then let a breath out slowly, now prepared for the rest of the meeting.

Meg nodded to Vern. "On my tab."

Ellen took a smaller sip of coffee and set her cup down. "I apologize. I'm still on California time and my flight got in late last night. I didn't realize how long it took to drive from Minneapolis to Two Harbors until I put the address into my phone."

"You didn't fly into Duluth?" Meg asked.

"I looked at a map and Duluth is nearly in Canada."

Kerry glanced at me with his half-face smile. "And we're closer to Canada than Duluth is."

"I know that now." Ellen glared at him. "And the overnight blizzard was the icing on the cake. I tried to get someone to install tire chains in some place, maybe Pine City. The pimply-faced kid in the service station laughed at me."

Kerry was enjoying Ellen's monologue. "Chains are illegal on Minnesota highways."

"Chains are illegal? How in hell do you drive around when it snows?"

"It's snowed in Two Harbors every month of the year except July," Kerry said. "We've just learned how to drive in it."

The producer looked at Elena Svoboda. "It must be difficult to have continuity in your lesson plans with all the school snow days."

"We lost a few days this year, but the schools only close when the snow drifts are too deep for the buses to get through. Most snowy days we just delay the opening until ten o'clock so the plows can clear and sand the roads."

Kerry was preparing additional comments, but Meg put her hand on his arm. "Let's discuss the recipes, okay?"

Ellen looked at her pad and tapped her pen. "We like recipes with a backstory, not anything off the internet. Jonathan said there's a lot of ethnic diversity here and he'd like to tap into that." Ellen paused, looking at our faces. "I don't see a lot of diversity represented here."

Elena looked shocked. "My family is Slovakian. Meg's English. Jackie is Swedish. I think Chief Stone is Welsh. I don't know Peter's ethnicity."

"But you're all White."

Meg leaned back. "I think a brief history lesson is in order. Two Harbors was originally a fishing community, established by Norwegian immigrants. After the discovery of iron ore on the Mesabi Range, miners arrived from eastern Europe and Scandinavia to work in the mines and to build and man the railroads. As a way of keeping the workers from unionizing, the

127

mine owners assigned crews who didn't speak the same language. The towns built across the region had ethnic neighborhoods with people who spoke the same non-English language and cooked foods from their home countries. We may all have white complexions, but we're as different as Chinese people are from Koreans and Japanese."

Ellen considered that, then nodded. "Okay, give me examples of some ethnic foods."

Svoboda smiled. "Pasties are a savory filled pie crust. Each ethnic group had a version of that recipe. They look the same, but depending on their ethnic origin, they can be filled with veal, lamb, beef, pork, onion, potatoes, rutabaga, or any combination of the above."

I chuckled and everyone looked at me. "And heaven forbid you ask for a pasty served with gravy."

Ellen looked confused.

"Most ethnicities eat them without any condiment, or they use ketchup." Mary smiled at me. "Only Protestants and heathens want gravy."

Picking up her pen, Ellen wrote pastry. "So, you have a pastry recipe for me."

Elena Svoboda shook her head. "No, no. It's pronounced like nasty. The nasty pasty."

Ellen looked annoyed. "Okay, give me the nasty pasty recipe."

Meg's eyes sparkled. "We don't have one."

"But you just said they're a favorite ethnic food. I think that's exactly what we'd like for the show."

Returning with the coffee pot, Vern poured and explained. "We can't choose one pasty recipe for the show. There are dozens, maybe hundreds, of pasty recipes. Everyone thinks their recipe is the *correct* and only one. You'd risk an insurrection if you had a Slovenian guest cooking her pasty recipe. The people with Cornish, German, Slovak, and Scottish recipes would boo and throw rotten eggs." He looked around the table, grinning. Meg nodded emphatically.

Ellen gripped her coffee cup tightly, tossing down the last of the liquid quickly, she handed the empty cup to Vern. "Cognac without the coffee."

Kerry leaned close to me and whispered, "She's going to need a designated driver."

Overhearing us, Meg pointed to herself and nodded.

"Okay, pasties are out," the producer said as she put a line through the note. "Give me a non-controversial ethnic food."

I flipped through the recipes I'd brought to the meeting. "One of the Whistling Pines recipes is for Irish stew with Guinness stout. The recipe came to this country with a family from Scotland. Jodi McCallie serves it with soda bread."

Ellen made a note but looked troubled. "Stew is so…passé. Do you have some other ethnic options?"

"A Finnish 'pulla' cardamon bread won the county fair baking competition in 2009. Sandy Ahonen said it was a recipe her grandparents brought from the old country."

Ellen made a note but hesitated. "Bread making is slow. It doesn't really fit well into a short television segment. What else do you have?"

Jackie Pearson leaned her elbows on the table. "Mary Beth Johnson's beet pickles won at the county and state fair, but she won't share the recipe."

The producer started to write, then paused. "The recipes are published on our website. Besides, pickles take too much time to prepare." Ellen pulled out her cell phone and touched the screen. "Jonathan had a suggestion. Let me look at his email."

Vern brought Ellen a cup that I assumed contained only cognac. He topped off the rest of our coffee cups while Ellen paged through her emails.

"Here it is. Jonathan says his grandmother used to make something called poteka. Does anyone have that recipe on their list?"

"Hang on," Elena Svoboda said as she flipped through her notes. "One of my teachers suggested poteka. It's a recipe for a nut-filled Slovenian bread her grandmother used to make."

Ellen made a note. "Since this was submitted by a teacher, I assume she speaks English and has something dressier than jeans and a sweatshirt to wear."

"Hailey Evers teaches English, is attractive, and dresses professionally."

"Perfect!" the producer exclaimed, circling poteka on her notepad. "We have an ethnic food."

We all sipped coffee while Ellen threw back her cognac like a cowboy drinking whiskey in an old-time western. I slid the Irish stew recipe to the bottom of my stack.

"Okay," Ellen said. She looked at the bar and raised her cup, signaling for another shot. "We try to have one outrageous dish and one dessert on each show. What've you got in those categories?"

I pulled out the Polish fish aspic recipe and was about to speak when Meg's booming voice cut me off. "I don't know what the rest of you have for outrageous recipes, but I was approached by a local commercial fisherman who'd like us to consider his recipe for Norwegian fried herring roe in butter sauce."

Ellen cocked her head. The recipe intrigued her. "Is herring roe like caviar?"

"Well, sort of. Rolf said he collects the roe sacs from the herring when he cleans them. They're not cured like caviar, just the fresh egg sacs. He batters and fries the roe in butter and spices, then serves them on dark bread with butter sauce drizzled on top."

Ellen coughed like she had something stuck in her throat. She took the cup of cognac from Vern's hand and threw it back, savoring the burn. She closed her eyes, then looked up at the bartender. "I'll need another."

Vern looked at Meg, who nodded and mouthed *I'm driving.*

Ellen wrote herring roe and looked around. "Does anyone have something equally…disgusting?"

"I have a recipe for a Polish aspic made from fish broth. It's served with cubes of cooked fish, carrots, and hard-boiled eggs in fish broth gelatin."

Coughing erupted around the table and Kerry leaned close. "That's really a thing?"

"I couldn't make that up."

Ellen appeared to be gagging. She looked frantically for Vern, who trotted to the table with a glass of brown liquid. Ellen swished it in her mouth before swallowing it. "I think that tops the live baby octopus Jonathan ate in Korea. He asked me to never do that to him again." She tapped her pen on the paper. "I think the herring roe might fit the bill. Tell me about Rolf. How will he look on television?"

"He'll be a hoot," Meg said. "He's a first generation Norwegian-American, so he speaks with a pleasing Norwegian accent. He's a hulking guy with wild blond hair, piercing blue eyes, and a face ruddy from years of fishing on Lake Superior. I've never seen him in anything but a flannel shirt, but it fits his persona perfectly."

Ellen smiled. "It'll look like the segment we did in Sweden with the fishermen and farmers. Jonathan liked the optics of that segment a lot."

We all watched while the producer made notes. Kerry leaned close. "What do you have left of the Whistling Pines recipes?"

I held out the black magic cake and Christmas rice pudding recipes for him to read. "I don't think the Swedish rice pudding has a chance, but the Czech cake might be a winner."

Ellen completed her notes about Rolf. "We usually prepare something sweet, like a dessert. What do you have?"

"Czech black magic cake," I blurted out before anyone else could speak.

"What is it?"

"A retired woman submitted a recipe her mother got from a Czech woman while she was recovering from childbirth. It's a moist chocolate cake. Holes are poked in the top and then warm frosting is spread so it seeps into the holes. I'm told it's like eating a candy bar."

Ellen smiled and made notes. "So, it's a wonderful recipe and it has a story. Tell me about the woman who submitted it."

"She's a delightful petite woman with a sparkling personality."

Ellen continued to make notes. "Does anyone have something better?"

Joan Pearson looked through her recipes. "I have a pudding cake that won the county fair competition in 2017. It's cake and pudding mixes combined to make a heavenly moist cake."

Ellen wrinkled her nose. "It's made from boxed mixes?"

Joan read the recipe. "Yes. It's very simple, and it'd be easy to make on the show."

Ellen looked at me. "Is the black magic cake from a mix?"

I picked up the recipe. "It's cake flour, cocoa, eggs…"

Ellen stopped me. "We're using that black magic cake, the fried herring roe, and the poteka." She closed her notebook. "Let's look at the potential venues."

Chapter Eight

Meg stood. "I thought the VFW would be a nice spot. The kitchen is this way."

Ellen closed her portfolio and stood. Sitting across the table and watching the amount of cognac she'd consumed, I expected her to either stagger or puke. She did neither, making me wonder if she was a hardcore drinker with an incredible tolerance.

Setting his newspaper aside, Vern walked to the kitchen door and held it open. Ellen stopped at the door, looking at the long galley where three women were preparing to serve lunch.

Ellen shook her head. "This won't work. There's no room for the camera crews to set up. Take me to the next place."

Meg gestured toward the front door. "The next two places are Lutheran churches across the street from each other."

The comment caught Ellen by surprise. "Why do you have back-to-back churches?"

"They were founded by two different ethnic groups. They each conducted their services in Swedish or Norwegian until the 1940s."

Ellen grabbed the doorframe to steady herself as she stepped out of the dark VFW building into the bright sunshine. "I thought they all spoke Scandinavian."

Laughing, Meg guided Ellen to her car. "Scandinavia is a sub-continent of Europe, and the countries staunchly maintain their independent languages, currencies, foods, and traditions."

"Ahh," Ellen said, as Meg unlocked the car door. "Like Japan, Korea, and China. We can sometimes read each other's written ideograms, but each country speaks differently."

Kerry nodded to his police car. "Ride with me."

"What do you think?" I asked.

"About what? The recipes or Ellen Vang's alcohol tolerance?"

"She's only five feet tall and can't weigh a hundred pounds, but I just watched her pour down five or six shots of cognac without apparent effect."

Kerry contacted the dispatcher and asked if there were any emergencies. Then he followed the caravan of cars the five blocks to the Swedish Lutheran Church. He locked the car then paused as the others gathered near Meg. "I got the BCA report on the murder scene. The house is incredibly clean, which made their job much easier.

Nearly all the fingerprints they lifted belonged to the victim. The smudges on the knife used to kill her were left by a leather glove with a slight cut on the right index finger and an imperfection in the leather of the right ring finger. If we find a glove, they're sure they can match it to the knife. The only other trace evidence left behind were footprints. Again, they said the clean crime scene helped us out there. The killer walked across the sparkling kitchen floor wearing boots gritty from the driveway. There were sandy marks on the first half dozen footprints, but also waffle patterns left by a woman's boot on the shiny floor. The waffle-patterned prints don't match the victim's winter boots. The heels are slightly worn but the tread pattern is crisp, and the right boot has an imperfection in the sole. The BCA tech said the boot prints might be easier to explain to a jury than a fingerprint."

"We'd better get going, the entourage is almost to the church."

Kerry and I hustled across the sidewalk and followed the others downstairs to the basement kitchen. Ron Olafson, one of the recipe judges and pastor of the Swedish Lutheran Church, met us at the bottom of the steps with hearty handshakes. "Welcome to our church. Our Women of Tomorrow group is here to show you around the kitchen."

Scanning the gray-haired women lined up in a reception line, I wondered how they considered themselves the women of tomorrow when it looked like several of them might keel over at any moment. Especially concerning, was a woman at the end of the line struggling to stay upright even with the help of her walker. I decided these women must've formed the group in the 1950s and never changed the name.

Halfway down the line, a woman was holding a leash attached to a dachshund. The small black and brown dog wore an orange and red vest identifying him as a service dog. Seeing all the unfamiliar faces, he yipped and tugged at the leash.

Elena Svoboda whispered to Kerry, "That's the first dachshund guide dog I've ever seen."

I chuckled and Kerry leaned forward. "I think he's more of a companion dog."

Meg introduced Ellen Vang to Patty Gustafson the first woman in the line.

Patty smiled broadly and shook Meg and Ellen's hands. "Welcome." She hesitated, then looked at Meg. "Does your Japanese guest speak English?"

I couldn't do anything but grimace. I glanced at Kerry who was shaking his head at the huge gaffe. To her credit, or perhaps due to the cognac, Ellen stood her ground. "Ms. Gustafsson, I was born in California, I graduated from UCLA, and my heritage is Chinese, not Japanese."

Patty was unabashed and unapologetic. "How wonderful! We love Chinese food. Just last week, we prepared chow mein for the men's club when they put up the Christmas decorations."

Claire Soderstrom was the next person in line, and she offered her hand. "It's so nice to meet you. There really aren't any Chinese people in Two Harbors. How tall will you get when you're fully grown?"

Kerry couldn't stand it anymore and covered his laughter with a coughing fit.

"Ma'am, I'm thirty-three years old."

Claire stiffened and turned to Patty, speaking in a voice meant to be heard in their cheap hearing aids, "She's got an attitude for a foreigner."

That comment even got to Meg, who was usually a model of decorum. "Let's look at the kitchen."

Ron Olafson put his hand on my arm and whispered, "I'm so sorry."

"It's not your fault," I said. "I work among senior citizens. Nothing they say or do surprises me anymore."

"I really thought they'd be more..."

Kerry was still chuckling. "I think the phrase is politically correct."

Ellen surveyed the kitchen and the small pass-through to the dining room. She walked back and forth, the Lutheran Women of Tomorrow on her heels asking questions and trying to get a word of approval. The producer stopped in the dining room and rocked her head from side to side. "We could make this work, but the logistics of moving people around and getting the camera angles would be challenging."

Meg nodded her agreement. "Let's look at the other church."

Clare stiffened. "You're not going to look at the Catholic Church, are you? They play bingo in their dining room and the place stinks from the ink in the scoring markers for days."

The pastor stepped past Claire before she could insult the Episcopalians, Methodists, and Presbyterians, too. "If the Norwegian Lutheran Church doesn't meet your needs, please keep us in mind."

Meg led the procession across the street to the other Lutheran church. Pastor Hal Norgaard greeted us inside the door. "Welcome to the Norwegian Lutheran Church." He directed us toward a room off the sanctuary. The dining room's large stained-glass windows let the late morning sun beam in on the light-colored birch furniture. Through two long pass-through windows, I saw glistening stainless-steel appliances, oven doors, and countertops.

Ellen took it all in from the doorway. "This will do nicely. The cameramen can set up in the dining room and shoot through the pass-through window. The doors on each end of the kitchen will allow the guests to flow through without bunching up and causing delays."

A nicely dressed man walked in behind the pastor. "Ms. Vang, this is Preston Marshall, chairman of our facilities committee. His people are at your disposal to make whatever arrangements you require."

Ellen walked over to Preston, someone I recognized from the Chamber of Commerce meeting as the owner of Preston Commercial Construction. "What have you got for power in here?"

"The dining room and kitchen are electrically up to code, with a separate two-hundred-amp circuit breaker box and twenty amp one-twenty-volt outlets every twelve feet. If you need more than that, I can have an electrician here this afternoon."

For the first time, the producer smiled. Ellen turned to Meg. "Yes, this will do nicely." She turned back to Preston Marshall. "Give me your cell phone and I'll enter my MCR operator's number. He'll be able to explain exactly what we need for the electrical, broadcast, and transmission equipment."

Preston accepted his phone back with a smile. "I'll call him immediately and arrange whatever is required."

Ellen nodded and turned to Meg. "Is there somewhere in town we can get a drink with lunch, or do I have to drive back to Minneapolis?"

Meg smiled. "We've got several nice restaurants that serve wine, beer, and liquor. Is there something special you'd like to eat?"

Ellen drew a breath. "Anything is fine as long as they don't try to feed me that herring roe shit. Just the thought of it makes me gag."

Meg winked at me as she and Ellen walked past. "There's a really nice restaurant at the stoplight. They serve wonderful steaks, seafood, and salads. Their wine list is extensive, and the service is excellent."

Ellen flipped her hand. "No wine. I need a stiff drink."

Kerry and I followed them out the door, Ellen still chattering. "What's with the old bats at that first church? Were they trying to impress or depress me? Haven't they ever seen an Asian woman before?"

I stopped at Kerry's car. "You don't need to drive me back to the VFW. The walk will do me good."

Kerry leaned on the top of the car. "If I wasn't on duty, I'd suggest we go back to the VFW for lunch and a beer."

"How about a VFW lunch and a Diet Coke?"

Kerry slapped the top of the car. "I'll buy."

The VFW was half full, with two women scurrying around taking orders and delivering plates of food. Kerry steered me to the table we'd sat at earlier where he sat with his back in the corner. Vern brought two cans of Diet Coke without prompting.

He set the soda cans in front of us. "Did you find an acceptable kitchen?"

"The Norwegians won. The Norwegian Lutheran Church's kitchen was great, and Preston Marshall charmed the producer. He promised to do whatever was needed to whip things into shape for the TV crew."

"Preston has a good head. He's a little intense for my tastes, but a reasonable guy who knows how to make a living, but still treats his people well. I assume whatever work his crews do will be a donation to the church. He's good about that."

We both ordered the special of the day, a hot turkey sandwich with stuffing, gravy, and cranberry relish on the side. With everyone out of earshot, Kerry leaned close. "I don't have a clue where to go with the Reggie Sandberg murder case."

"What are the usual murder motives?"

"Love and hate top the list. She was a widow, and by all accounts, her children loved her. Next is money. She's a retired cook living off her Social Security and modest savings. Whoever killed her took her purse, but her son said she rarely kept more than thirty or forty dollars in cash around the house. The last is revenge, and by all accounts, everyone liked Reggie."

Shaking my head I said, "Don't discount the money thing. Convenience store clerks get killed for less than a hundred bucks."

"C'mon Peter. No one kills a widow for twenty bucks. There's something else I'm missing."

I thought about the crime scene. "Her recipe box was stolen."

"Really? Why would someone steal recipes they could download from the computer in the library?"

"She had the recipes from Oscar's Lunch. Maybe someone wanted them badly and Reggie refused to give them up."

Our steaming turkey sandwiches arrived with gravy dripping from the edges of the plate. We thanked Hannah, our waitress, from the VFW auxiliary. She'd once told me she'd been a field hospital nurse in Viet Nam, patching up the Marines after the Corpsmen, like me, had done our best.

Kerry inhaled deeply, savoring the aroma. "It smells like Thanksgiving."

"I can't tell Jenny this is what I had for lunch."

"Why not?"

I waved my fork, having taken a bite of hot stuffing that burned my mouth. "She assumes I'm eating a peanut butter and banana sandwich in my office."

"I'll buy you a beer after work if you'll brainstorm some more with me."

"That would get me a week or more of sleeping on the couch. I can't leave Jenny home alone with Jeremy and the baby two nights in one week."

Kerry nodded. "I was deployed a lot when Jacob was an infant. Deb had it pretty tough."

"Deb's a tough lady. Hell, she continues to put up with you."

Kerry smiled with the unscarred half of his mouth. "If you keep that up, you'll be buying your own lunch."

After bussing a nearby table, Hannah walked over and surveyed our plates. "I guess you two enjoyed the turkey. It looks like you licked the plates." We handed her our plates and she smiled. "Jeff's making meatloaf tomorrow. It's his secret family recipe."

As Hannah left, I could see the flash of an idea cross Kerry's face. "The BCA delivered all the papers they collected from Reggie's house. Someone needs to sort through her recipes. If a stolen recipe is the motive, maybe we can narrow the field of suspects."

I thought it was a rhetorical comment, but Kerry stared at me like he expected a reply. "It's an interesting thought."

"That's an enthusiastic reply."

"What did you expect me to say? 'Gee Kerry, that's absolutely inspired. I think you're right, looking through a pile of recipes to determine what's not there is brilliant!'"

"I get enough sarcasm from my family. I don't need it from you."

"It's an impossible task. You can look at all the recipes, but there's no way to know what's missing." I struggled to give an analogy but came up empty.

"Are you going back to work?" Kerry asked as he stood.

"I've got to put in a few hours there unless you're going to start paying me for my consultations."

"You know…"

I put up my hand, realizing I'd opened the door to discussion of a job with the police department. "I'm kidding. I'm not going to take a job as a city cop."

"You have a standing invitation." We walked to the door and Kerry held it open for an older couple who were entering. We stepped outside and he stopped. "My other cops are green and don't seem interested in learning how to conduct an investigation at this point in their careers. I could use your sense of curiosity and intuition."

"You can buy me coffee or lunch any day to pick my brain, but I don't want to be a cop."

Kerry opened the trunk of his car and took out a small cardboard box. The sealing tape was printed with an *evidence* logo. "Cut the tape to open the box and sign the log on top. Don't let it out of your control or leave it in an unlocked space. You may be called into court to verify that the contents haven't been tampered with."

He held out the box, but I didn't take it. "What's in it and why are you giving it to me?"

"These are the papers from Reggie's kitchen floor. I need you to determine if any of the Oscar's Lunch recipes are missing."

"Oh no, I'm not the person to sort them. I didn't even arrive in Two Harbors until years after Oscar's was closed. Hell, the building was demolished and replaced before I moved here."

Kerry shoved the box against my abdomen, and I grabbed it reflexively. "I moved here after you did, and I don't have a resource to tap into historical knowledge. You have two hundred resources. Please."

"What? You just told me not to let the papers out of my control. In the next breath you're telling me to show them to the Whistling Pines retirees. Which way should I handle it?"

Kerry's eyes lit up and the right corner of his mouth curled. "I want it both ways." He left me holding the box and got into his car.

There goes the rest of the day and heaven knows how much more, I thought to myself.

I pulled out of the VFW parking lot and turned toward work. The Whistling Pines van was parked two blocks ahead and I visualized the activities schedule but couldn't think of a reason the van would be downtown. Consumed with curiosity, I parked behind it and locked the box of recipes in my trunk. I walked the sidewalk, checking the business names on the door. I passed the 3M museum, wondering if someone had arranged a tour of the original home of the global Scotch Tape conglomerate. There was no crowd in the small museum, so I moved on.

The adjacent accounting and legal offices were equally quiet, as was a storefront converted into a flower shop. The next door belonged to a photo studio. I stopped and listened to the murmured voices from inside. Opening the door, I found a group of female Whistling Pines residents sitting in a waiting area reading magazines and chatting. Their hair and makeup looked like they'd just come from the beauty salon.

Alice Oliver looked up with surprise. "Peter, I thought you weren't going to be involved in the fundraising calendar. Did you change your mind?"

Before I could answer, Hulda Packer pushed her walker through a door leading to the deeper recesses of the building as a strobe flashed behind her. She shuffled into the waiting area, stopped, and eyed me with suspicion. "Wendy drove us here. You're a wet blanket and you don't need to hang around."

The shuffling sound as Hulda walked made me look at her feet, usually shod in orthopedic shoes that made a clopping sound. Seeing her feet in bedroom slippers I froze. I was going to ask what was happening when I realized I knew the answer.

Wendy swept through the door as the strobe flashed again, apparently synched to a camera. She had a fur coat draped over her arm and a roster in her other hand, apparently ready to summon the next photographic subject. Looking guilty, she said, "Peter, I think you should leave."

"Really? This is happening?"

I looked toward the door behind Wendy. She backed up, blocking it. "You shouldn't go into the studio right now."

The fur coat Wendy was holding sparked a memory of the naturist cruise during Buccaneer Days. Alma Kotter had worn it and treated me to the view she said Ava Garner had given Frank Sinatra. I'd looked away, but not in time to prevent seeing Alma pulling the coat open to reveal her…altogether.

"Alma's being photographed?" I asked.

Alice leaned forward. "It's all very tasteful, Peter."

Wendy's Cheshire cat grin told me all I needed to know. I spun around, walked out the door, and nearly ran to my car.

I called Jeri Westfall from my office and asked if I could visit her apartment. She answered the door, nicely dressed, wearing a long skirt and printed blouse.

"Come in, Peter. It's always nice to have visitors. Can I make you a cup of coffee?"

"Thanks, but no." I sat on the sofa across from the overstuffed chair she usually occupied. A book lay open on the table next to her.

"I just met with the producer of the *World Eats* television show. She'd like to feature your black magic cake recipe."

Jeri's eyes lit up and she clasped her hands. "That's wonderful."

"They're filming it live from the Norwegian Lutheran Church kitchen. They want you to tell the story of how your mother received the recipe as a gift as you prepare the cake with Jonathan Edwards."

Concern passed over Jeri's face. "I think that show is only an hour long and it takes longer than that to make and bake the cake, cook the frosting, and ice the cake."

"I'm sure they know how to deal with that. They'll probably just mix the batter with you, then produce the finished cake, or something."

That news didn't allay Jeri's concern. "The frosting has to be cooked in a double-boiler and stirred constantly. It's not something you can set aside for later use."

"Trust me, the television people will know how to deal with it. I'm sure they've broadcast shows with more complicated and time-consuming recipes. They'll handle it."

Jeri let out a breath like she was relieved but was obviously unconvinced. "That's an evening show, right? I hope it's not too late. I'm not a night owl."

"I think it'll be broadcast live in the central time zone. I believe it's scheduled for seven o'clock."

"That would be perfect. I could go to the church after supper and be back by nine." A new wave of concern flooded her. "Oh dear, I don't drive after dark, and the sun sets before dinner this time of year. I don't think I can do it."

"Trust me, Jeri, someone will arrange a ride for you. It'll be fine."

She looked around nervously. "I'll need to go to the grocery store. I don't have any cake flour and I'm sure I don't have enough eggs or cocoa powder."

"I'll give the producer the recipe and they'll have all the necessary ingredients at the church. You don't have to do anything."

Jeri lit up. "I'll have to call my children. I hope they'll be able to watch it. What channel will it be on?"

"I'm not sure. It's a channel that broadcasts cooking shows. I'm sure your children will be able to find it on their local channels"

"They all have cable television with a thousand channels. I suppose they'll be able to find it when they know what time it's broadcast."

I stood up, then remembered the producer's admonition. "The show puts all broadcasted recipes on their website, so black magic cake will be known to the world. Are you okay with that?"

"It was given to my mother as a secret family recipe in the 1930s. Mother and the woman who gave it to her are dead, as are most of their children. I think it's about time for the world to know about black magic cake, don't you?"

"I think it's the perfect time to share it with the world."

I picked up the box Kerry had given me and stood.

"What are you carrying around in the box, Peter?"

"These are the recipes that were strewn around Reggie Sandberg's kitchen when she was killed. I need to look through them."

Jeri shuddered. "That seems like an eerie job. Looking through a dead woman's recipes seems rather intrusive. Recipes are very personal, hand-written records of something the owner valued. I write out my favorite recipes, put my name and the date on the top, and give them to my children and dearest friends. I'm literally giving them a part of me as an eternal gift that will be passed to their children after I'm gone."

I weighed Jeri's words as I waited for the elevator. The weight of the box seemed to increase as I held it. I reflected on a Christmas cookie recipe my college roommate's mother had given me after I raved about her melting moments cookies. That recipe was tucked away in an envelope, and every Christmas I made a batch of Mrs. Kunkel's cookies and thought of her arthritic fingers mixing the dough, forming the cookies, and baking them to golden brown. I could barely read the recipe, written in her shaking hand. But I had a vision of her and the smell of cookies in her kitchen whenever I made the recipe.

I was holding Reggie's life legacy. When I returned the recipes, I'd have to advise Kerry to make sure this box of treasures was passed on to Reggie's children.

I got out of the elevator on the first floor and walked to the nurses' office. Jenny was at her desk reading something. She looked up when I sat in her guest chair.

"What's in the box?"

"Reggie Sandberg's recipes. Kerry asked me to sort through them. He hopes I can determine which recipes are missing."

Jenny nodded. "Good luck with that. If that box is full, there must be a thousand recipes."

"Jeri Westfall is going to make her black magic cake on the Jonathan Edwards cooking show."

"That's wonderful! She's so fun and perky, they couldn't have found a better guest."

"Jeri said it was time for the world to share that recipe. She's been writing down her other recipes and sending them to her children, as a legacy." I paused. "I don't remember my mother cooking much of anything after my father died, but I'm sure she has recipes from her mother. We should talk to our mothers and ask for copies of their favorite recipes."

"I can find any recipe I want on the internet."

"Do you remember the melting moments I make every year for Christmas?"

"Sure. You have the recipe in a kitchen drawer."

"I think of my roommate's mother and the aroma of her kitchen every time I make that recipe. I want our mothers' favorite recipes and the recipes we remember from our childhood. I want to be able to touch a recipe card my mother wrote out in cursive, with her name on the top, not a sterile recipe I read off the internet that's gone after I turn off the computer."

Jenny hadn't heard Jeri's monologue, so wasn't as emotionally affected as I was. "I'm sure Mom would be happy to give us a few of her favorite recipes. Give her a call."

I reached out and squeezed Jenny's hand. "What's your favorite, the one you'll always associate with your mother?"

The weight of what I was saying connected and Jenny squeezed my fingers. "On very special occasions, Mom made Yankee pot roast. She'd have Dad or me whip the potatoes and she'd use a pastry bag to pipe them around the edge of the serving platter."

"Perfect! I'll call Barbara later and ask for that recipe and any others that are special to her."

"What's your favorite?"

I thought back to the years before my father's untimely death, trying to remember my mother cooking in the kitchen. "This sounds stupid, but my mother made a dish she called porcupine balls. It was meatballs made with rice baked in tomato soup. It was nothing special, but I can smell the aroma of the soup just thinking about it."

"Call her and ask for the recipe."

"She hasn't made it in decades. I wonder if she even had a recipe, or if it was just something she whipped up from memory."

Jenny squeezed my hand again. "Trust me, she'll be delighted to write it down for you."

* * *

With Kerry's evidence box tucked under my arm, I walked toward the dining room. Howard Johnson beckoned me from the aviary. "Are you planning to take a vanload of mourners to Reggie Sandberg's funeral?"

"I hadn't thought about it."

"Reggie had a lot of friends around town. Post a signup sheet and see how many people show interest."

I nodded. "I'll take care of it."

Mary and Kathy were holding recipes while Karla worked on her laptop at a dining room table. I assumed they were continuing to work on the cookbook.

"Good morning, ladies."

Looking haggard, Karla looked up from the computer. "I had no idea putting together a cookbook would be so difficult."

Kathy held up a printed sheet and a recipe card. "It's the teaspoon vs. tablespoon thing. People write Tbsp on some recipes, and we know that means tablespoon, but others capitalize the letter T for tablespoon and use a small t for teaspoon." She handed me a recipe card. "Look at this recipe and tell me, does it call for a teaspoon or tablespoon of vegetable oil?"

I looked at the recipe and based on the shaking handwriting, I couldn't determine if the writer's T was a tablespoon or teaspoon. "I think you'll have to ask Gloria Kroeger which it is."

Kathy sighed. "I've already chased down three people this morning to get clarifications. Two of them couldn't tell what they'd written and had to look up the original recipe." She stood. "I'll find Gloria and be back."

I looked at Karla. "Can't you guess and call it good enough?"

"No, Peter! People are going to prepare these recipes and we need them to be correct. A tablespoon is three teaspoons. That's a big difference in spices, leavening, salt, or sugar. It needs to be right."

Mary was staring at the box tucked under my arm. "It looks like you've stolen something from the police evidence room."

An idea flashed. "Could you take a break for a bit? I have Reggie Sandberg's recipes. Chief Stone asked me to look through them hoping I'd be able to determine which are her personal recipes, which are from Oscar's Lunch, and speculate on what's missing."

Karla closed her laptop and sighed. "I'd be happy to do anything other than correct recipes for a while."

I carried the box to another table and cut the tape with a pocketknife. Inside were hundreds of recipe cards. I looked at the cards and then at Mary and Karla. "I don't know where to start."

Mary lifted a handful of recipes out of the box and quickly sorted through them. "These are mostly entrées. Here's crockpot chicken with white wine. That's not one of Oscar's recipes."

"How can you tell?"

"Oscar never served anything as exotic as chicken with wine, and I'm sure nothing was cooked in a crockpot at the restaurant. He used big pans he could roast in the oven."

"I could hug you," I said.

Mary laughed and winked at Karla. "That would start some rumors."

Karla picked up a handful of recipe cards and flipped through them. "Put the box on a chair and we'll do what we did with the cookbook recipes; we'll sort them into piles of entrées, side dishes, breads, and desserts. Then we can look through each pile and do another sort of Reggie's vs. Oscar's recipes."

I set the box on the chair as Karla and Mary started sorting. "Do you think you'll be able to sort Reggie's recipes from Oscar's?"

Karla handed a recipe to me. "This is probably one of Oscar's, it's for five gallons of sloppy Joes. I can't imagine anyone preparing that volume of one food item for personal use."

Piles were forming when Mary handed me another recipe. "Here's another one of Oscar's recipes. It's for a sheet pan of carrot cake."

Kathy returned with a Post-it note stuck to Gloria's recipe. "It's a tablespoon of oil. Gloria says it won't come out of the pan if you only put a teaspoon into the batter." She looked at the growing piles. "Are all of these for the cookbook?"

I explained the source of the recipes and how we were sorting.

Kathy put Gloria's recipe on the laptop computer and joined us. "This looks like fun."

It took less than fifteen minutes to do the first sort. Karla brought a box of rubber bands to the table and we bound each stack, then split up the pile of entrées.

"Most of these are Reggie's recipes," Mary said, putting cards in a growing pile. "Here's Oscar's recipe for ten gallons of chili." She set that in a smaller pile.

Kathy set a recipe in the small pile. "Here's Oscar's recipe for ten gallons of chicken and wild rice soup."

Pausing, Karla took the soup recipe off the small pile. "I loved Oscar's wild rice soup." She read through the recipe. "Aha! He added sour cream to thicken it and add tang. I'll have to add that to my recipe."

Mary nodded. "I saw Oscar's Swedish pancake recipe. He used buttermilk."

The women nodded, knowing what buttermilk would add to the recipe.

With the entrée recipes sorted, we stepped back. Karla looked at me. "There was nothing to that. The volume of the recipe made it obvious which were Reggie's personal recipes, and which were from Oscar's."

I bound Reggie's entrée recipes and set them into the box. "The chief thinks someone may have stolen one or more of Oscar's recipes. Can you determine if any are missing?"

Karla, Kathy, and Mary exchanged questioning glances. Mary broke the silence. "I ate at Oscar's in high school, but my menu choices were limited to hamburgers and fries."

Something Mary said had Kathy chuckling. "What?" I asked.

"My boyfriend used to take me to Oscar's Lunch when we first dated. Because I'm a year or two older than Mary, my menu choices were more…mature. I remember a few menu items, but certainly not all of them."

I looked at Karla, who put up her hands. "Mary and I are close to the same generation. I remember hamburger baskets with fries. On the rare occasion our family went out to eat, my parents often ordered liver and onions. I remember eating Oscar's carrot cake and blueberry pie ala mode."

Karla's comments reminded me of a menu I'd seen on Reggie's kitchen floor. I looked in the box, and on the bottom was an Oscar's Lunch menu in a red plastic case, probably as it had been used by his customers.

"Look what I found," I said, holding it up. I opened it to the inside pages and set it on the table.

Karla ran her finger down the list of entrées. "Here it is, liver and onions served with home-fried potatoes. It brings back memories."

Mary choked and coughed into her elbow. "Ugh. Liver and onions. Just the sound of it gags me."

A warm smile passed over Kathy's face as she examined the menu. "This takes me back. I can picture myself sitting in a booth, placing my order, then staring dreamily into my future husband's eyes." She sighed. "I can't believe how stupid and naïve we were back then. No thoughts about raising kids or paying a mortgage, just talking about getting married and moving into our own apartment."

"I hate to interrupt your trip down memory lane," I said. "But let's finish sorting the rest of the recipes so we can compare what's here with the menu."

Karla picked up the menu. "Let's split the effort. I'll start matching the entrées with the menu while you three finish sorting the rest of the recipes."

The sort went quickly, and we handed the larger quantity recipes to Karla as we found them. "Uh oh," Mary said.

"What's the problem?" I asked.

"I've got a couple dozen pie recipes that could be made one at a time or in multiples." Mary spread a stack of cards on the table. "Some were obviously made in larger quantities. He'd make batches of filling large enough to fill several pie crusts, like this lemon pudding recipe. But here's a recipe for Dutch apple pie that's just enough for one pie. It could be Reggie's, but I suppose it could be Oscar's, too."

Karla brought the menu from the other table and set it in front of us. "The pies are going to be a problem." She put her finger on the desserts. "The menu just gives the price of a slice of pie or a piece of cake. There's no list of the choices."

"I suppose it was a seasonal thing," Kathy said. "He had strawberry pie in the spring, blueberry pie in August and September, and apple pie in the fall. I suppose he used commercial pie filling for cherry pie, and the custard pies could be prepared year 'round."

Mary pulled aside eight or nine recipes. "These recipes are for large batches of filling, so they're obviously Oscar's recipes. Most of the other recipes are…" She paused, flipping through the remaining recipes, comparing them to the larger batches. "All of Oscar's recipes were written by the same person, presumably Oscar. Many of the recipes to make a single pie, are written by different people. A few have a name written on the top, like they'd been given to Reggie by someone."

The women quickly sorted out Reggie's recipes, leaving only the recipes in Oscar's writing. Karla handed me the small stack. "There you go, Peter. Here are Oscar's pie recipes."

"Are any entrée or side dish recipes missing?" I asked Karla.

She laughed. "The menu is from a point in time. There are about a dozen of Oscar's recipes that aren't represented on the menu. It's impossible to tell if the others are from an earlier or later time."

Kathy shook her head. "Or some, like the sweetened sauerkraut salad, weren't a hit and were probably dropped after a short, failed trial."

I pinched the bridge of my nose. "So, we have too many recipes, not missing recipes?"

Kathy picked up the pie recipes and sorted them into custard and fruit pies. "There's at least one fruit pie recipe missing. Oscar served gooseberry pie when the berries were in season. I remember people grumbling about gooseberry pie running out before he closed." Kathy did another sort and looked at me. "The sour cream raisin pie recipe is missing. Oscar won awards for that pie, and he made it every single day."

"Are there any other missing recipes?" I asked.

"There's roast turkey, turkey gravy, cranberry and orange relish, but no stuffing recipe."

Kathy's eyes lit up. "Of course! Oscar always served turkey and stuffing the whole month of November."

Mary reached into the box and lifted out a recipe card with the tip of one finger and thumb. "No one stole Oscar's lutefisk recipe."

I gathered the menu and recipes as we laughed.

* * *

After posting a signup sheet for a van ride to Reggie's funeral, I called Kerry and reported the missing recipes.

"Why would someone steal those three recipes?" He asked.

"They were apparently some of Oscar's signature dishes. The sour cream raisin pie won prizes."

"I'm still missing a motive. Someone stole those three recipes, and is going to do what, serve them to their family for Thanksgiving dinner? There's no motive there."

"Kerry, you asked me to determine if any recipes were missing. My part is done. You have to figure out if or why that ties into Reggie Sandberg's murder."

"I'm just thinking out loud, hoping I was missing something."

"Kerry, I think you're looking for a demented cook who's making enough dressing to stuff fifty turkeys."

"You do realize that's not at all helpful."

I smiled. "Maybe if I'm bad enough at this, you'll stop asking for my help. That worked with Jenny when I helped paint the nursery. She sent me packing after I splattered paint on the hardwood floor and windowsills."

Kerry sighed. "Tape up the recipe box, sign the tape with a Sharpie, and keep it locked up until I can pick it up."

"Oh heck, Karla was rifling through the recipes. There were some she wanted to use in the fundraising cookbook."

"Okay, now I know you're yanking my chain. Have a nice evening. Say hi to Jenny and Jeremy."

I was signing the tape on the box when Hazel Johnson swept into my office. "I'm so glad you're still here," she said breathlessly. "I heard the television people narrowed the field of recipes to three, and one of them is making Slovenian poteka."

"That's right. The producer chose fried herring roe, black magic cake, and the poteka nut roll. They're having three local cooks prepare them on live television with Jonathan Edwards."

"I heard Hailey Evers is making poteka. You have to stop her."

"Stop her? Why?"

"Hailey's mother's sister got dumped by Jonathan back when he was Donny Koloski and they were in high school. She'll probably poison him to get even for him dumping her aunt."

I'd been struggling with small town dynamics since I'd moved to Two Harbors, but this declaration ranked right up there with the woman whose garbage service stopped because her daughter had a fight with the garbage man's wife's best friend. All I could say was, "Huh?"

"It was a messy break up. I don't know all the details, but Jonathan left town without saying goodbye or even sending her a Dear John letter."

"I think it's called a Dear Jane letter if the guy sends it to a woman."

Hazel waved her arm in the air. "That's not the point! Jonathan burned Hailey's aunt and she'll be out to poison him on national television."

"Hazel, how many years ago did that happen?"

Hazel recoiled. "What's that got to do with it?"

"This isn't Kentucky and we're not talking about the Hatfields and McCoys. I'm sure Hailey's aunt was hurt and upset, but it's been decades. I'm sure she's moved on with her life."

"Peter, you're not from here. Those old vendettas just fester. You mark my words;

she's going to poison him." Hazel hesitated. "You'd better have your friend the police chief set up a metal detector so Hailey can't sneak in a gun or bomb."

I was going to continue the argument, but Hazel left before I could point out the stupidity of her case.

Sighing, I dialed Kerry's cell phone. "Have you changed your mind about having a beer?"

"I wish." I relayed the essence of Hazel's story. "She thinks one of the cooks is going to poison, shoot, or bomb Jonathan Edwards during the broadcast."

"How credible is this woman?"

"I don't know. She's hardly said a word to me before."

"Should I be frisking everyone coming through the door for a bomb, or is she another of your elderly crackpots?"

Reflecting on Hazel's story, I made a judgement. "I think she's right in the middle. Not crazy, but with a crazy story."

"That's not helpful, Peter."

"I don't know! You told me to keep my ears open and this is what I heard. I'm just the messenger."

"Easy, Peter. Would you be worried if you were the police chief?"

"I wouldn't take the police chief job for a million dollars a year."

"Listen, I don't have a metal detector or bomb-sniffing dog at my disposal. Should I be concerned?"

"She actually mentioned poison first."

"Peter…"

"Yeah, I know, it's nuts. This whole thing is nuts. The supposed threat is nuts."

"What food is supposedly being poisoned?"

"A Slovenian nut roll called poteka."

"Okay, now you're pulling my leg. The threat is nuts, then you tell me a nut roll is going to be poisoned."

"Ironic, isn't it."

Kerry sighed. "I've seen episodes of this show and the person submitting the recipe eats the finished product at the same time as Jonathan, the host. I'm going to assume we don't have a suicide poisoner, so I'm discounting the poisoning risk. I'll keep an eye on the woman making the nut roll to see if she's carrying in a knapsack that looks like a bomb."

"What if she's got a gun?"

"If she's got a gun or knife, Jonathan's on his own."

"That seems calloused."

"Peter, I'm in the middle of a murder investigation and I don't have time to follow-up on a half-baked threat from a senior citizen who probably heard the story third hand. Can you live with that?"

"Hey, you're the police chief. I defer to your extensive experience and superior judgement."

"Now you sound like my wife. Have a good night."

Chapter Nine

The Norwegian Lutheran Church dining room and kitchen were filled with people, cables, cameras, and sound equipment. Some people were speaking softly, and other voices carried urgency as the broadcast approached. A buffet of sandwiches and coffee for the crew and guests was set up along a wall with the windows overlooking the parking lot. Ellen Vang wore a long shirt with tails that hung down over her tight yoga pants. Her petite stature, slender build, and choice of clothes made her look like a teenager. She wore a headset over her hair and spoke into the mic as she rushed from one group of people to another. Technicians were testing microphones, adjusting lights, moving cameras, and taping cables to the floor.

The black magic cake and poteka were baking in the oven so the finished product could be removed from the oven at the appropriate time. The aromas were mouth-watering.

Meg Cochran's authoritative voice carried over the murmured conversations of the workers and crowd. Meg was a force of nature, and her voice fit the persona. After a couple of Meg's laughing outbursts, Vang shushed her.

In the heat of battle, I'd yelled at Marine Corps officers, but I wouldn't shush Meg. She smiled and took Vang's direction well, lowering her voice.

Jonathan Edwards, wearing a dark blue apron over a light blue dress shirt and black pants, was sitting in a corner of the dining room where a makeup artist was spraying something that smelled like lacquer on his hair. The artist put on some finishing touches as the seven o'clock broadcast time approached. I knew Jonathan had to be in his fifties, but the makeup and hair style took ten or more years off his appearance. I'd spent some time stationed in San Diego and seeing Jonathan in makeup reminded me of California where everyone was trim, tanned, and dressed to look like they were twenty-five years old. I'd learned to look at people's hands to estimate their age. The hair, plastic surgery, and clothing hid a lot, but people's hands gave away the passing of time. Jonathan's hands had age spots and the skin looked almost translucent. He wasn't the young man portrayed in his television ads.

Joyce DuBois, a local beautician, had been hired to put the finishing touches on the guests' hair and makeup. She was in a corner touching up Jeri Westfall's lipstick. Dressed in a tasteful mid-calf blue skirt and ivory flowered blouse, Jeri noticed me watching and winked. If she was at all rattled by the upcoming TV exposure or the hubbub of the pre-broadcast preparations, she was hiding it well.

Rolf Atkinson, dressed in jeans and a plaid flannel shirt with the cuffs rolled up, looked like he was ready to climb onto his fishing boat. He ate sandwiches at the buffet while flirting with the cute female technician who was trying to attach a microphone transmitter to the back of his jeans. Joyce made an attempt to tame his wild blond hair without success. After consultation with the Hollywood makeup artist and the producer, it was decided he'd wear a knit cap to cover his mass of unruly hair. Rolf suggested a black cap, but someone produced a stocking cap with Norwegian-themed colors as bright as Rolf's personality.

In her early thirties, Hailey Evers, was the youngest featured cook. She waited patiently in the corner talking to an older woman. Her dark hair was combed back and tied in a ponytail. She clasped and unclasped her hands nervously in front of her khaki knee-length skirt. The armpits of her light-yellow blouse already damp, she bit her lower lip, glancing at the clock near the kitchen as her older friend offered reassurance.

The producer clapped her hands to quiet the crowd. "Okay folks, we're five minutes from broadcast. Everyone who's not part of the crew or a guest has to move to the rear of the room." She pointed at Meg. "You cannot talk during the broadcast. The rest of you, we'll signal when we want you to clap and laugh. If you need to cough or sneeze, leave. Are we clear on the rules?"

A woman ushered Jonathan into the kitchen, whispering in his ear. She pointed to a spot on the counter where she'd apparently placed a crib sheet with the names of the guests and the recipes they were preparing. Jonathan, being the perfect jerk, rolled his eyes in annoyance at the coaching.

Ellen waved to the corner where Joyce was brushing Jeri's hair. "Jeri Westfall, you're up first."

Jeri walked to the kitchen where a technician helped her step over the cables. A young female technician helped Jeri string a microphone wire under her blouse, then clipped it to her lapel. She held two fingers up to the sound man who studied the gauges and switches in front of him, apparently ready to switch on mic number two.

Ellen announced thirty seconds to airtime and the crew moved back from the counter and took their silent positions away from the camera. Ellen put her hand to the headset and mouthed *ten* to Jonathan, then started counting off the seconds to airtime on her fingers. At two fingers she backed away and a smile spread across Jonathan's face. Ellen finished the countdown. A technician signaled for the crowd to clap, then Ellen pointed to Jonathan, who smiled.

"Ladies and Gentlemen. It's my pleasure to host a special live holiday edition of *World Eats* from my hometown of Two Harbors, Minnesota, on the scenic north shore of Lake Superior. We've found three cooks who are going to share their favorite recipes with us. My first guest is Jeri Westfall who's going to share her Czech Black Magic Cake recipe."

Jonathan moved next to Jeri who was a foot shorter than the host. A technician had her stand on a wooden box so the cameraman could frame them together. "Jeri, tell us the story of your cake."

Jeri recited the same story we'd heard at Whistling Pines. Jonathan smiled and nodded. He appeared immensely interested in Jeri's story as they cracked eggs, added ingredients, and mixed the batter.

Pushing the bowl of batter aside, Jonathan smiled. "And now, through the magic of television, we're going to remove Jeri's cake from the oven."

One of the technicians waved uplifted hands, signaling for the crowd to laugh.

Jonathan donned oven mitts and removed the cake from the oven. Jeri explained the process of making a stirred frosting in a double-boiler. Jonathan poked holes in the cake, then spread it with pre-prepared frosting.

With great ceremony, Jonathan sliced the cake and slid two perfect pieces onto plates. He handed a plate and fork to Jeri, then cut off a bite and put it into his mouth. His eyes lit up like he'd never tasted anything as delicious in his entire life. He stepped behind Jeri, wiped his lips with a napkin and smiled. "Jeri's recipe is on the *World's Eats* website."

The technician clapped his hands over his head and the two dozen of us clapped as Jeri nodded and curtsied.

Ellen spoke into her mic and the lights on the set dimmed. "And we're on a commercial break."

To his credit, Jonathan hugged Jeri and whispered something to her that brought a smile to her face. The technician helped Jeri down from her box and off the set as another member of the crew led Rolf into the kitchen and removed the box Jeri had been standing on.

Ellen made sure Rolf was on his mark, then announced, "twenty seconds." She stepped back and repeated the countdown to the end of the commercial break.

Jonathan smiled at the camera. "Our next guest is a Lake Superior fisherman sharing his favorite recipe. Please welcome

Rolf Atkinson." The technician signaled the crowd and we clapped.

Ellen had been distracted until Rolf was nearly on camera. She glanced at Rolf's jaunty Norwegian hat and flinched, then spoke urgently into her mic. "Someone get that ridiculous hat off his head. It makes him look like he's ready for the ski jump competition."

The young woman who'd strung the mic cord through Rolf's shirt had to jump to reach Rolf's stocking cap. When she pulled the cap off, Rolf's blonde hair sprung out, making him look like someone had run a mixer over his head. The only other hairdo I'd seen that wild was a picture of Albert Einstein.

Ellen rolled her eyes, but frantically waved Rolf onto the set. He stepped next to Jonathan, who looked small next to the hulking fisherman. The producer had mentioned the "optics" of featuring someone like Rolf on the show. Jonathan's beaming face said Rolf was perfect, from the flannel shirt to his wild blonde hair and piercing blue eyes.

Jonathan moved Rolf to a spot marked on the floor. The cameraman framed them, and Jonathan looked directly into the camera. "Rolf, please tell the audience about your herring recipe."

Rolf smiled, and speaking in Norwegian-accented English, sounded like he was straight from the set of the movie *Fargo.* He explained that the recipe had been brought from Norway when his grandparents emigrated in the early 1900s.

Jonathan pulled a large stainless-steel pan out of the refrigerator, revealing dozens of silver herring, each about a foot long. Rolf picked up a filet knife, then deftly sliced open each herring. Herring entrails oozed out with the egg sacs and drooled over the remaining fish.

Ellen had been watching intently, but the sight of the egg sac harvest appeared to be too much for her. She covered her mouth and turned away from the scene.

Rolf handed Jonathan a sac of herring eggs, his hands dripping with fish slime. The roe sac looked like an elongated chicken egg yolk. "Are we saving these?" Jonathan asked, apparently unaware of Rolf's recipe.

"Oh ya! These are the main ingredient. I'll take the rest of the herring home and smoke them."

Jonathan's smile faded slightly. He glanced at Ellen, who was still turned away from the scene. His eyes widened as the pile of roe sacs grew on the plate in front of him. Seeing no escape, he looked skeptically at Rolf. "I've never seen these in the store."

Rolf laughed. "No, they don't freeze. You can only get them fresh."

Rolf pushed aside the pan of gutted fish, then described the mix of herbs used to season the roe sacs. He dredged them in seasoned flour, then set them in a pan of sizzling butter. "My friend Walter (the W pronounced like a V) caught these herring himself and hand-delivered them to the church for the television show. You can't get herring any fresher than this."

Jonathan looked at the roe sacs curling into the shape of shrimp as they fried. "Rolf, why are we eating the roe and not the fish?"

Rolf puffed up. "Oh, these are the filet mignon of the herring. We fishermen sell the fish, but we bring the roe home to treat our families. Not many people know the roe is edible."

The odor of the frying herring roe didn't reach the television viewers, but as it mixed with the sweet aroma of Jeri's cake and baking poteka, the crew turned their heads and covered their mouths. That move wasn't lost on the crowd in the back of the dining room. The few snickers were met with the technician's threatening glare and a cutting his throat gesture. The smell of the frying herring roe reached him, and he closed his eyes and put his hands on his knees. This was apparently the unscripted part of Jonathan's cooking show. The authentic crowd response to whatever disgusting thing Jonathan was about to eat had become a signature of the *World Eats* show. It was the highlight of each broadcast and the home audiences loved it.

I'd eaten roasted camel in an open-air Baghdad market with fresh goat manure in the streets and livestock all around, but even that didn't prepare me for the smell of frying herring roe mixed with the sweet aroma of chocolate cake. I started breathing through my mouth. A few other people with more delicate stomachs left during the herring "cleaning." More raced for the bathrooms as the smell of frying roe reached them. Ellen, the producer, seemed to be gagging, her face buried in her elbow to muffle the noise.

Jonathan ignored Ellen, the fleeing crowd, the smell of the roe, and commotion among the techs who were grimacing and choking. Rolf scooped the fried morsels out of the frying pan and Ellen turned to face him, preparing for the commercial break. Jonathan smiled as Rolf slid the fried roe on top of dark Norwegian bread. Rolf deglazed the pan, adding his secret spice and capers, then he scraped the capers, browned crusty bits, and butter sauce over the fried roe. At some point, Jonathan's smile faded, replaced by a look of impending doom. He glanced at the producer to convey a silent message.

"Mmm, doesn't that look delicious. Rolf's recipe is on the *World Eats* website." Jonathan cut a bit of toast and roe, slid his fork under it and put it in his mouth. Rolf picked up the slice of toast and took a huge bite, grinning ear to ear as he chewed and swallowed.

Jonathan continued to smile but didn't chew. He nodded to Ellen. The technician cued the crowd to clap, and Ellen immediately cut to a commercial. Once sure the camera was off, Jonathan spit the fried roe into a napkin.

"Water! Get me something to wash this taste out of my mouth!"

Rolf, laughing heartily, pulled a flat, pint bottle of clear liquid out of his back pocket. He uncorked it and handed the bottle to Jonathan. Tipping up the bottle, Jonathan took a large swallow. His eyes went wide seconds before he started coughing.

Rolf snatched the bottle as it slipped out of Jonathan's hand, then he slapped the countertop. The crowd roared with laughter as Jonathan coughed and gasped.

Grinning ear to ear, Rolf asked, "Not a fan of aquavit?"

Jonathan finally caught his breath. "What is that, turpentine?"

Rolf laughed and slapped the table. "It's aquavit, elixir of the gods."

Jonathan grabbed a stack of napkins and wiped the aquavit dribbling from his mouth and chin. "Elixir of the gods? I think you could use that to strip paint."

A technician guided Hailey to the kitchen while others struggled to get Rolf, the herring roe cooking utensils, the pan of gutted herring, and the bottle of aquavit out of the kitchen.

Hailey hadn't gained any confidence and was nearly shaking as the crew readied Jonathan for the final segment. She glanced at the woman in the corner, getting a nod of encouragement in return. I watched the exchange and thought, *Hailey's fortunate to have such a supportive friend along.*

Ellen shouted into her mic to run another commercial while the crew wiped up the aquavit Jonathan had spewed onto the counter. The herring situation was apparently not unprecedented because a production team member appeared with a bottle of air freshener. She sprayed the area liberally while other crew members replaced Rolf's utensils and ingredients with a countertop mixer, small containers of pre-measured ingredients, a large spatula, and a rolling pin. Hailey stiffened as a female sound tech ran a wire through a sweater that nicely accentuated Hailey's attractive figure and clipped the mic to Hailey's collar.

Jonathan, finally composed, watched the wire being threaded, his eyes lingering on Hailey's figure a moment too long. He stepped next to her and put his hand on her arm. To everyone watching, Jonathan was trying to calm her. The move caused Hailey to jerk like she'd been shocked. He removed his hand and whispered something to her. She relaxed slightly and nodded as Ellen repeated the countdown. We were cued to clap as the lights came up and the camera started.

"Our final guest tonight is a local teacher preparing one of the comfort foods from my childhood. Hailey Evers is going to share her grandmother's Slovenian nut roll recipe with us. Hailey, tell us about your grandma's poteka."

Hailey drew a breath, then spoke softly. Ellen waved her arms, gesturing for Hailey to speak louder while the sound man adjusted dials to capture Hailey's soft-spoken words. She gained confidence as she spoke and relaxed a bit when Jonathan said he'd attended the school where Hailey taught. She relaxed more when Jonathan suggested they start making the dough. Hailey described each ingredient as she and Jonathan poured the premeasured items into the mixer's bowl.

With all the ingredients added, Jonathan turned on the mixer. He smiled at the camera as a technician slid the mixer aside. A different crew member handed Jonathan a metal mixing bowl. "Again through the magic of television, we've got dough that's risen and is ready for the rolling pin."

One of the crew members cued the audience, and we laughed.

Jonathan sprinkled flour on the counter and gestured for Hailey to continue her explanation of the dough preparation.

Hailey used a spatula to scoop a ball of dough out of the metal bowl and onto the table. "We sprinkle flour on the table and work the dough into a rectangle with our fingers before rolling it." She held up another bowl. "We'll spread this seasoned nut and butter filling on the dough."

Jonathan joined Hailey in the spreading of the dough with his fingers. He smiled at Hailey. "You probably didn't know this, but I made poteka with my grandmother when I was a boy."

Hailey nodded to the woman who'd been talking to her before the broadcast, now standing in the corner. "My mother told me she'd made poteka with you and your grandmother."

Jonathan hesitated for a fraction of a second, surprised by Hailey's comment. He followed Hailey's gaze to the corner of the room. I realized the woman who'd been comforting Hailey was her mother, the pregnant girl left behind when Jonathan departed to find his fortune in Las Vegas.

My mind flashed back to my conversations about Donny Koloski's liaison with his girlfriend's sister and his surreptitious departure from Two Harbors, leaving behind a pregnant teenager to raise a baby girl alone. I remembered Hazel Johnson's warning that Donny/Jonathan might be poisoned, shot, or tarred and feathered. Hailey's mother's sly smile seemed to rock Jonathan. I looked for Kerry, hoping he'd jump in before the impending poisoning, stabbing, shooting, or tar and feathering. I spotted him near the door. His arms were crossed, and he was smiling, apparently unaware or unconcerned about the impending threat.

While Jonathan was distracted, Hailey reached for the rolling pin. "And now we roll the dough." Her finger struck the rolling pin and it spun across the counter, falling to the floor.

Jonathan regained his composure and reacted quickly, bending down to retrieve the errant utensil. His head disappeared. As soon as his head was out of sight, Hailey's eyes went wide and she shrieked. "Get your hands off me!"

She shoved the star, who was off balance reaching for the rolling pin. We couldn't see behind the counter, but it appeared Jonathan had sprawled on the floor with a thud. The sound technician reacted quickly to silence Jonathan's mic as he spewed profanities. Hailey moved from behind the counter where she lifted her skirt, briefly exposing a white handprint on her upper thigh, the fingertips apparently extending under the elastic of her red panties.

The producer was taken by surprise and paused a second before signalling for a commercial break. Hailey pulled down her skirt, ripped the mic cord from her blouse, and fled the dining room, followed closely by her mother.

Jonathan got up from the floor. His hands, covered in white flour, were raised in the air. "I didn't touch her. I swear I didn't touch her!"

Kerry watched, grinning as the television crew raced around the dining room and kitchen. Ellen was talking to the technician at a console, apparently finding commercials and programming to fill the remaining six or seven minutes of airtime. A young woman was being berated by Jonathan after she'd handed him a towel to wipe the flour off his hands. Television monitors in corners of the dining room showed commercial after commercial being broadcast.

Jeri Westfall was standing in the center of the dining room with her hands held to her face. I escorted her to the back wall where we were out of the hubbub and somewhat shielded from Jonathan's profane tantrum. I smelled a whiff of smoke seconds before the kitchen smoke detector started screaming. A young female technician wearing a headset grabbed a pair of potholders and pulled the smoldering poteka out of the oven. The precise ballet of items magically appearing as they were needed for the show had fallen apart, and the finished poteka was left in the oven well past the golden-brown stage.

In her rush to deal with the smoldering poteka, the technician left the oven door open and smoke continued to rise to the ceiling. The screeching smoke detector distracted me and everyone else from the sprinkler head over the oven. The heat rising from the open oven melted the fusible link and released a spray of water over the kitchen.

The cameramen swept up their tripods and cameras, shielding them from the sprinkler spray with their bodies. Sparks flashed in the kitchen and Preston Marshall, who'd arranged for the additional electrical outlets required for the television crew, dashed to a corner, threw open the circuit breaker box, and flipped breakers, quelling the sparks and throwing the kitchen into darkness.

I heard people in the kitchen cursing as they tripped over cables while trying to pull expensive electronics out of the water spray. Jonathan staggered around, looking like a drowned rat. His hair was plastered to his skull, and his makeup was running onto his shirt. He took one step toward the dining room, then he slipped and fell on the wet kitchen floor where a technician had apparently spilled herring slime. Ellen trotted to him, apparently offering words of encouragement and reassurance as she helped him to his feet, her words and his profane response lost in the smoke detector's screech.

Kerry walked over to me with his cell phone to his ear. He ended the call, shaking his head. "The fire department responded to the flow alarm in the sprinkler system. The first fire truck and an ambulance are already halfway here from the station. It's probably just as well. The firemen have the key to shut off the sprinkler water and turn off the smoke alarm."

Jeri was looking past me at the left-hand kitchen door. "They can probably hose down the herring slime, too."

"What?" I asked.

She pointed to the large pan that held the herring. It had flipped over in the rush to get the electronics out of the kitchen. The slimy herring and their innards slid around the kitchen floor in the water accumulating as the sprinkler system continued to spray.

Preston Marshall's feet flew out from under him like he'd slipped on ice. He crawled across the kitchen, tried to stand, but fell again. He finally gained his footing on the carpeting but was wet and covered with herring slime. He shook his hands, then wiped them on his sodden pants.

Catching us watching him, Preston walked over. "The herring smell isn't going to come out of the carpeting. It'll have to be replaced."

Kerry held his hand over his mouth to hide his grin. "I suppose a quick scrub won't do it."

Preston shook his head. "I hope the fire department shuts down the sprinkler water before the puddle reaches the sanctuary or Sunday's service may have to be held outside."

Reverend Norgaard joined us for the end of Preston's observation. "Maybe I should keep a couple herring and do my sermon on the loaves and fishes. The herring odor will make it poignant."

I tried not to laugh, but a snort escaped.

Firemen burst through the front door. The chief, in a white helmet, accessed a panel in the coat closet to shut off the water flow and alarm. Preston was unable to process what had happened. "I was outside the kitchen door. I heard a scream, then all hell broke loose." His eyes went wide. "Um, sorry pastor. All heck broke loose."

Norgaard waved off the apology. "I think the devil had a hand in this, so a reference to hell is probably warranted."

I replayed the series of events for Kerry, ending with Hailey's scream, the white handprint on her leg, all leading to the fire alarm and sprinkler going off.

Kerry looked at me. "Why did Hailey do that?"

"Why did she do what? Jonathan groped her behind the counter, and she reacted."

Kerry shook his head. "The mark on her thigh was white paint, not flour."

"What?" I asked.

"Hailey set Jonathan up. Do you know why?"

"Um, maybe. She kept glancing at her mother in the corner."

Ellen, still sodden, with the headset now around her neck, rushed over to Kerry looking flustered. "We'll take care of her. It's just a misunderstanding. Our people will contact Hailey and set this right." She saw Norgaard's clerical collar and added, "And the damage to the kitchen. We'll pay for that, too."

Kerry nodded. "Jonathan's done this before with other women?"

"Well, um, never on the set, and certainly not on live television…"

"Usually in dressing rooms, I suppose."

Ellen froze, staring at Kerry's badge. "I…can't comment. Just have Hailey contact the studio. We've got lawyers who'll want to speak with her. There's no need for you to arrest anyone or do anything. It'll all be taken care of." She turned to Preston and the minister. "And the other damage too. We're insured. It'll all be covered."

Ellen rushed away and Kerry shook his head.

"What are you going to do?" I asked.

"She asked me not to arrest anyone, so I guess I won't do anything," Kerry took a breath. "What's Hailey's backstory?"

"I suspect Hailey is Jonathan's illegitimate daughter. Her mother has a twin sister who was Jonathan's high school sweetheart. Shortly before Jonathan's departure from Two Harbors, Jonathan got his girlfriend's twin sister pregnant. I think the twins just made good on their promise to tar and feather him if he ever came back to town. Maybe the lawyers will offer Hailey the child support her mother never received."

Jeri Westfall was standing opposite Kerry. Shaking her head she said, "This is all too bad. Jonathan seemed like such a nice boy."

Chapter Ten

Jeri chatted continuously on the drive back to Whistling Pines. She was wound up over the end of the television show, but the conversation quickly diverted to familiar comfortable topics.

"I don't understand how people can work from home. My son, Jim, worked from home. How did his company know what he was doing? I mean, was there a camera on his computer so they knew he was sitting there eight hours a day?"

"I imagine they had some way to measure his productivity."

Wrinkling her nose, Jeri paused. "He sold industrial computer systems, so I suppose they tracked how many computers he sold and installed. But still, maybe he would've sold more if he hadn't been sitting at home."

"The world has changed, Jeri. Computers and the internet have turned the world upside down."

"Some people still have to go to work every day. There aren't any internet barbers or restaurants." She paused. "I saw an ad for an internet café. What is that? Does someone deliver coffee to you?”

“It's a coffee shop with wi-fi that allows you to be connected to the internet while you sip your latte.”

“That seems strange. Why go to a coffee shop alone and stare at your computer while you're drinking coffee? Why not go to a café with a friend and talk?”

“Why indeed,” I said as I pulled up under the Whistling Pines portico. I opened the car door for Jeri and escorted her into the lobby where we were met by a half dozen women who immediately started questioning her about the television show, Jonathan Edwards, the herring roe recipe, and the abrupt end of the broadcast.

I retreated to my car and called Jenny. “I just dropped Jeri off. Is there anything I need to pick up on the way home?”

“We need to talk.”

I froze. “Um, about what?”

“I'll tell you when you get here.” Jenny ended the call before I could request clarification.

My stomach churned as I drove the few miles to the house, my mind tossing the possible issues I might've unknowingly created. I couldn't come up with anything, which made me reflect on one of Jenny's comments to Gail, one of the nurse's aides. She'd told Gail I was clueless about relationship issues.

Putting on a brave front, I stepped in the back door and hung my coat on the peg. "I'm home," I said, not too loudly in case Amy was asleep.

Jenny, in a flannel nightgown, bathrobe, and slippers, walked into the kitchen with Amy asleep in her arms. She looked more concerned than angry, so I relaxed a bit.

"What's up?"

"Tim and Zoey came over."

"Our neighbors?"

Jenny nodded. "They brought Rambo, too. He rushed through the door and checked out the entire house. They apologized when he lifted his leg on the stairway post."

Hanging my head, I took a deep breath. "I hope they cleaned it up."

"Tim was very apologetic and grabbed a dish towel to sop up the puddle."

"A dish towel, not a paper towel?"

Jenny shook her head. "It's in the washer with the rags I used to clean up all of Rambo's muddy footprints."

"Was it just a neighborly call, or did they have something specific in mind?"

Biting her bottom lip, Jenny drew a breath. "Zoey offered to babysit if we want to go out some night."

"Um, that was nice of her."

Jenny clenched her eyes shut. "She, Tim, and Rambo could come over here, or we could bring the kids to their house."

I opened my mouth, but I couldn't verbalize a single thought. After a second, I asked, "What did you say?"

"That we really appreciate the offer, but my mother loves to babysit. We'd be robbing Grandma Barbara of time with Amy if we had anyone else watch the kids."

I didn't realize I'd been holding my breath but let it out and closed my eyes. "Good answer. I'd have probably said, 'hell, no!' and regretted it."

"Zoey looked disappointed but accepted that answer. Then they dropped another bombshell. Their band is playing at Hugo's Saturday night, and they invited us."

"I think we're busy."

Jenny chuckled, which caused Amy to stir. Nodding to the stairs, we put Amy in her crib and walked to the bedroom. "Did you politely decline?" I asked as I stripped off my shirt and pants.

"It's a bit more complicated," Jenny replied as she watched me change into nightwear. "They asked if you'd play lead guitar with them. I guess their guitarist is missing in action."

"No way. I'm not interested in being part of their band. My plate is full."

Jenny hung her bathrobe behind the door and slipped into the crisp sheets. Although the house had a boiler that provided heat, the bedroom radiator never got more than warm, leaving the bedroom chilly all winter.

I turned off the lights and snuggled into Jenny's warm back. I felt tension in her body. "What's wrong?"

"I was afraid you'd want to play with the band. I'm sure you miss being onstage."

"I don't need to be onstage, and I've heard their music. I'm not into heavy metal. I'd rather play oldies to the Whistling Pines residents." Jenny didn't relax, even with my reassurance. "There's something else."

"Kerry called."

"Yeah, he wanted me to go out for a beer after the television broadcast. I declined."

"He asked me how I felt about possibly being a cop's wife."

"I also declined that offer."

"Kerry said he needs you, badly. He asked if I could encourage you to consider his offer."

"I'm not going to be a cop."

"You're sure?" she asked.

"Working at Whistling Pines is all I need or want."

Jenny relaxed. "But you've enjoyed helping Len and Kerry with investigations. Kerry says you're every bit as good an investigator as he is."

"I told him I can talk about investigations over a cup of coffee anytime, but I don't want to be a full-time cop."

Jenny rolled over so we were nose-to-nose. "Thank you. I don't want to be a cop's wife."

I hugged and kissed her. "The kids are asleep."

Jenny touched my cheek gently and giggled. "You smell like fish."

"I'll take a quick shower."

"Yes, you will. And by the end of your shower Amy should be awake for another feeding."

"But after…"

Jenny pushed me away. "I'd really like to get more than four or five hours of sleep tonight."

Climbing out of bed, I grabbed my bathrobe, a fresh t-shirt and sleep pants. "You're prioritizing sleep over romance?"

"I'm prioritizing reality over a sailor's horny ideas."

Amy started to cry as I stepped into the shower. *So much for romance tonight.*

Chapter Eleven

Day 5

We'd reset the alarm so it played a soft rock radio station, with the volume low, in the hope it wouldn't wake Amy and at least one of us would be able to shower and dress before her first morning feeding. It was a nice theory on many levels. This morning, the radio woke Amy before either of us responded to the music. I rolled over to shut off the music, only to realize it had been playing for over ten minutes. Both Jenny and I were too exhausted to hear it. As much as I hated to admit it, the need for sleep had rightfully won over passion.

Jenny rolled over and stood. "Jump in the shower and dress while I feed Amy. You can entertain her while I'm in the shower."

Amy was all smiles, happy to listen to the gurgling coffee pot while I poured bowls of cereal for Jenny, Jeremy, and me. I set the bowls and spoons on the table, then fetched the milk carton. Jenny walked downstairs, fluffing her hair.

"What are you chuckling about?" she asked, sitting down in front of her cereal as I set Amy's seat on the floor.

"Remember when you used to sniff the milk before pouring it on your cereal?" I asked.

"Do you miss your bachelor days, when your refrigerator was a petri dish of moldy food and spoiled milk?"

"Hey, there was beer in the fridge, too. It never went bad."

Jeremy thundered down the stairs and threw himself into his chair. He stared at the cereal in his bowl. "Can we get kids' cereal sometime? I don't like brown flakes with bits of dried fruit and raisins."

Glancing at me with a smile, Jenny answered. "Would you like the sugar-coated flakes or the cereal with the marshmallow stars?"

"Either would be okay." Jeremy looked at Jenny's smile and rolled his eyes. "My teacher was talking about using irony. Was that an ironic comment?"

"I think your mom was actually using sarcasm."

"Does that mean you're not buying frosted cereal?"

"Yes, that's what it means."

Emanations from Amy's diaper ended the cereal discussion. Jeremy looked at his sister sternly. "You've got to stop pooping in your pants while we're eating. It's disgusting."

Amy wiggled her arms, oblivious to Jeremy's admonition.

I took a swallow of coffee, then scooped Amy into my arms. "It's too bad you don't know how to change diapers, Jeremy."

He thought for a second. "It's ironic that you've never taught me how to change Amy's diapers." He looked at Jenny. "Is that the correct way to use ironic?"

"It'd be better if you'd said, 'It's ironic that you'd like me to change her diapers but haven't shown me how.'"

Jeremy shook his head. "That's what I said."

I left the semantics discussion and went upstairs. I returned to Jeremy restuffing his backpack with homework and a lunch bag. He closed the zipper and looked at me. "Are you going to be a cop like Jacob's dad?"

"No. He likes being the police chief. I prefer working at Whistling Pines with your mom."

"Is it because you get to play music at work this way?"

"That's part of it. There's a lot less stress in my job than being a cop. I like mine better."

"Are you going to play in the band with Tim and Zoey?"

"Don't you think I've got all I can do with work and taking care of you and Amy?"

"Mom told Tim that you really miss playing music."

I knelt down to Jeremy's level. "I really like playing music, but I have other things that are more important right now."

"Like what?"

"Being your dad."

Jeremy searched my eyes. "That doesn't take a lot of time, does it?"

Wrapping him in my arms, I gave him a hug. "It doesn't take a lot of time, but I don't want to miss a minute of it because I have to play music with a band."

"Mom, Amy, and I could come along. I like to hear you play music." He paused. "Maybe Mom could sing with you like she did at Buccaneer Days."

The comment caught Jenny by surprise. "That was a one-time event. Now, go brush your hair and teeth."

"Yeah, you could sing with me again."

Jenny shook her head. "I've retired from my professional singing career."

"You got a standing ovation."

Jenny's eyes got misty. "*You* got a standing ovation. I was standing next to you."

"Honey, I've experienced a moment like that maybe three times in my life. We were alone on that stage, like there was no one else in the world. The band and crowd both sensed it."

"Forget it, sailor. My career singing with the band is over. I sing solo, and only in the shower."

My cell phone buzzed and I handed Amy to Jenny. "This is Peter."

"Are you out of the house?" Kerry asked.

"I was just going to put my coat on. What's up?"

"Put your coat on and step outside."

I pulled my coat off the peg and slipped it on. "Okay, I'm on the back step."

"The Bureau of Criminal Apprehension just called with two more tidbits they gleaned from the Sandberg crime scene. The tread pattern is from a knee-high women's boot sold primarily through Fleet and Farm stores. It's marketed as a barn boot that's popular with dairy farmers and horse people."

"Let me guess, the second tidbit is that they found traces of manure in the footprints."

"You should work on your stand-up comedy act."

"It seemed logical."

"They found traces of cutting oil and tiny metal fragments."

"I don't know what cutting oil is."

"Machine shops use it to lubricate and cool their cutting equipment."

"What's the connection to barn boots?"

"Maybe some farmer's wife picked up a machine part from a shop that was repairing it."

"And on the way thought, 'Gee, I think I'll make a side trip, kill Reggie Sandberg, and steal some recipes on the way home.'"

Kerry sighed audibly. "Can you be serious for five minutes?"

"I'm freezing. Hang on while I get in my car and start the engine."

The car was no warmer than the back steps, but at least there was no windchill. The engine cranked over and started, followed by a blast of cold air from the vents. I stared at the frost covered windshield and thought, *maybe Kerry will talk long enough so the frost melts and I won't have to scrape the windshield.*

"Are you in the car?"

"I feel like I'm inside a bottle of milk. It's cold and all I can see is the white frost on the windows."

"We buy cartons."

"What?"

"Cartons of milk. The kids would think I'd lost my mind if I talked about a bottle of milk."

"I assume that means I'm sitting here freezing my butt because you've run out of things to tell me about the murder."

"Pretty much. It was you who said you wanted to sit in the freezing car. I really didn't have anything else."

"So, the oily boots and metal chips didn't tell you anything else?"

"Not really. The BCA was just updating me on their analysis of trace evidence from the crime scene. They didn't provide any insight into the source of the contaminants."

"The killer wore leather gloves and oily barn boots. There are no fingerprints, no hairs, no other trace evidence."

"Nada."

"Every criminal leaves trace evidence and takes some traces with them."

Kerry laughed. "I loved that line from *CSI: Miami.* Horatio Caine said that right after Calleigh Duquesne told him a crime scene was devoid of evidence."

"It's true, isn't it?"

"I suppose there's an element of truth to it, but you have to remember the line was written by some guy sitting in a room dreaming up witty comebacks for a fictional crime show. They always caught the bad guy, usually after a gunfight, and did it in one hour."

"Yeah, yeah. It was fiction. But still…"

"Peter, we're not going to solve this in an hour, the lab won't have DNA evidence in ten minutes, there's not going to be a car chase or shootout, and I won't pull a bottle of expensive Scotch out of my bottom desk drawer to celebrate the end of the case."

"That's *Law and Order.*"

"What's law and order?"

"At the end of every *Law and Order* television episode Fred Thompson pulled out glasses and a bottle of Scotch to celebrate the conclusion of the case."

Kerry sighed again. "They're all fiction, Peter."

"There's an element of truth to them."

Chuckling, Kerry paused. "If we arrest a suspect, I'll bring you into the interview room to be the bad cop to my good cop."

"Why am I the bad cop?"

"Because the good cop stays behind after the bad cop stalks out. The suspect breaks down and confesses to the good cop while the bad cop watches through the one-way mirror."

"Think about it. Can you see me as the bad cop? What am I going to do, torture them with sad guitar songs until they go insane?"

"There's the solution! You bring the accordion to the interview. They'll probably confess when you take it out of the case."

The frost was melting, leaving trickles of water streaming down my windshield. "I'm going to work now. You can buy me coffee later if you want to talk about something."

Kerry didn't disconnect. "Did Jenny tell you I'd called last night?"

"Nice flanking maneuver, soldier. Trying to use my wife to talk me into being a cop was underhanded."

"You're wasting your talent playing guitar for the senior citizens and driving them to Judy's for pies and pastries."

"I am NOT wasting my time. I'm maintaining my sanity." I paused and softened my voice. "I'm also able to sleep at night."

"Think about it."

I was going to say no when I realized I was listening to a dial tone.

* * *

I hung up my coat, turned on the computer, grabbed my coffee cup, and walked to the dining room. I noted that eleven people had signed up for a ride to the Sandberg funeral, meaning, I had to arrange my schedule to accommodate the funeral and travel time.

My plan was to catch Karla, Kathy, and Mary to see if they'd completed the cookbook edits. Instead, I was greeted by a mob of people standing in a circle around a table. My first thought was that someone was having a medical emergency, so I rushed to the group. Instead of a medical emergency, Jeri Westfall was surrounded by women firing questions at her about the television show.

"Did Jonathan really grope that woman?"

Someone in the crowd, not Jeri, replied, "Of course he did! Didn't you see his handprint on her thigh?"

"I can't believe she'd lift up her skirt, so people saw her red panties. On national television, no less!"

"I think it was a ploy to improve his ratings. They say there is no bad publicity. I bet every newspaper has a picture of Hailey's panties on the front page."

"I almost threw up when Rolf was gutting those herrings. Ugh, that was a terrible thing to show on TV."

"It's no worse than when they opened that can of Swedish surströmming and Jonathan turned away, pretending to gag."

The conversations flew around like machine gun fire, the women talking over each other, throwing out disgusting scenes from Jonathan's other broadcasts. Jeri sat at the table with her hands folded, occasionally answering a question, usually about the events during and after the poteka segment.

Peggy Lipton was busily writing on a stack of recipe cards. She'd finish one, hand it to someone in the crowd, and immediately start writing on another. Karla was standing to the side, and I took her away from the gathering crowd.

"How long has this been going on?"

Karla looked at her watch. "Jeri came down for breakfast about half an hour ago, and she's been mobbed ever since."

"Does Jeri ever say anything, or is she just the topic of discussion?"

Karla slid her glasses down her nose and looked over the top of them at me. "Have you ever known Jeri to indulge in the idle gossip around here? She occasionally gets a question, and she replies quietly, and factually."

"What's Peggy Lipton doing with the note cards?"

"She's copying Jeri's black magic cake recipe for anyone who wants it."

I looked back at Peggy, who was carefully copying the recipe." I could run copies off in the lobby."

Karla looked at Peggy, then back at me. "She's smiling. Let it be."

"How's the cookbook edit going?"

"I proofread it for the final time last night. I'm going to deliver it to the printer this morning."

"That's been quite an undertaking."

Karla rolled her eyes. "If I ever volunteer to do something like this again, please slap me. All the 'Ts' drove me nuts! I'm ninety-nine percent sure I've got the teaspoons sorted correctly from the tablespoons. I wrote Tbsp where appropriate, instead of using upper and lowercase Ts. It was a royal pain."

I patted her shoulder. You, Kathy, and Mary were troupers."

Karla laughed. "I'm sure we'll be rewarded in heaven."

"What's your marketing plan?"

"We're going to set up a table in the lobby and anyone who wants a cookbook can buy one from us."

"That's it? No sales in town or on the internet?"

Karla ran her tongue around the inside of her mouth like she had a seed stuck in her teeth. "Those are marvelous suggestions. How many extra copies will you need when you set those things up?"

"Um, never mind."

Karla nodded. "Good plan. If you find some other computer literate sucker, er, person, who's willing to take that project on, just let me know how many cookbooks they'll need."

A roar of laughter came from the crowd around Jeri. Then she stood and put up her hands. "Excuse me," she said, pushing aside her breakfast dishes, "I need to talk to Peter."

Jeri, smiling, walked to me and looped her arm around mine. "Let's walk over to the aviary."

I wondered what private thought Jeri wanted to share as we separated from the crowd in the dining room. Out of earshot, Jeri released my arm and smiled at me. "The cooking show was…fabulous. Thank you for including me."

"Your recipe was a winner, the backstory was charming, and you were absolutely wonderful during the filming. The crowd loved you."

She put her hand on my arm. "Those are very kind words, but I know you had a hand in the selection and sale to the television people. Thank you."

"Have you answered all the questions from the crowd?"

Jeri peeked past me into the dining room. "To be frank, I've answered every question about three times. That's why I steered you out here, so I could escape the crowd. They're into speculation about Hailey's incident, the fire alarm, and the fire sprinkler. The consensus is that it was all staged to add drama to the end of the show."

"Is that what you think, Jeri?"

She shook her head. "We were there. There's no way they could've planned all that. And that poor woman, the producer, was frantic. I thought she was going to have a heart attack."

I looked over Jeri's head into the dining room. "It looks like the mob has dispersed. You can finish your coffee."

Jeri turned and smiled. "There are still two people waiting for Peggy to copy the black magic cake recipe. I hope they all enjoy it as much as my family has."

"It's a wonderful legacy, Jeri."

I was walking past the sign-up sheets when my cell phone rang.

"Can Deb and I come over tonight?"

I recognized Kerry's voice, but the only reason for him to visit with his wife was probably to twist my arm more about taking a job. "You know, we're not getting a lot of sleep. This weekend might be better."

"Deb wants to see the baby and she has a solution for your lack of sleep."

"She's bringing over sleeping pills, or is she taking Amy home with you?"

"You know how marriage is. I haven't been clued in on her sleep solution. I was just told to call you and invite ourselves over. I'll bring a six-pack of beer and a chilled bottle of wine. What time are you through with supper and is it okay if Jacob comes along?"

Lacking an excuse, I said, "Jeremy usually has his homework done before supper and we're through eating and have the dishes washed by six o'clock. Jacob and Jeremy will disappear so we can have adult conversation, so that's an advantage."

I reversed direction and walked to the nurse's office. Jenny was having a conversation with one of the aides, so I waited by her desk to respect the privacy of the information.

"What's up, husband?"

"Kerry, Jacob, and Deb are coming over after supper."

Jenny closed her eyes. "Please call him back and beg off. I'm dead on my feet and I'd rather collapse in front of the television."

"He was insistent. Deb wants to see Amy and she has a sleep solution for us."

Jenny blew out a breath. "Fine. I'll put ice cubes under my eyes so they're not so swollen and I'll try to smile."

"Kerry's bringing beer and wine."

Jenny's sad eyes fit her sarcastic response. "Whoopee. Tired *and* hungover tomorrow. That'll be just wonderful."

* * *

I was reading emails and eating a sandwich when Jenny walked in and closed my office door. She pulled her breast pump out of a satchel and started up the pump and I looked away.

"My office is now the lactation room?"

"Your office has a door that locks and has the least traffic of any spot in the entire campus. You've been gone at lunch time for most of this week, so you didn't even know I've been here pumping."

"To be honest, I didn't know you'd been pumping."

Jenny raised her eyebrows. "Where did you think the milk you've been feeding Amy has been coming from? It's not next to the cream in the dairy case."

"Sorry. I haven't thought about it. I've had a few distractions."

"What did Kerry want when you went outside to talk this morning?"

"There was new analysis of the evidence from the murder scene. The killer wore

211

women's barn boots contaminated with oil and metal particles."

"Does that point him toward a suspect?"

"Apparently not, or he wouldn't have called me."

Jenny capped the two small bottles of milk, arranged herself, and packed up the pump. "Did you have any insights for him?"

"I'm half asleep all the time. So no, I didn't have a coherent suggestion."

"But now he knows the killer was a woman or a man with small feet."

I nodded. "A woman who maybe lives on a farm, then walked through a puddle of oil with metal particles in it."

"I'm not a farm girl, but I don't think farmers keep oil in their barns."

"Yeah, I had the same conclusion."

Someone knocked on the door. Jenny stood and opened the door to Howard Johnson's smiling face. "I thought maybe you two were napping."

Jenny shook her head, not offering an explanation except, "I wish." She slid past Howard.

"People are lining up for the movie. Are you planning to make popcorn?"

I got up, nodding. "Sorry, I'm running behind." I grabbed the DVD of *It Should Happen to You,* a Judy Holliday and Jack Lemmon comedy.

I explained the mystery of the oily barn boots to Howard as we walked to the community room. He had no insights to offer but promised to think about it.

Half the seats were already taken, and people were streaming in as I put oil and popcorn in the popper, then loaded the movie into the DVD player. A female voice called from the back, "Can you replay the cooking show from last night? I want to see the part where Jonathan Edwards pretends to slip on the herring and fall down. Maybe you have a copy where we can hear what he was saying."

That brought a round of laughter from the crowd. I scooped up bags of popcorn and handed them out as Howard dimmed the lights and the movie started to play. I stood in the back corner watching the opening credits. The suggestion to replay the cooking show teased some thread in the back of my brain. I'd been there, watching in real time, but I'd only seen many of the events peripherally. Jonathan was already on the floor when I looked his way, so I hadn't seen him fall. I'd only seen a flash of Hailey exposing the handprint on her thigh, which had distracted me from whatever else was happening in the background. It had almost been like a magician's sleight of hand; nothing up my sleeve, but while you're distracted, I palmed the ball hidden under the second shell with my other hand.

I stepped out of the room and did a Google search for *World Eats.* I got a menu of recent shows and a YouTube link to last night's show. I clicked on the arrow in the YouTube screen and the cooking show opening played.

I was startled when Nancy asked, "Is that the cooking show from last night?"

I held my phone higher so she could see the screen. "I just found it on YouTube."

"Let's go back to my office. I didn't see it last night and we'll be able to watch it on my larger computer monitor."

Nancy left for her office, and I looked in on the movie crowd. They were laughing and everything was under control, so I felt comfortable leaving for a while. Nancy had the YouTube search screen up when I walked in.

"Close the door. I don't want people thinking we sit around watching videos all day." She sat with her fingers poised over the keyboard. "What search did you use to find the show?"

"The program is called *World Eats.*"

The menu of recent episodes flashed on the screen, and I pointed to the recording from the previous night. She touched the arrow to start the program, then closed the blinds.

The show's logo appeared, followed by Jonathan Edwards walking onto the set as the crowd clapped. Jonathan nodded to the crowd, then introduced Jeri Westfall. She walked in from the right and stepped onto the box next to Jonathan.

"Jeri looks very nice," Nancy said as Jonathan asked her to explain the backstory of her recipe.

I was intrigued, seeing the broadcast without all the peripheral preparations. "This seems so strange. There were dozens of people scrambling around frantically but all we see is Jonathan speaking with Jeri like they're alone in his kitchen."

Jeri and Jonathan mixed the cake batter, then Jonathan took a finished cake out of the oven and said the line about the magic of television and the crowd laughed, on cue. He brought out a bowl of frosting and poked holes in the cake. Jeri explained that the frosting melted into the holes and made it almost like eating a candy bar.

Jonathan finished icing the cake, cut two slices, and handed one to Jeri. The camera zoomed in on his face as he put a bite of cake in his mouth. He got a dreamy look and made a yummy sound.

"Oh, Jeri, this is heavenly." He explained that Jeri's recipe was available on the show's website. The scene changed immediately to an insurance commercial featuring a talking duck.

Nancy looked at me. "Jeri looked wonderfully composed and photogenic."

"Jeri was wonderful, and she had a good time."

"I heard laughter and clapping. Was there an audience?"

"Not so much an audience as the people who were helping with the show and a few other people who'd accompanied the featured cooks."

Nancy looked puzzled. "I didn't see any of them."

"Actually, there was pandemonium behind the cameras. It's interesting for me to see what was broadcast because I spent a lot of time watching the offscreen commotion. It was a chaotic ballet orchestrated by the show's producer. She was speaking into her mic all the time, coordinating the whole thing."

The commercial ended and Jonathan introduced Rolf. Nancy glanced at me. "Did they mess up his hair intentionally?"

"Not really. Someone put a multi-colored stocking cap on his head while they were doing his makeup and the producer told them to pull it off a second before he stepped on-screen."

Rolf told the story of his recipe, then the pan of herring was delivered by someone off camera. Rolf explained the harvesting of the roe from the herring. I'd been focused on Rolf's knife as he sliced open the herring. The camera zoomed in on Jonathan's face. He glanced at the camera and wrinkled his nose, like Rolf's gutting of the fish was disgusting. The camera then focused on Rolf dredging the roe sacs in flour and sliding them into hot oil.

The camera missed the reaction of the crew and crowd to the smell of the frying roe. Jonathan looked interested and undisturbed by the smell of the preparation. Rolf slid the fried roe onto bread and drizzled seasoned butter on top. Jonathan announced where to find the recipe, put a piece of roe in his mouth, and the view changed to a commercial with hamsters driving a compact SUV.

Nancy turned to me. "That all seemed professional, and Rolf's accent made it really charming."

I laughed. "The frying herring smell was so disgusting that the crew covered their faces and several people in the crowd ran for the bathrooms. When the camera cut away, Jonathan yelled for water. Rolf handed him a bottle of aquavit that must've burned his mouth because he spit all over the table. They ran a second commercial so the crew could clean up before he introduced the third cook."

Nancy shook her head. "Ah, the magic of television."

"Yes, I'll never watch a cooking show the same ever again."

"The third guest is Hailey Evers?"

I nodded as the second commercial ended. "Yes. I'm really curious about how they handled the end of her segment."

Nancy turned to the monitor as Jonathan introduced Hailey. "You can't see how nervous Hailey is. I swear she was about to wet her pants as they introduced her."

Jonathan gave no hint that anything untoward had happened at the end of Rolf's segment. He was all smiles and charming. Hailey seemed nervous and looked offscreen a couple times before relaxing.

"What was she looking at offscreen?"

"Her mother was in the dining room and had been reassuring her before they called Hailey up."

"Her mother, Cecelia?"

"I didn't hear her mother's name," I said as Hailey gained confidence.

Jonathan and Hailey started working the dough as Hailey explained the next step, spreading the filling before rolling and baking it. Jonathan mentioned making poteka with his grandmother. Hailey glanced offscreen and mentioned that her mother remembered making poteka with him. The camera caught Jonathan's quick look at the woman offscreen, and his flash of recognition. At that point, the show cut away from the live broadcast and rolled over to a list of the recipes, and then the credits.

Nancy stopped the playback. "That's odd, that he didn't taste Hailey's finished poteka. He always samples the dish and makes comments about how wonderful it is while the cook smiles."

"The last few minutes of the show were chaotic, and the production company must've had a time delay so they could cut away or bleep if a guest uses a profanity. The director must've decided not to air the show's ending." I paused thinking about the comments made about Hailey's red panties. "There must be another version of this that some of the residents have seen." I pointed to another icon on Nancy's YouTube display. "Let's watch this one. The counter says it's had 103,970 views and the ticker just keeps rolling."

Nancy clicked on the other icon, and we waited while a circle spun in the middle of the screen. A video started, but it wasn't the official broadcast. The camera shook and captured the entire kitchen area, much as I'd seen it live, not just Jonathan's smiling face as captured in the televised broadcast, but the entire kitchen area, with audience, cameramen, producer, and technicians. I pointed to a box in the lower right corner. "Click there to view this on your full screen."

Nancy clicked the box, and the video filled her large computer monitor. The recording began while Rolf was being prepped, apparently during the commercial after Jeri's segment. Vang was frantically directing people and a female technician was arranging a colorful stocking cap on Rolf's head.

"Who took this video, Peter? The view is from behind the television cameras filming the segment we've just watched."

I thought back, trying to picture the people in the room. I had a vague recollection of someone in the back corner, next to Hailey and her mother, with a cell phone aimed at the set. "There was a woman in the back with a cell phone. She must've started recording after Jeri left the kitchen."

The lights came up and Jonathan smiled, as he had in the previous video, and started Rolf's introduction. Rolf was standing at the kitchen door, ready to move into the scene. Ellen said something unintelligible into her mic and the female technician, who'd been arranging Rolf's hat, held her hand to her ear, then jumped up and ripped the stocking cap off Rolf's head, leaving his wild blond mop of hair sticking up. Rolf was irritated, but someone pushed him into the kitchen and told him to smile.

As he walked next to Jonathan, a woman's voice, apparently the videographer, said, "Oh, Gawd, look at what they did to his hair."

The video continued, but at a broad angle, capturing all the activity around the images shown during the official television show. Instead of the narrow view of Jonathan's happy smiling face listening to Rolf's explanation of the roe recovery, we got a broader view of Rolf slicing open the herring, with guts running out and Rolf's slime-covered hands gently separating the roe sacs from the other entrails, as he spoke about the man who'd delivered the fresh herring to him.

Chuckling, Nancy shook her head. "The director and camera crew did a nice job of focusing away from the messy gutting of the fish. I'm sure some people with delicate stomachs would've changed channels if they'd shown the slimy guts running into the herring pan."

A technician reached out and pulled the pan aside as Rolf dredged the roe sacs in flour. Another person used a hot pad to pull a cast iron frying pan off a burner and set it next to Rolf. Jonathan watched the process, smiling, and Rolf put the roe into the frying pan of hot butter.

Within seconds, the crew started turning away from the smell of the frying roe, covering their faces and turning green. The view swung wildly away from Jonathan and Rolf, focusing on a man and two women who fled the room, gagging. The woman taking the cell phone video laughed. "Oh man, can you believe the stink?" She coughed. "And the combination of the chocolate cake and frying herring is about enough to gag a maggot."

The recording swung back to Jonathan and Rolf just as Jonathan spoke to the camera, telling the viewers where to find Rolf's recipe. Jonathan lifted a piece of fried roe to his mouth, made his furtive signal to the producer, then smiled until he heard the producer say, "and we're in commercial."

The television production had then shown a commercial, but the cell phone videographer continued her recording as Jonathan spit the roe into a napkin and yelled for water. The laughter of the crowd echoed in the dining room as Rolf handed Jonathan the aquavit. The crowd roared when Jonathan spit the aquavit on the table, the laughter drowning out what was apparently Jonathan's profane tirade. The producer ran to Jonathan with a roll of paper towels while yelling into her mic, telling the studio to run another commercial.

Rolf, who was laughing, was shuffled out of the kitchen and a man waved his arm, signaling for someone to come to the kitchen. A woman's voice said, "They're ready for you, dear. Take a deep breath. It'll be fine."

Hailey's back appeared in the video as she walked across the dining room, stopping at the kitchen door. Jonathan had regained his composure as the makeup artist touched up his face and ran a comb through his hair. The camera centered Hailey in the view as a woman spoke with her and threaded a microphone cord through her form-fitting sweater, hooking the transmitter behind her back. The video moved to Jonathan, who was watching Hailey's microphone being arranged. His on-screen smile was gone, replaced by a lascivious grin as his eyes ran up and down Hailey's body, then focusing on her chest as the mic cord was run beneath it.

"Look at that lecherous old shit eyeing her like a piece of meat," a woman standing near the camera said.

"He's the same horn-dog he was in high school. No one in a skirt was safe around him."

Hailey was guided to a spot next to Jonathan. His smile changed to warm and engaging as he leaned close to Hailey and whispered something to her. A second later he looked into the camera and introduced the third segment of the show.

The whispered videographer's voice drowned out the activity in the kitchen. "What do you think he whispered to her?"

The other off-screen voice whispered back. "I'll bet you ten bucks he invited her to his hotel room for a drink after the show."

Nancy looked at me. "Whoever's recording this doesn't like Jonathan much."

I nodded. "I think the end of the show is going to look very different from what we saw in the official broadcast."

The poteka dough was prepared and set on the flour-dusted table. Jonathan commented about making poteka with his grandmother. Hailey's response and look into the corner was captured. Jonathan's momentary surprise caused the video to jiggle as the videographer laughed. "I think he just recognized you."

A moment later, the rolling pin rolled off the table and Jonathan bent down to pick it up. Hailey jumped away from him and yelled, then rushed to the end of the counter where she was framed in a doorway. She lifted her skirt, exposing the white handprint on her thigh, ending under the hem of her red panties.

Vang was screaming into her mic, "CUT. CUT. CUT. Go to a commercial."

Hailey pulled down her skirt, pulled the microphone off and handed the electronics to a technician. The video went back to Jonathan who was waving his arms and protesting his innocence to the producer. Behind them, the smoke detector started screeching and a technician pulled the smoking poteka out of the oven. A few seconds later, the sprinkler started spraying. People ran from the kitchen to escape the spray. The pan of herring and entrails was knocked over. Jonathan slipped in the slimy mess and fell down. The video bounced as the woman holding the cell phone laughed.

The videographer abruptly swung left, capturing Kerry walking into the dining room. I recognized my back as Kerry stepped next to Jeri and me. The camera got closer to us as the producer ran to Kerry. We heard Ellen's plea to Kerry that no one be arrested and her assurance that the show's lawyers would contact Hailey and pay for the kitchen damage.

Hailey stepped past Jeri and me, then approached the camera. A soft voice said, "It's okay, honey. You were perfect." It was followed by Hailey's sobbing. Then, the video ended.

Nancy's screen switched back to a bunch of icons. The video of the official show was in the top left corner and the counter under it said a few hundred people had watched it. The counter under the unofficial version clicked up by tens and passed 250,000 views as we watched.

Nancy shut down YouTube and turned to me. "Well, the second video was much more damning. What happened after that?"

"The firemen arrived. They shut off the fire alarm and sprinkler. The television people wound up their cables and dried off their cameras, then I drove Jeri back here."

"Jeri was quite a star this morning."

I nodded. "She nearly begged me to save her from the crowd of people asking questions."

Nancy leaned back. "I feel sorry for Hailey. That was terrible."

Something nagged at me as I thought about the crowd around Jeri. "Someone commented on the handprint, the one on Hailey's thigh."

"I suppose they saw the second, unofficial video."

I shook my head. "That's unlikely. It was first thing in the morning. I wonder if an unofficial video had even been uploaded yet."

Nancy shrugged. "How else would they know Jonathan grabbed Hailey's leg leaving a handprint in flour?"

"Kerry, the police chief, said it was paint, not flour. I wonder if someone here knew about the plan to set up Jonathan before the show?"

Knocking on Nancy's door interrupted my musing. Howard Johnson stuck his head in. "Am I interrupting?"

"Come in, Howard," Nancy said, standing and signaling the end of our conversation.

"The movie ended, so I put the DVD in its case."

"Thanks, Howard," I said, accepting the plastic box.

Howard looked at each of us. "You look somber. Did someone die?"

Nancy waved off his concern. "We just watched a replay of the cooking show from last night."

"Jeri looked very cool and collected," Howard said.

"The broadcast was cut short before Jonathan sampled the poteka," I said.

"Yes, I thought that was odd. They cut away to the recipes and commercials rather abruptly."

Howard's face betrayed no knowledge of anything but the televised ending of the show. "Did you hear about the commotion in the kitchen after the broadcast cut away?"

A hint of a smile crept onto Howard's lips. He closed the door and leaned against it. "I haven't seen it, but the rumor mill says there's a bootlegged video that continues after the network switched from the live broadcast to the recipes."

I nodded. "And you've heard there was an embarrassing incident."

Howard chuckled. "There are always rumors about embarrassing incidents. Some are true. Many are not."

Nancy crossed her arms. "We just watched the privately recorded video. It continued to record after the network cut away from the broadcast. Jonathan bent down to pick up a rolling pin and groped the final cook under the counter."

Raising his eyebrows, Howard considered his response. "I heard Hailey Evers had a handprint in a…compromising location."

Nancy nodded. "We can confirm that. It's no longer a rumor."

Howard opened the door, then paused. "If asked, I'll confirm that information."

"What are you planning to do, Peter?"

"It's not really our issue."

Nancy sat down, drew a deep breath, and let it out slowly as she thought. "You'd better call the police chief and make him aware of the unofficial video."

"I'm sure dozens of people are going to call to demand that he arrest Jonathan Edwards."

Leaning forward, Nancy looked at me earnestly. "This is an instance where my curiosity is overwhelming my sense of propriety. Please call Chief Stone. I want to know what he's planning to do."

"Like I said, it doesn't really involve Whistling Pines."

"Let's say, having that information will…quell the rumors that are certainly swirling about Jonathan's legal situation."

I closed the door. "You want me to use my relationship with the chief to get inside information on what may be an ongoing investigation."

Nancy smiled and stood. "That's an impolite way of putting it, but you got the gist of my request."

I closed my office door and called Kerry's cell phone, knowing I'd never get past the receptionist who screened incoming calls. He answered after the third ring.

"Do you have a second?"

"Hang on while I close my door." I heard his footsteps and the door latch. "What's up?"

"I just watched a video of the cooking show, taken by someone on their cell phone. It captured a few more minutes of activity, past the point where the network stopped broadcasting the live program."

"How much more?"

"The videographer was standing right behind us when the producer asked you not to arrest anyone and said their lawyers would contact Hailey, and the show would pay for the damage to the kitchen."

"That's good news. We've got them agreeing to pay for the kitchen damage. It'll make it harder for them to weasel out of the repair costs."

"Um, Kerry, it captures the moment when Hailey lifts her skirt, exposing the handprint. Are you going to arrest or charge her?"

"Charge her with what, embarrassing an arrogant jerk?"

"I...guess it could be extortion or something."

"I'm not aware of Hailey extorting money from anyone. As a matter of fact, you said there's a video of the producer saying their lawyers are going to contact her. I took that as an admission of guilt and they're offering to make things right with her. That's not extortion."

"But they posted a video."

"Millions of people post embarrassing videos every day. It's not illegal to post an embarrassing video online unless it involves a child, and even that hasn't been tested in the courts."

"So, Hailey did nothing wrong."

"I didn't say that, Peter. What she did is highly immoral, and if she used the video to extort money from Jonathan Edwards, she'd be guilty of extortion. I suspect the show's lawyers will negotiate a settlement with the stipulation they're not admitting guilt. There will certainly be a non-disclosure clause so neither party can reveal the details of the settlement. That's perfectly legal and takes it out of the courts. No laws are broken and there's nothing to prosecute."

"Really?"

"I'm sure there are millions of situations resolved this way. I think it's a part of Hollywood lore that went with the casting couch. There's nothing I'm going to do about it."

"But there's a video of the producer asking you not to make an arrest. It looks like you're colluding in a coverup."

Kerry chuckled. "You and I both know she didn't want me to arrest Jonathan Edwards. We also know he's not guilty of anything, so there's no collusion. I'm just doing my job."

"But…"

"It's over, Peter. No arrests are going to be made. No one is going to be charged. I have a murder investigation and that's where I'm going to focus."

I blew out a breath. "Okay."

"Okay. We'll see you at six."

I looked at the clock and realized my workday was over and it was time to make supper and check Jeremy's homework. I shut down the computer, grabbed my coat, and turned off the lights. I stopped at Nancy's office to inform her there weren't going to be any arrests resulting from the television filming and left.

Chapter Twelve

There was an unfamiliar car in my driveway when I arrived home. In a big city, I'd probably panic because Jeremy might've opened the door to a stranger. In Two Harbors, crime was limited to speeding, littering, and DWIs, with an occasional murder.

I walked in and heard Brian Johnson's voice coming from the living room. He was sitting at the dining room table with Jeremy, holding a worksheet. He glanced up, smiled, then turned to Jeremy. "Number six is correct, but you didn't show your work."

"I know the answer, Mr. Johnson. Why do I have to show my work?"

"Because the teacher won't give you credit for solving the problem unless you show your work."

Jeremy snorted and took the worksheet. Brian got up from the table as Jeremy erased something and started writing out his pathway to solving the problem. He nodded toward the kitchen.

"Thanks for helping Jeremy with his homework."

"The hard part was trying to remember how to convert fractions to decimals. It's been a while since I've used that skill."

"That's my nightly dilemma. I did all that as a kid, but those skills are rusty and many of the math skills they're teaching the kids are different from the approaches I was taught."

"Why didn't the sesame seed want to leave the casino? Because he was on a roll." Brian was disappointed when I didn't laugh out loud. "Jeremy had to think about it, but he thought it was funny after I explained casinos and gambling to him."

"A joke doesn't really work if you have to explain a backstory to the recipient."

"It's a cute joke. I bet his friends will laugh at it."

I walked to the refrigerator and pulled out a casserole, hoping Brian would take the hint and leave so I could prepare supper. "Did you come over just to tell me the joke?"

"I thought I'd update you on the damage to the church."

"From the fire sprinklers?"

"That wouldn't have been a big deal if the pan of herring hadn't been flipped over. The fish slime got washed out of the kitchen and dining room onto the carpeting in the narthex and a little way into the sanctuary. An army of people showed up this morning with shop vacuums and carpet scrubbers.

They sucked up all the water and scrubbed the carpet."

I popped the casserole into the microwave and set it for three minutes. "So, there really isn't any damage?"

Brian laughed. "The water's gone, but the whole church smells like a herring."

"That's bad."

"Oh, most of the congregation grew up eating fish, so it's not terrible. We'll have the normal Sunday service. Pastor Norgaard is going to use the story of the loaves and fishes to leverage the fishy smell. The problem is going to be next week when the slime in the carpet pad starts to get gamy."

The mental image of two hundred Lutherans walking into a building that smelled like rotting fish flashed through my mind. "That won't be good."

"Preston Marshall has a carpeting sub-contractor who's searching for enough commercial carpet to replace what's soaked with fish slime. I heard he found a wholesaler in Fargo who got a shipment of greenish-yellow carpet intended for a school. The principal said it was too much the color of summer cow pies and refused to accept it. I guess there's more than enough to replace the sodden carpet and the Sunday school rooms too."

"The church is willing to accept that color of carpeting?"

"Well, there's only one thing a Norwegian likes better than fish, and that's a good deal. We're basically getting the carpet free, and Preston and his contractor are donating the installation labor."

"I thought the television show was going to pay for the repairs."

Brian snorted. "They sent an insurance adjuster who said the carpet was worn past its useful life and needed to be replaced. So, he refused to pay for the replacement."

"But the producer said…"

"Ellen Vang is no longer an employee of *World Eats,* and her replacement knows nothing about promises made to repair the damage."

The microwave beeped, so I stirred the casserole and put it back in for another three minutes. I pulled out my phone and found the amateur video of the show. I cued it up, moved to portion when the producer asked Kerry not to arrest anyone, and handed it to Brian. He watched and smiled.

"This is on YouTube?"

"Yes."

Brian handed the phone back. "Preston has a lawyer on retainer. I think he'll find this video useful." He lifted his coat from the back of a chair and pulled it on. "Have a nice evening, Doc."

"You too, Brian."

I was setting the table when Jenny and Amy appeared. Jeremy, having finished his homework, was stuffing the worksheets into his backpack.

"I should check your homework," I said, setting out silverware.

"Mr. Johnson checked it. The only thing I needed to do was show my work on the math problem."

Bless you Brian, I thought. *As much as you are a pain in the butt, you have a heart of gold.*

Jeremy walked into the kitchen as Jenny lifted Amy out of the baby carrier. "Mom, why didn't the sesame seed want to leave the casino?" He grinned and waited expectantly.

"I don't know. Why didn't he want to leave?"

Jeremy started to laugh and struggled to get out the punchline. "Because he was on a roll!"

Jenny chuckled, but that wasn't good enough for Jeremy. "Do you get it, Mom? If you're in a casino and you're winning, it's called being on a roll."

"Got it."

The microwave beeped and I retrieved the casserole.

"Mr. Johnson, the tuba player, was here. He checked my homework."

Jenny smiled at me. "Ah, the source of the sesame seed joke. He must've run out of tuba jokes."

Jeremy's eyes lit up. "He switched to food jokes. What's orange and like a parrot?"

Jenny shook her head. "I don't know."

"A carrot! Get it? It's orange and it rhymes with parrot."

"Got it. Thanks."

I picked up the casserole with hot pads. "Supper is ready. Jeremy, pour milk for everyone."

As if on cue, Amy started to fuss. Jenny looked at me and drew a breath. "I guess all four of us will eat supper together tonight."

Jeremy took the glasses down and opened the refrigerator. "Isn't it embarrassing to feed Amy when you're around people, Mom? I told Jacob you were breast-feeding Amy and he thought it would be embarrassing for you to feed her with other people watching."

Jenny glanced at me, acknowledging the fact that sexual awareness had arrived. "I'm not embarrassed, but other people are sometimes uncomfortable seeing me feed her. I cover Amy's head with a baby blanket when I'm feeding her in public."

Jeremy went ahead with pouring milk and putting the carton away as if we were having any other conversation. I was proud of Jenny's answer. I hoped it would stick with Jeremy when he encountered other breast-feeding women.

Jenny was droopy during supper. Amy ate happily while Jeremy prattled about school and Brian Johnson's homework assistance. He looked at me, holding his fork halfway to his mouth. "Mr. Johnson was really helpful, Dad. He showed me how to fix my math problems. You just tell me they're wrong and need to be corrected." Jeremy shoved another forkful of tater-tot hotdish into his mouth.

"You shouldn't let strangers into the house when we're not around," Jenny said, trying to make it a suggestion, rather than scolding.

"It was Mr. Johnson, Mom. He isn't a stranger."

Jenny nodded but glanced at me signaling this was a topic for later discussion.

Jeremy cleared the dishes and Jenny put Amy into her living room playpen. I ran the dishwater into the sink and rolled up my sleeves. Washing dishes and showering were the two mindless things I did every day that allowed my thoughts to ponder items outside my normal life. Sometimes I sang in my mind. Other times I thought about the future. That night, the excitement of Jeri Westfall's television appearance ran through my head. More than a dozen people were gathered around her when I came down for coffee. They were buzzing about her on-screen appearance, her polite demeanor, her recipe, and what a jerk Jonathan Edwards was.

A flash struck me as I handed Jeremy the casserole. The broadcast had cut away when the rolling pin rolled off the table, switching to a display of the recipes, then broadcasting a commercial. Hailey's reaction to Jonathan's alleged impropriety wasn't broadcast, but one of the women in the morning gathering mentioned the handprint on Hailey's thigh and her red panties.

I tried to picture the group of women, then tried to focus on who'd mentioned the handprint. I couldn't picture the person who'd made the comment. Had she seen the bootleg video? Had Jeri mentioned it? Or had she known the incident had been planned?

The doorbell interrupted my thoughts. Jeremy tossed the dish towel on the counter and raced to the back door. Jacob Stone stepped in, kicked off his snow boots, threw his coat over the back of a chair, then raced upstairs with Jeremy. I heard Jeremy ask Jacob, "Do you know why the sesame seed didn't want to leave the casino?" The reply was lost when Jeremy closed his bedroom door.

A huge gift box, wrapped in pink paper with pastel balloons, preceded Deb Stone into the kitchen. "Peter, can you hold this while I take off my coat?"

The box was lighter than I expected, and it jingled. I was about to ask about it when Kerry followed Deb carrying a six-pack of beer in one hand and a bottle of wine in the other. "Where's your corkscrew?"

"Second drawer left of the sink, probably buried way in the back. It doesn't get much use."

Deb sat in a chair next to the door to remove her boots. Laughing, she said, "We're about to change that. Where are the wine glasses?"

"Left end of the cabinets, top shelf, way in the back."

With her feet in woolly slippers, Deb padded across the floor and opened the cabinet. She was a petite woman, slightly more than five-feet tall, with short dark hair. She stared into the open cabinet. "Kerry, I'd need a stepladder to reach the wine glasses, can you take two down, please?"

Kerry, who was a foot taller than his wife, reached past her and took down two glasses. He handed her the mechanical corkscrew and twisted the lids off two beer bottles, putting the rest in our refrigerator.

Jenny walked into the kitchen, watching the activity. "Hi guys. Thanks for coming over."

Deb poured wine, then gave Jenny a hug. "I know the last thing you want is company right now, but I also know you needed a boost." She released her hug and turned to me. "Give Jenny the gift."

Jenny's eyes were barely visible above the box. "What's this?"

"It's a baby shower gift. I'll bring the wine. Carry it into the living room and open it."

Kerry handed me a beer and leaned close. "Prepare for the three most dreaded words a parent can hear." He looked at me, expecting a recitation of those words.

My mind raced. "'Your daughter is pregnant,' is four words. What are those three words?"

"Some assembly required," he said, tipping his beer bottle to me. Then he reached in his pocket and pulled out a 4-pack of batteries. "You'll need these after you assemble the gift.

I accepted the batteries and laughed. "Now I'm worried."

"Don't be. This will help you get more sleep."

Like a kid at Christmas, Jenny ripped wrapping paper off the box, while Deb held their wine glasses and smiled. The now-visible picture of an infant in a seat had me baffled.

I held up the batteries for Jenny to see. "It apparently requires these."

Deb laughed. "You really don't know what this is?"

Jenny ripped the tape off the top of the box. "Um, no."

"It's a baby bouncer with a vibrating seat. I'd put Jacob in one of these and he'd be happy and sleep for hours. It was the only thing that quieted him down other than riding in the car."

Pulling instructions from the box, Jenny looked at me. "You need a pair of pliers and a Phillips screwdriver."

Kerry nudged me with his elbow. "Some assembly required."

Amy reacted to the voices and woke up, fussing. Deb set the wine glasses on the end table and went to the playpen. "May I pick her up?"

Jenny smiled. "Sure!"

Deb and Jenny sipped wine and played with Amy while Kerry and I assembled the vibrating baby seat. With the assembly complete, I installed a battery, and the seat began to hum.

Deb pulled the seat next to the couch. Having fussed for several minutes, the seat seemed to immediately quiet Amy. Deb pushed on a corner, and the seat bounced as it vibrated. Amy's eyes lit up.

Jenny let out a breath and leaned back. "If this continues to work magic, I may nominate you to be the next Mrs. Homemaker."

The women laughed as Kerry and I broke down the cardboard box and stowed the tools away.

We were into the second round of wine and beer when Jeremy and Jacob came down the stairs. Jeremy surprised me by handing me the guitar. "I told Jacob you could play anything."

"Not tonight, we've got company."

Deb leaned forward. "You play guitar?"

Jeremy lit up. "He plays in a band and everything!"

I was about to deny the claims, but Deb stopped me. "Please play something."

I set my empty bottle on a coaster and put the guitar strap over my shoulder. "Any requests?"

Deb looked apprehensive. Do you know 'Lyin' Eyes'?"

I played the opening riff and started the first verse. When I got to the part where Don Henley joined Glenn Frey in the Eagles version, Deb closed her eyes and started singing harmony. Jacob turned from watching me and looked at his mother with wonder. Jenny and Kerry sang along on the chorus. Jeremy and Jacob looked at each other like they'd been transported into a sci-fi movie.

Deb looked at me as the chorus ended and I nodded. She sang the second verse with all of us joining her singing the chorus. I sang the third verse with Deb humming harmony until the chorus.

When the song ended, Jacob couldn't contain himself. "Mom, you can sing?"

"Honey, I sing in the church choir every week."

"But, Mom, I can't actually hear *you*. I hear all the voices."

"Have you sung professionally?" Jenny asked.

"Just in the high school and St. Olaf choirs."

I smiled. "The St. Olaf choir is no slouch outfit. Their annual Christmas concert is broadcast by PBS."

Deb changed the topic. "Jeremy said you played in a band. Do you know any George Strait songs?"

I played the opening of "Amarillo by Morning" and stopped a bar into what is normally the vocal. "You're not singing," I said to Deb.

"Can you play it in C? George's tenor G key is at the low end of my vocal range."

I replayed the opening in the higher key and Deb sang three verses. When we ended, she blew out a breath, "I haven't sung that anywhere but in the car. I usually sing the harmony to George's CD."

Jeremy hopped up and walked to the piano in the corner. He lifted the fallboard, "Dad plays the piano, too."

I put up my hand. "I wasn't planning to bore the Stones with music."

Deb looked at Kerry. "Peter, this is a treat for us. Would you play something?"

I sat on the piano bench with my wrists resting below the keys. I had dozens of songs running through my mind and couldn't decide what to play. Jenny leaned close, "Play 'Faithfully'."

I played the piano opening as it's performed by the band, Journey. "Highway run…" Deb joined in, singing harmony through the rest of the song. I turned and held up my hands. "Sorry, that's the end of the piano concert."

Jeremy jumped up. "I'll get the accordion."

"Not tonight, Bud. I need a little more practice before I play the accordion in front of other people."

"The piccolo, Dad?"

"Not the piccolo or the flute. I'm done." I held out the guitar. "Please put this in its case."

The boys went back upstairs. Kerry brought two more beers and refilled the wine glasses. Deb had something on her mind and waited until she was sure the boys were out of earshot. "The television show was quite a production. We watched the unofficial show and saw the real ending."

Jenny was confused. "What real ending?"

Deb pulled her cell phone out of her purse and fingered through pages. Kerry shook his head. "The broadcast was cut short because…it cast the star in a poor light."

I snorted. "It was way past a poor light. He…"

Deb put up her hand to stop my explanation as she passed her phone to Jenny. "Watch this. It picks up where the broadcast stopped."

Kerry knelt next to me and whispered while the women watched the insane moments after the broadcast cut away. "You don't seem comfortable that I didn't respond to Jonathan being set up."

"There's something more to it. I overheard a group of women yesterday, and one of them mentioned the handprint and Hailey's red underwear. None of those women were at the church and it was early in the morning, before people began chattering about the uncensored internet video. I think there was a broader conspiracy to set up Jonathan Edwards. I think several people knew about it before the broadcast."

"Was Jeri talking to that group of women?"

"Not to that immediate group."

"Is it possible that Jeri mentioned it and the information spread through Whistling Pines?"

"Ah, the rumor mill is legendary. I'm sure Jeri mentioned it and the word spread."

Kerry stood. "Leave it, Peter. Some non-judicial justice has been meted out."

"But..."

"It's done, and it's a payback for an old injustice. Remember, we have a murder to investigate."

"*We* have a murder to investigate?"

Kerry's eyes lit up. "I found a note in Len's files. He deputized you when we were trying to solve the time capsule murder. I'm activating you."

"No. I turned in my badge. I'm not a cop."

"You're a member of the police reserve and I'm calling you to active duty."

Jenny and Deb were laughing, replaying the part where Jonathan slipped on the herring slime after the sprinkler was soaking the kitchen.

"Fine, what are we investigating?"

"We need to find a pair of oily barn boots and some bloody leather gloves."

Jenny handed the phone back to Deb and they listened to me. "I don't know how to do that. It's not like we can drive from farm to farm asking to see their barn boots and gloves."

Kerry put his hand on my shoulder. "It's not that complicated. Keep your eyes and ears open. Whoever did this is going to let it slip to someone. Or, we'll spot someone walking around town in a pair of barn boots."

I glared at Kerry. "Farmers don't wear their barn boots into town. That's the point. They leave their boots in the barn so they don't track manure into the house or their vehicle."

Pausing a second, I caught his meaning. "Ah, someone wore their boots into town when they killed Reggie Sandberg."

Deb and Jenny overheard our discussion. Jenny cocked her head. "Farmers don't wear their barn boots into town, but not everyone who wears rubber boots is a farmer."

Kerry raised his unscarred eyebrow. "From the mouths of babes."

Jenny laughed. "Ooh, I'm a babe." Her uninhibited laugh was a little too loud and Amy started to fuss.

Deb covered her mouth to hide her laughter. "I think it's time for us to leave," she whispered. "Will you get Jacob from upstairs, Kerry?"

As soon as Kerry was on the steps, Deb grabbed me in a bear hug and kissed my cheek. Having become accustomed to Jenny's mother who hugged by gently touching shoulders, I was taken aback. "Oh, Peter. The Kerry I married is back. Thanks for your part in arranging the chief's job."

"I had nothing…"

"Bullshit," Deb said in a whisper as she released her hug. "Len Rentz called before he hired Kerry. He told me you were the person who suggested Kerry for the job."

"I only introduced Kerry to him."

Deb scooped Amy out of the vibrating seat and hugged her. "You're just adorable…and I'm so glad I'm past this point in my life. I'm giving you back to Mommy."

Deb passed Amy to Jenny and kissed her on the cheek. "You two are a cute couple with wonderful children. I hope the vibrating seat helps your sleep issues."

Jenny pulled Deb close with her free arm. "Are you and Kerry doing okay?"

Deb glanced at the stairs, then whispered. "Kerry grumbles about the job but he's sleeping nights and actually smiles sometimes. We're getting there."

Thundering footsteps preceded Jacob and Jeremy's entry to the living room. "Do we have to go now, Mom?"

"I'm afraid it's time for Amy's bedtime meal. By the time we get home, and you unwind, it'll be your bedtime, too."

Kerry followed behind the boys, holding a giant Lego pirate ship. "Look what the boys built while it was quiet upstairs."

"Very cool," I said.

Jeremy glanced at Jacob, who rolled his eyes. "Dad, no one says 'cool' anymore."

There was a knock on the back door as the Stones were putting on their boots and coats. Our neighbor, Tim, was standing on the back steps looking sheepish. "I'm sorry."

"Sorry for what?"

"We were kind of in the moment and lost track of time. I looked out and saw the Chief's car, so I figured I should apologize."

I pulled Tim inside. "Chief Stone, this is our neighbor, Tim. He just apologized for playing music so late into the evening."

Kerry put out his hand. It took Tim a second to register the gesture, pull off his mitten, and shake hands. "It's nice to meet you, Tim. You aren't in any trouble. My family was just visiting Peter and Jenny."

Tim bobbed his head. "Um, great. Thanks. I guess I'll go."

"Tim, this is my wife, Deb and my son Jacob. We're just regular people. It's not my job to harass you or the other members of your band. If I see you in town, I'll say hi. I hope you feel comfortable doing the same."

There was another, faint knock on the door. Zoey was on the step looking even more uneasy than Tim. "Um, did the cop arrest Tim?"

I gestured for her to come in. "No one's been arrested. I just introduced Tim to our friends, the Stone family. Kerry is the police chief. This is Zoey, Tim's girlfriend."

Kerry put out his hand and Zoey reluctantly shook it. "Everything is okay. We're visiting socially, not arresting anyone."

Zoey bobbed her head. "Okay."

Deb patted Zoey's arm. "We're just on our way out. It's Amy's feeding time."

Zoey looked at Amy cradled in Jenny's arms and smiled. "Remember, I'll babysit any time. Just let me know."

Tim and Zoey left as Deb hugged us both again. "Zoey offered to babysit?"

Jenny looked past Kerry to make sure Zoey and Tim were gone. "That's not going to happen."

Kerry pushed Jacob out the door, then leaned back inside. "Let me guess; it was the smell of marijuana smoke on their clothing that turned you off."

Deb pushed Kerry out the door. "You don't have to be a cop all the time."

I heard Kerry protest as they walked down the sidewalk. "Hey, I didn't arrest them. Hell, I didn't even hassle them about it."

I sent Jeremy upstairs to pick up and brush his teeth. Jenny fed Amy while I sat next to her and relaxed. "That was nice."

"It was," Jenny replied. "And Deb has a lovely voice. You two sang some beautiful duets."

"She knows how to sing harmony. Not all singers can do that without music in front of them and some practice."

Jeremy bounded downstairs, catching the end of our conversation. "Yeah, maybe you and Mrs. Stone could be in Tim's band together."

I got up and patted his head. "That's not happening. What are we reading tonight?"

"Mom and I started *Stormbreaker* last night. It's really good. The main character is Alex Rider."

"Oh, boy!" I said, in mock excitement. "Maybe we should start over so I can catch up."

"No, Dad. We quit just before an exciting spot."

Chapter Thirteen

Day 6

Morning came too early and a mild headache from the beer gnawed at my head. The shower felt good, but in the interest of family harmony, I didn't stand in it until the water heater was empty.

The overnight dusting of snow made clearing the windshield easy. Drivers were being unusually cautious, slowing so they didn't slide through the slippery intersections. The Duluth weatherman said a low-pressure front was coming through. With moisture streaming up from the Gulf of Mexico, his model predicted the North Shore would receive 3 to 6 inches of snow starting after the evening rush hour.

Karla swept into my office. "The cookbooks are here! We're having the grand opening of the first box in the cafeteria. Please come down and watch."

I closed my computer screen and stood. "Of course!"

Kathy and Mary were standing next to a table stacked with a dozen shipping boxes. Another fifteen women were gathered around them, all looking excited. Karla led me to the table and waved her hand over the cartons. "I thought a hundred cookbooks would be more boxes, but this is what Anders Printing sent."

Mary pushed a box toward me. "You usually carry a penknife, Peter. Will you do the honors?"

More people gathered as I cut the tape. A walker bumped into my ankle and I looked down at Hulda Packer, who was making a path like Moses parting the Red Sea. She glared at me. "I have to be in the front, or I won't be able to see over all these people!"

I opened the flaps, then froze. "These aren't cookbooks. They're calendars."

Hulda jammed her walker against my leg, shoving me aside. "Why did they send our calendars to you? They're supposed to be shipped to Wendy."

Hulda yanked a calendar out of the box and held it up so she could see it through her thick glasses. "This is a horse! We didn't take any pictures with horses." She flipped through the pages. "Bah! These women all have clothes on. We're naked in our calendars."

I gently took the calendar from Hulda. "This is the Minnesota Paint Horse Association calendar. See? MPHA."

Hulda scowled. "Paint horse association? Who ever heard of people painting horses? That's just stupid!"

Hulda yanked her walker back, rolling over my toes and several other feet.

"I think they call them paint horses because of the white markings on their dark coats," I said to her back.

Hulda waved her hand dismissively as she stalked away. Karla had her cell phone in hand, dialing a number. She stepped away from the crowd with the phone to one ear and a finger in her other ear. I carefully replaced the calendar in the box and closed the flaps.

Kathy edged up to me as the crowd cleared. "It's my fault. My daughter Anna is coordinating the MPHA calendar fundraiser. I asked the printer if they'd send me a copy. I suppose the addresses must've been mixed up."

Karla's relieved expression as she approached us told me she'd sorted it out. "Anders is sending a truck. The cookbooks were mistakenly labelled for shipment to the MPHA in Hinckley, but UPS hasn't picked up the order yet. They'll be here in fifteen minutes to reclaim the boxes of horse calendars and deliver the cookbooks."

With the cookbook and calendar problem solved, I returned to my office. Nancy walked in and closed the door—never a good sign. She sat for a second, composing her thoughts. "We may have a problem."

"We, as in you and me? Or, we as in me?"

Nancy smiled, knowing she'd often invoked the "royal we" when directing me to take care of something. "Whistling Pines may have an issue," she clarified. "I inadvertently saw the proofs of the pictures for Wendy and Hulda's calendar."

"They're bad?"

"They're delightful, if we were running a senior citizen's bordello."

I closed my eyes, trying not to envision the naked, wrinkled, sagging flesh I'd glimpsed when the naturist cruise had departed the previous summer. "That bad?"

"I'm not comfortable having Whistling Pines associated with the photos in this calendar."

"You know, the movie *Calendar Girls,* was based on an actual garden club fundraiser. It was a booming success, and the women became very famous."

Nancy wrinkled her nose. "That was a group of garden club volunteers, not senior citizens who live in a small-town retirement community."

"It might attract a lot of future residents."

"It might attract a bunch of old perverts, too."

"That bad?" I asked

"Has Alma Kotter ever told you about Ava Gardner flashing Frank Sinatra?"

I bit my lip.

"Exactly. And then there's Marilyn Monroe's picture standing over the air vent."

"That too?"

"They tried to recreate a number of…memorable Hollywood photo shots. I have the proofs in my office if you'd like to see them."

"Um, no. I really don't need to see senior bordello photos of people I know."

Nancy sighed. "I wish I could unsee them."

"Yeah, that would be a problem." I paused, hoping Nancy had a plan. When she didn't offer anything more or stand up, I threw out the first thing that came to mind. "Talk to the photographer. I bet he or she can photoshop some…scenery into the pictures."

Nancy perked up and pulled a business card out of her pocket. "Here's the photographer's card. Her name is Janice Coggins: please give her a call."

I hesitated. "I think you should have Wendy do this. She's been coordinating the calendar effort."

"Wendy got us to this point. I need your sensible approach to rectify the situation."

Nancy left and I felt the weight of the monkey that had been on her back transfer to my shoulders. Reasoning that nine o'clock was too early to call the photographer, I grabbed my coffee cup and walked to the dining room.

A line of five women stood next to the table where Karla and Kathy were selling cookbooks. Karla was handing out books while Kathy made change for the eighteen-dollar purchases.

"It looks like sales are going well," I said to Karla as I passed.

"I hope it holds up. We've got to sell forty to break even."

Kathy leaned over. "We're up to eleven and most people are buying two."

"I'm sure it'll turn out fine," I said, touching Karla's shoulder. I took a step, then turned around. "Don't forget Nola Saarvala. She prepaid for two cookbooks when she got copies of the recipes."

"Thanks!" Karla said. "That slipped my mind in the excitement. I've got her money in my jewelry box. Do you have her phone number?"

"She didn't leave it with me. Ask the receptionist to look it up."

I filled my coffee mug and scanned the room. Breakfast was in full swing, with people at most every table. Wendy and Hulda were avoiding eye contact with me. Normally, I'd consider that a blessing and I'd slip out before Wendy flagged me down to help with a crossword puzzle. With Nancy's mission, I decided it'd be best if I faced them head-on. "Good morning," I said, sitting in the third chair, across from Wendy.

Hulda glared at me. "I hear you're going to be a spoilsport."

"What do you mean?"

Wendy crossed her arms. "Nancy doesn't like our calendar pictures. She told us she was going to have you resolve the problem."

Clicking her dentures in disgust, Hulda sneered at me. "What are you planning to do about it?"

Wendy put her hand on Hulda's arm. "The pictures are actually tasteful. Have you seen them, Peter?"

"Nancy told me they looked like an advertisement for a senior citizens bordello."

Hulda frowned and tapped her hearing aide. "What? No one brought a cello!"

"Not a cello, a bordello." Seeing the confusion on Hulda's face I said, "A bordello. A brothel."

Hulda got angry. "You're married and you're going to a brothel?"

Because Hulda never spoke in an inside voice, several nearby heads turned. "I'm not going to a brothel. I was trying to tell you that the calendar pictures look like an advertisement for a..."

Smiling, Wendy waited for the next bordello synonym.

"The calendar looks like an ad for a house of ill-repute."

Hulda shook her head. "Why were you beating around the bush, talking about cellos?" The conversation finally connected with Hulda and she smiled. "Really? Someone thinks our pictures look good enough to advertise for a house of ill-repute?"

"Hulda, that's not a good thing. We need to tame them down a bit."

"Are you going to cover up our boobies?"

I clenched my eyes. "Not having seen the pictures, I'm not sure what is required."

Wendy reached down and I put up my hands. "I'll talk to the photographer. I do NOT need to see the pictures."

Wendy's Cheshire grin unnerved me as she pulled something out of her bag. I turned my head. "Don't worry. It's just the crossword, Peter."

I turned back as Wendy spun the photo of Alma Kotter around to face me. My mind was convinced there was a crossword puzzle on the table and the photo in my peripheral vision didn't match what I expected. I looked down to understand the difference and was staring at Alma's open fur coat, never to be unseen again.

"Dammit, Wendy."

Chuckling, she slid the photo off the table and into a large envelope. "Would you like to see the others, too?"

"No. I didn't want to see that one."

Wendy slipped the envelope into her bag. "It's not that bad. Her coat is strategically covering her…assets. You did see that, right?"

"I didn't look that closely."

Wendy reached for the envelope, but I put up my hands. "Don't. I'll talk to the photographer about it."

"Really, Peter, the photos are glamour shots, not pornography. The photographer chose very tasteful poses."

"Then, why does Nancy think they look like they're ads for a…house of ill-repute?"

"She needs to loosen up."

"She's the director and she sets the operating standards. It's like asking you to not show your tattoos here."

Hulda turned to Wendy. "Nancy didn't like the picture of the tattoo on your…"

Wendy put her finger to her lips before Hulda could blurt out the location of Wendy's tattoo.

"No," I said, holding up my hands. "Tell me that you're not in any of the pictures."

"Sharon Cross couldn't hold her pose so I had to steady her. The photographer thought it would be wrong for me to be wearing a sweater and khaki slacks in a glamor shot."

"Geez, Wendy. What were you thinking?"

"I thought it was playfully fun."

At a loss for words, I stood and walked away.

"Peter!" Wendy called.

"What?"

"You forgot your coffee."

* * *

The pile of cookbooks was shrinking and there were still four people waiting to buy one. "It looks good, ladies."

Kathy pointed to the cash box in front of her. "We've covered the printing costs and everything else is profit going to the fundraiser."

Mary sidled up to me, smiling. "Thanks for your support. We were stressed out for a while, but it looks like it'll all work out." She smiled, leaned close, and whispered, "And it'll be less controversial than the calendars."

"Far less controversial than the calendars."

* * *

The wet footprints leading to my office presaged a non-resident visitor. Kerry looked up from a sports magazine that had been on the corner of my desk. "You know, this is like five years old. I think the Raiders franchise moved from Oakland to Las Vegas in 2019."

"I keep it for my visitors to read."

261

"Your visitors might appreciate a recent magazine, even if it's *Today's Baby*." He reached into his pocket and handed me some small slips of paper. "You're going to a church fundraiser tonight."

I looked at the slips printed in black and white, apparently made on a copier. The shapes were irregular, hinting that they'd been cut apart with scissors. "You guys were over last night. I think two nights of excitement would be more than we can handle."

I tried to hand the tickets back, but Kerry stood without accepting them. "It's a concert to raise money for the church's new carpeting."

I saw the five-dollar price printed on the three tickets and reached for my wallet. "Let me pay you."

Kerry stepped away. "Deb had to buy ten and you're the beneficiaries of three."

"I thought the church was getting surplus carpeting."

Kerry's head came around the door. "That was Preston Marshall's very benevolent plan until the choir ladies saw it being unrolled in the Narthex. The new plan is for a very expensive commercial carpet with a floral pattern." He paused. "I'm not surprised. Are you?"

Kerry didn't wait for my answer. His years of marriage trumped mine and if he knew enough to not be surprised that the women of the choir could change the carpeting plans, I wasn't going to argue. I filed that information away, hoping it would save me from some future marital pitfall.

I carried the tickets to Jenny's office. She looked up from a medical file, the dark bags under her eyes visible from ten feet away. "Kerry brought us tickets for a fundraiser at his church tonight."

"Deb called me a few minutes ago."

"Can I give them to someone?"

Jenny shook her head. "I'm afraid we can't."

I sat in her chair. "Why not?"

"How many close friends do we have as a couple?"

It was a trick question, but I couldn't determine the expected response. "I don't know. How many?"

"Two. Kerry and Deb are the sum total of our joint friends."

"Okay. That means we can't give away the tickets?"

"You're catching on."

The tiredness in her eyes made me physically ill. "I'll take Jeremy. You stay home with Amy."

"*We're* going, Peter. All four of us."

"What do you want me to do?"

"Do what you usually do. Go home after work. Make sure Jeremy's homework is complete and correct and make supper."

I stood up. "You're sure?"

Jenny stood up and rounded the desk. She took my hand and squeezed it. "I'm not Emily Post, but I know this is an obligation we can't refuse. We'll suck it up tonight and we'll take turns napping this weekend."

I returned to my office, conflicted and sad we had to go out. My phone chimed an unusual tone and I looked at the screen. *The National Weather Service has issued a special weather statement for your area. A blizzard watch has been issued for your county from 7 P.M. tonight through 2 P.M. tomorrow. Hazardous conditions may include heavy snow and gale-force winds causing periods of zero visibility. All unnecessary travel should be cancelled.*

"Great. That's the icing on the cake."

I'd tucked the photographer's business card in my computer keyboard, and it caught my eye. Checking my watch, I decided to call hoping to catch her before she got into a photo session. She answered on the first ring.

"Hi, I'm Peter Rogers, from Whistling Pines. Our director asked me to speak with you about the calendar pictures."

"Oh, great! I think they're wonderful. The ladies have so much energy and it really came through the lens. Don't you agree?"

"I'm sure it does. The problem is there are…physical assets that also came through. There's some question about the appropriateness of the photos for a community fundraiser."

"Oh. Wendy thought they were flirtatious, but tasteful."

"Wendy has a bear tattoo that peeks out of her blouse and ends…somewhere farther down her anatomy. She thinks it's flirtatious and tasteful too. Most people disagree."

"Wendy's bear is adorable."

I sighed. "Is her bear tattoo visible in one of the photos?"

"It is! I turned her so the entire tattoo is exposed."

"Is Wendy entirely exposed too?"

"No! Her right leg is bent to hide…"

"Um, I don't need any more detail."

"Your name is Peter, right?"

"Right. Peter Rogers."

"I've got some time at noon. Come to the studio and I'll show you the pictures. There are many more than the few proofs I gave Wendy. We can look through them and you can see if some are more in line with your director's tastes."

"No," I said a bit too sharply. "Can you do some photoshopping to insert some tasteful shrubbery in front of whatever might not be considered tasteful."

"I think they're all tasteful. I'd be proud to display any of them in my studio."

"Would you feel good about showing them to my fourth-grade son?"

"Oh, we're using a grade-school boy as the arbitrator of taste?"

"We're using him to set the standard of decency for calendars the women will be giving their children and grandchildren."

"But there's wonderful artistry displayed in these photos."

"There's also some physical attributes we might not want on display in the grocery store magazine rack. Can you make the photos more…PG rated?"

"I can easily dial them back to PG-13."

"No more than PG, please."

"Do you realize how much time this will take?"

"Do you have any idea how many uncomfortable conversations will take place when children see grandma's wrinkled…body parts?"

"Fine. But you have to call the shop to stop the print run."

"They're already printing?"

"I think they started printing them yesterday."

I looked up the number for the print shop and punched in the numbers incorrectly twice before getting the number right. "Are you printing the Whistling Pines glamour shot calendar today?"

"Um, no."

I exhaled. "Great. The photographer is going to redo the pictures and send you a new file."

"Wait a second. What do you want?"

"I want you to hold the printing of the calendars until you get new pictures."

"I think you're confused. We printed yesterday. They're in boxes and on the shipping dock."

"Are you shipping them to Wendy, at Whistling Pines?"

"Hang on."

I waited while computer keys clicked. "One box is going to Whistling Pines. The rest are going to other destinations."

"Give me an example."

"One's going to the historical society, one to the grocery store, and one to a Christmas bazaar in St. Cloud. The others are going out of state."

"Out of Minnesota?"

"Yeah, there's a couple boxes going to a bookstore chain and one going to a company that sells playing cards and calendars."

"Please pull them off the shipping dock until I can get someone down there."

"Hang on." I listened to silence and some muffled conversation. "The truck just left."

"Can you get them back?"

The man laughed. "I think it's a federal crime to remove mail from a postal truck."

I closed my eyes, then walked to Nancy's office with the bad news.

* * *

Nancy said she was disappointed. I almost wish she'd yelled and screamed, but saying she was disappointed, hurt. We walked out of her office together. "Wendy and I are having a discussion," she said. I'm sure Nancy was going to tell Wendy she was *very* disappointed.

Howard was leafing through his mail when I walked past the boxes. "You look like your dog just died, Peter."

"Nancy gave me a mission and I came up short."

Howard nodded toward the aviary where a pair of lovebirds were sitting on a branch billing and cooing. "This is about the calendars?"

"Nancy asked me to intercept those photos before they were made into calendars. The calendars shipped before I got the message to the printers."

"When did Nancy ask you to take care of this?"

"A couple hours ago."

"Peter, the calendars were shipped before Nancy asked you to intervene. It was an impossible task. Don't beat yourself up."

"Thanks for the words of encouragement. I'm still frustrated I couldn't stop it."

Howard cocked his head. "It'll be fine. The calendars will show up. No one will be hurt, and they'll get a few laughs."

"I think there will be some embarrassed families."

"So what, Peter? It's not your problem."

Feeling slightly better, I walked back to my office. I passed a window and noted a few snowflakes swirling, a harbinger of the coming storm. I stopped outside my office door because someone was having a conversation inside. I listened to one side of Brian Johnson's conversation with someone in his band. When it ended, I walked in.

"What brings you to Whistling Pines?"

Brian looked up, smiled, and ignored my question. "I left my tuba in the car and forgot to lock the doors."

"And?" I asked.

"I rushed back in a panic and my worst fear came true. There were two tubas in the car."

I chuckled. Brian had broken my depression. "Thanks, I needed a laugh."

Brian leaned back, looking surprised. "You actually liked one of my jokes?"

"It's been a tough day. You helped me end on a high note."

Digging in his pocket, Brian pulled out three slips of paper. "Here are tickets to the Lutheran Church fundraising concert, my treat."

I held up the tickets Kerry gave me. "You're a couple hours too late. Chief Stone beat you to the punch."

"I hope you can make it. I'm playing with a polka band and it's always more fun to play for a full house."

"I hope the weather forecast improves. I'm not excited about driving around in a blizzard."

Brian stood and put out his hand. "I'll see you tonight, Doc."

Chapter Fourteen

Supper was a blur. I threw together a salad and fried a ham slice. Jeremy assured us he'd finished his homework and it was all fine. Kerry called as we finished washing dishes to make sure we were coming to the concert.

Amy was fussy. Snow continued to swirl outside the window, and the wind was picking up. I put the last plate into the cupboard and walked into the dining room where Jenny was packing spare diapers and baby wipes into a bag.

"Let's stay home. The weather's starting to get worse and we're both dead on our feet."

Jenny looked over her shoulder at me. "I promised Deb we'd be there, and you just told Kerry we were coming."

"I know, but it's not worth the risk of driving in the snow."

Jeremy turned off the TV and listened to us. "Jacob said I could sit by him."

Jenny straightened Amy's winter suit and shook it out. "We're going."

"But…"

Jenny's family didn't argue or raise their voices. When they were angry, they got very quiet and spoke in clipped sentences. She glared at me. "We. Are. Going."

"I guess I'll warm up the car."

We drove to the church in silence except for Amy's giggling as Jeremy played peek-a-boo with her. Jenny stared out the side window without speaking, a sure sign I was in the doghouse. Wind buffeted the car and the anti-lock brakes chattered at every stop sign.

The church parking lot was filling when we arrived. I spotted Brian carrying his tuba into the church, followed by a man with an accordion case. Jeremy saw Jacob, and I had to restrain him to keep him from running headlong across the busy parking lot.

We hung our coats in the huge narthex closets, and Jenny changed into tennis shoes, leaving her snow boots with our outerwear. "Let's sit near the back in case Amy gets fussy," she said as we entered the sanctuary.

A small combo of high school students tuned a saxophone, guitar, and bass, while another student arranged a drum set behind them. Jeremy raced down the aisle and sat next to Jacob and Kerry. Deb wasn't in the row with them.

Pastor Norgaard carried a microphone to the front of the sanctuary at precisely 7:00. "Ladies and gentlemen, thanks for coming out in this weather. I promise that the music will make it worthwhile. Speaking of worth, we greatly appreciate your ticket purchase. In case you hadn't heard, there was a mishap during the filming of a TV show that necessitated the replacement of our carpet. The old carpet has been removed, along with the herring smell." That brought a round of laughter. "And the new carpet will be installed next week, assuming the choir women approve of the color and pattern." That brought another round of laughter. "Our opening entertainment is the Two Harbors High School Jazz Combo."

A round of applause rippled through the full sanctuary. The musicians were surprisingly good, playing a variety of jazz styles through three songs, then finishing with what I knew was a very challenging song called, "Take Five", made famous by the Dave Brubek quartet at the Newport Jazz festival.

Brian Johnson walked out with his tuba and picked up a microphone as the jazz combo packed up. "Most of you know me. For those of you who don't, you may have heard me practicing my tuba in the yard. One of my neighbors came over and watched me play. I asked him if he'd heard my last concert. He said he hoped so." Laughter echoed through the sanctuary. "I'm playing a few polka songs with the Crazy Eights tonight." Brian turned around and pointed to each of the band members as he counted. "Correction. I'm playing with the Crazy Sevens tonight," the joke got more laughter.

They played five polkas and a few couples drifted into the side aisles and across the back, dancing to the music. When they were done, Brian introduced Andrea Maki who performed "Memory" from the musical *Cats.* She was followed by two women who sang two beautiful country duets.

I was surprised when Deb Stone walked onstage carrying a guitar and a stool. She picked up the mic and smiled at the crowd. "Hasn't tonight been fabulous?" The crowd clapped and she nodded, then waited for the applause to stop. "We've got one act left and I have to apologize, because I'm only half of it. My partner is a talented musician who's played professionally with several bands." She glanced to the sides, as if she expected someone to walk out. Then she looked into the crowd, smiled, and locked eyes with me. "Please welcome my friend, Peter Rogers."

The crowd clapped. I looked at Jenny who was grinning.

"You knew she was going to do this," I hissed.

"Quit playing coy and get down there. Deb can only stall so long."

I smiled as I walked to the front but was steaming. Deb handed me the guitar.

"Is it tuned?" I asked as I put the strap over my shoulder.

"I don't know. Didn't you tune it last night when we were over?"

I looked at the guitar and realized she'd picked it up, probably from Jeremy before I got home. I strummed it, tuned one string, and looked up. She nodded and whispered, "George Strait."

I played the opening of 'Amarillo by Morning', then sang the first verse. Deb sang harmony as she had the night before, then sang the second verse alone.

We sang two more duets, then Deb stepped forward. "I have to tell you, I shanghaied Peter to get him here. He's a tremendously talented musician and has played any song I've mentioned. I'm going to stretch his talent a bit with this next Johnny Cash number. Can you play 'I'll Fly Away'?"

I searched my memory and picked a few tentative notes before nodding to Deb. She sang the first verse and the crowd started to clap to the beat. I sang harmony to the second verse, then Andrea joined us from the right aisle for the third verse as her accompanist started playing. We started the last verse and the pipe organ started playing as more voices joined behind us. The sanctuary was filled with sound, and everyone was on their feet clapping as the choir filled the loft, singing along and clapping. We played the chorus again as Deb urged the rest of the crowd to join us.

The cheering standing ovation went on for more than a minute as we bowed and acknowledged the crowd. When the clapping died down, Pastor Norgaard took the mic. "We're serving hot cider and homemade cookies in the dining room."

Deb approached me with her head hung down as people started filing out of the sanctuary. "I'm sorry to have blindsided you, but Jenny warned me you'd say no if I asked you to play a duet with me."

"What would you have done if we hadn't shown up?"

Deb smiled. "Jenny promised you'd be here if she had to drag you by the ear." She pushed the guitar aside, hugged me, and kissed my cheek. "Will you forgive me?"

I unstrapped the guitar and smiled. "You're forgiven. But, please don't do it again,"

I worked through the crowd of people shaking my hand. Jenny met me in the back of the sanctuary. "You were really good."

"That was devious."

Jenny just smiled. "Do you want cider and cookies?"

"I'd rather duck out now and avoid the crowd in the parking lot later."

Jenny followed me to the closet, and we searched for our coats. "I've got my coat," she said, "but I can't find my boots."

The floor was a jumble of snow boots, overshoes, and slipover rubber shoe covers. I saw a pair of brown farm boots. They were my size, much larger than a woman's boots. I went the length of the closet, searching through the piles of boots. A pair of pink boots caught my eye. I picked one up, noting it was women's size 8. I touched the tread, then rubbed my fingers together feeling the slippery oil residue. I held the sole up and saw the sparkle of dozens of metal particles reflected in the light.

Jenny was putting Amy's snowsuit on at the other end of the closet. I raced down to her. "Change of plan. Have cider."

"Where are you going?" she asked as I trotted past.

"I've got to find Kerry."

The narthex/atrium was filled with people talking and sipping cider. I scanned the area, without seeing Kerry. A line snaked from the narthex into the dining room, waiting for cider. The dining room was jammed shoulder to shoulder with hundreds of conversations going on. Kerry was nowhere in sight.

I waded into the crowd, carefully avoiding elbows and cups of cider. Round tables surrounded with chairs dotted the room, each surrounded by the gray heads of senior citizens. Babies cried and children yelled as they chased each other around the room.

Stepping onto an empty chair, I looked around the room, finally spotting Kerry and Deb in a far corner. Kerry's back was turned to me, but I caught Deb's eye and waved. She motioned for me to join them. I tried to gesture to Kerry but she shrugged, not understanding my gestures. I stepped down from the chair and waded toward the last spot I'd seen Kerry.

"Peter!" Deb exclaimed. "Meet Andrea Maki. She's the soprano who sang the aria and joined us in the last song."

I nodded and shook her hand, then grabbed Kerry's elbow. "I found the oily barn boots," I whispered.

Cider had slopped from Kerry's cup onto his pants when I grabbed his elbow. He shook hot cider from his hand and glared at me. "What are you talking about?"

I raised my voice, trying to be heard over the hundreds of conversations. "The oily boots from the murder scene. They're in the coat closet."

"What?"

I nodded toward the exit. "Follow me."

The crowd was starting to thin, so our exit went faster than when I'd waded through the packed dining room. Kerry stopped me in an open spot. "Okay, what are you trying to tell me?"

"There's a pair of women's barn boots with oily tread in the coat closet. C'mon, I'll show you."

Kerry followed me through the crowd who all wanted to shake my hand. I got a glimpse of Jenny amid a group of women who were passing Amy from arm to arm.

The coat room was full of people pulling on coats and boots. We zig-zagged through the crowd to the spot I'd found the boots. There were still dozens of pairs of snow boots, but the pink barn boots weren't there.

Grabbing Kerry's arm, I pulled him toward the church's front door. "They're gone. She must've left for her car. Let's check the parking lot."

Kerry slowed. "Let's take a breath."

"No, she might be right outside the door."

The snow and wind had picked up. We stood on the top step in our shirtsleeves, the snow flying into our faces and the wind tugging at our shirts and pants. Dozens of people were walking to their cars, all bundled in their coats and struggling through the inches of snow that accumulated during the concert.

I saw a flash of pink boots to our left, just before they disappeared between two cars. "There!" I pointed.

Kerry squinted into the snow. "I don't see anything."

"She walked between the last two cars. She's wearing a teal down parka. There, she stopped by a SUV in the second row."

I started down the steps until I felt Kerry's hand on my shoulder. "She'll be gone before we get to her. Get in my car."

As all good cops do, Kerry parked in the front row with the nose of his car facing out, so he didn't have to back out of a parking spot. I swept the snow off the windshield with my bare hands while Kerry started the engine. I jumped into the car when he turned on the red and blue flashers.

"Where is she?"

"She turned toward Highway 61."

"What's she driving?"

"A snow-covered SUV."

Kerry glanced at me as he threaded between the people walking to their cars. Most tried to get out of his path, but an older man panicked and slipped, falling in the middle of the driveway, blocking our path. Kerry waited as he got to his knees. His wife helped him to his feet, then waved us past.

"What color is the SUV?"

"They're all covered with snow! Everything's white."

Kerry gasped in frustration. He turned onto the street, but when he accelerated the back of the police car fishtailed.

"There's only one set of taillights ahead of us. It must be her."

Kerry straightened the car and picked up the radio mic, announcing to the dispatcher that he was in pursuit of an SUV.

The dispatcher announced the pursuit, then asked for the license number and description of the suspect's vehicle. He looked at me, but I shrugged.

The SUV idled at the stoplights with it's left blinker flashing. Kerry was gaining, but every time he stepped harder on the gas the rear of the car slewed, causing him to steer it back. The stoplight turned green when we were still a block away. The SUV, probably with 4-wheel drive, eased around the corner.

"Can you read her license plate?"

"It's covered with snow, like her rear window."

Saying we were racing toward the intersection would've been a gross overstatement of our speed. I glanced at the speedometer and saw it creeping toward 20.

"I think she's driving a Jeep SUV," Kerry said, his knuckles white on the steering wheel."

"It's boxy, like a Jeep. It's hard to tell when it's covered with snow. I got a glimpse of gray or silver on the side when she turned."

Kerry announced our vague description of the vehicle, and that it was now southbound on Highway 61 driving through downtown Two Harbors.

The stoplight changed to red as we approached and Kerry turned on the siren but eased off the gas as two vehicles passed through, crossing the intersection ahead of us.

"We're going to lose her," I said, shivering, suddenly aware of the cold. Kerry was absorbed, putting on the brakes and preparing for the left turn. The one oncoming vehicle slowed when the driver heard the siren and saw Kerry's flashing lights. The car slid into the intersection, but Kerry was able to turn and continue the pursuit.

With three sets of taillights ahead of us, I tried to focus on the Jeep SUV. "She appears to be going straight."

We made slow headway toward the vehicles ahead. An oncoming pickup saw Kerry's flashing lights and eased to the shoulder as we left the old downtown area and the buildings thinned. The nearest vehicle, an older car, saw Kerry's flashing lights and braked, skidding slightly as it eased to the right edge of the road.

The radio sounded emergency tones and the dispatcher announced an accident north of Two Harbors and called out the fire department and ambulance. A Minnesota State Trooper asked if we were still in pursuit and where we were. Kerry responded as the SUV seemed to drift farther away, its taillights becoming less distinct in the blowing snow.

The car immediately ahead of us continued to be oblivious to the flashing lights and siren. It drove at a slow speed, appropriate for the conditions, blocking our path while the SUV got farther and farther ahead.

With no oncoming traffic, Kerry pulled into the left lane of the two-lane road and accelerated. When the hood of Kerry's car was even with the car he was passing, they panicked and locked up their brakes, the car twisting left and right as we passed. I saw the face of a bewildered old man and his wife as we continued past.

Kerry tried to accelerate to gain on the SUV, but the three or four inches of slushy snow made acceleration nearly impossible. Blue and yellow lights flashed ahead of us, as a plow truck approached from the other direction.

"Finally," Kerry muttered to himself. "We should be able to move to the other lane and catch up to the Jeep."

More tones sounded on the radio and the dispatcher announced a fender bender accident without injuries at the stoplight where we'd turned. Kerry glanced at me. "How sure are you that the woman in the Jeep is the killer? I could be responding to these accidents."

"I don't know. Her boots had oily tread and the soles had embedded metal particles. At a minimum, you need to talk to her."

We met the snowplow just before coming to the stoplights at a road that ran alongside a gas station and several fast-food restaurants. The light turned yellow, and Kerry tapped the brakes to slow down. The plow pushed snow to the side and spread sand on the slippery road, but also created a maelstrom of swirling white behind it. Kerry pulled into the newly plowed lane and his tires bit into the sand as he accelerated. His headlights lit nothing but the swirling snow behind the plow.

In those two seconds of blindness, a car pulled out of the crossroad. Kerry saw it and slammed on the brakes a second before he impacted the other car's right front fender. Our momentum carried us ahead, spinning counterclockwise down the road until the rear bumper hit something solid and jerked us to a stop.

The deployed airbags smashed me into my seat, protecting me from injury, but jarring me violently. I glanced at Kerry, who pushed at the airbag, trying to get it out of his face.

"Are you okay?" I asked.

Rolling his head, he paused. "I wish that Humvee in Iraq would've had airbags." He picked up the radio mic, announced the end of the chase, the accident location, and the need for a tow truck.

My phone vibrated and I pulled it from my pocket with shaking hands. "Where the hell are you? We're in our coats and ready to leave."

"Are Deb and Jacob with you?"

"Yes, she's been calling Kerry. His phone immediately rolls over to voicemail. She's left three messages."

I explained the boots, the chase, the accident, and our current location.

"OMG! Are you okay?"

"Yeah, tell Deb we're both fine, just a little shaken up. Can you drive her home?"

"Um, sure. Is Kerry driving you home?"

"Um, I don't think his car is driveable." I looked through the snow at the blue and white sign across the road. "Can you pick us up at Culver's after you drop Deb at home?"

"No problem."

"We'll be drinking coffee until you arrive."

"You're certain that you're okay. Do you need an ambulance?"

"No, the airbags deployed and left us shaken but uninjured"

"It's snowing hard. It may be a while before I get Deb home and back to Culver's."

I laughed. "We don't have many other options. It's not like I can call an Uber."

"Have you tried?"

Kerry overheard the discussion and laughed. "No and I'm not going to."

Kerry tapped my arm. "Ask her to bring our coats."

"Did you hear that?"

"I heard Kerry's voice, but not what he said."

"Please bring our coats."

I heard Jenny and Deb talking, then a laugh. "You guys ran outside without your coats?"

"We were a little rushed and afraid we'd lose sight of the woman wearing the pink barn boots."

"Deb asked if we should pin your mittens to your sleeves, so you don't lose them."

"Ha, just bring the coats and fetch us when you can."

There was a knock on my window as I ended the call. I tried to roll it down, but the engine died after the impact, so I opened the door a crack. A middle-aged man looked in. "Are you guys okay? I didn't see you until a second before you hit us."

"We're uninjured. How about you?"

"The light just turned green after the plow passed, so I was barely creeping. My wife and I are fine." He glanced at the front of our car. "I don't think you can drive this car. Can we give you a ride?"

"Our wives are picking us up at Culver's."

"Get in our car. A two-block walk is a long way without coats in this blizzard."

Chapter Fifteen

Day 7

The alarm music came on four hours after we'd gone to bed. Kerry and I drank too many cups of decaf coffee the night before. The manager took pity on us and stayed open past his normal closing time, refilling our cups liberally without charge. Jenny had demanded to check our heads and eyes, inspecting the few cuts and bruises caused by the airbags. She declared us free of concussions before allowing us to leave Culver's.

I got out of bed feeling aching muscles and stretched ligaments in my neck, back and arms resulting from the violent deployment of the airbags. I inspected the few scratches on my face as I shaved, then dressed and made coffee. I had to shake Jeremy to wake him from his short night.

He looked at me with sleepy eyes. "I'm still tired, Dad." He rolled over and closed his eyes.

"I am too, but there's only one more day of school before the weekend. You'll get through it."

"Can't I stay home? I don't have any tests today."

"Get up and get dressed. I'll set out a bowl, cereal, and milk."

He was grumbling as I walked out of his room. Jenny met me in the hallway on the way to the bathroom with a fresh uniform in her arms. She yawned, looked as if she was about to say something, then turned away. I heard the shower running before I got to the bottom of the stairs.

I looked out the kitchen window as the coffee maker burbled, signaling the end of the cycle. There was a fresh inch of snow on the roof of the car and a mini snowdrift on the hood. The snowplow rumbled past. That meant there'd be a foot or more of packed snow blocking the end of the driveway.

Jenny came downstairs with Amy in her arms. I'd set out coffee and toast with jelly for her. She put Amy in the vibrating chair, sat down, and looked at the toast. "I'm so tired I'm not sure I can eat."

"The plow just went by. I have to shovel the driveway before we'll be able to get the cars out."

Jenny yawned. "That should wake you up."

I sat down across from her and took a bite of toast. "I may have to shower again after I shovel. We got a lot of snow overnight and there are some drifts, too."

"There's an old snowblower in the garage. Can't you clear the driveway with it?"

"It's decades old, covered with dust, and I don't have any gas for it."

"You have lawnmower gas. Give it a try before you start shoveling."

I must've made a derisive sound because Jenny glared at me. "Listen, dozens of people die every year shoveling snow. Try the snowblower before you pick up the shovel, dear."

"Fine, but if I die of a heart attack pulling on the starter cord, you'll be sorry."

Jeremy came slowly down the stairs, his shirt buttoned unevenly and wearing a pair of food-stained jeans. "Why can't I stay home today. I'm really tired."

Jenny's phone buzzed and she struggled to get it out of her purse before the call rolled over to voicemail. "Hello. Oh hi, Deb. Yes, we're up although Jeremy thinks he should stay home from school today."

Jenny listened as I finished my toast. I was rinsing my plate and refilling our coffee mugs when she ended the call.

"Deb says the church posted a video of the concert on their website."

"I'll check it out tonight."

"Peter."

"What?"

"Deb said watching the finale brought tears to her eyes. I suppose you guys couldn't capture the enormity of it, singing down in the front, but with the pipe organ and the choir." Jenny paused searching for words. "Wow."

I smiled. "I'm pleased it came out so well."

"There was a donation basket set out in the serving line. Pastor Norgaard called Deb this morning and told her there were over three thousand dollars in the plate when they shut down the kitchen, including a check for a thousand dollars from the people who own the garden center. Between the ticket sales and contributions, they have more than they need to pay for the new carpet."

Jenny got up and hugged me. "Why the big hug?"

"That's from Deb. She said it wouldn't have come together if not for you."

"I think they would've done fine without me," I said, draining my coffee.

Jeremy stopped eating and looked at me. "The lady next to Chief Stone said she'd never heard anything more beautiful than the song you guys played at the end. I think it made her sad because she was crying."

* * *

I pulled the old snowblower out from under a pile of boxes and used a rag to dust it off. I didn't recognize the brand name, so I assumed whatever company made it had long ago gone out of business. There was oil on the dipstick and the inside of the gas tank was clean and rust-free. I poured gas in and hoped for the best. On the third pull the machine burped but died. On the fourth pull of the cord, it started. The engine sounded like it was going to tear itself apart and blue smoke poured out of the exhaust. When the snowblower died, I was tempted to push it back in the corner, then remembered the choke on the snowblower my father used when I was a kid. It restarted but chugged. I turned the choke halfway off, and the engine smoothed out. After a few seconds, I turned the choke all the way off, the engine sped up, and a roar reverberated inside the tiny garage.

Jenny waved from the house and gave me a thumbs-up sign as I made the first pass down the driveway. The old beast didn't throw the snow a hundred yards, but it pushed it far enough to clean the driveway and remove the mess the plow pushed off the street.

Rather than having Jeremy wait on a narrow street for the bus, or me wondering if he'd gone back to bed, I drove him to school. He stared out the window, acting like the sullen teens I'd seen getting out of their parent's cars at the school entrances.

"What's wrong?"

"People miss school all the time, Dad. All. The. Time. I haven't missed a day this year. I could've stayed home."

"If you were sick, I'd let you stay home. Tiredness is not a valid school excuse."

He sighed and rode in silence until I dropped him at the front door.

The plow was still clearing the Whistling Pines parking lot, so I took a spot already cleared rather than my usual space in the back row, which was still covered in snow. The lobby seemed hot after walking in through the brisk breeze. Karla's cookbook sale sign was still up on a table by the dining room entrance, so I assumed the sale was still underway. I considered buying a cookbook for my mother, then rejected the thought, remembering that she ate out, ordered delivered food, or opened a can for every meal. I wondered briefly if she'd donated her pots and pans to a charity.

I could see light coming out of my office from far down the hallway and I briefly wondered if I'd forgotten to switch everything off when I'd left yesterday. Walking through the door, I found Brian sitting in my guest chair. He was working a sudoku on his smartphone and kept at it while I hung my coat behind the door.

"Hi, Doc," he said, finally putting the phone in his pocket.

"Good morning. What brings you here so early?"

He reached into the pocket of the jacket he'd hung on the back of the chair and pulled out a DVD case. He handed it to me and smiled. "Pastor Norgaard has me delivering DVDs to all the performers from last night's fundraising concert. Did you hear we raised more than enough to pay for the new carpet?"

"Deb Stone called Jenny this morning with that news."

Brian handed the DVD case to me. "Cue it up to 1:17:00,"

"I need to check my email and see if there are any overnight emergencies."

Brian, looking as earnest as I'd ever seen him said, "Cue it up, Doc. Please."

I turned my computer on and put the DVD into the slot. The inside of the church popped up, with the pastor turning on the microphone. "Go to one hour and seventeen minutes."

I put my cursor on the time bar at the bottom of the screen and moved it to the right until I got to 1:15 and stopped. I watched Deb walk onstage and start her introduction.

"Why am I watching this?"

"Bear with me, please."

The camera must've been mounted in the balcony, looking down at the sanctuary. After Deb's coaxing, I walked down the aisle to the front, and she handed me my guitar. After tuning, she whispered to me, and although I couldn't hear her say George Strait, I knew that had been her request.

The congregation was silent as I picked the opening to "Amarillo by Morning." I sang the opening verse and Deb joined me for the chorus. She sang the second verse, her lovely alto voice filled the sanctuary, which had better acoustics than I'd expected. I joined her for the chorus, the sound of the acoustic guitar and two voices almost haunting in the sanctuary. Three hundred people watched in rapt silence. I glanced at Brian who gestured for me to continue watching.

We watched all the songs Deb and I'd sung in a duet. I was reaching for the mouse to stop the playback, but Brian put his hand on my arm. "Not yet, Doc."

Deb picked up the microphone and asked if I could play, "I'll Fly Away". I plucked a few notes then nodded to her. The sanctuary was filled with our voices, then someone in the audience started to clap to the beat of the music. By the second verse, the entire congregation was on its feet clapping when Andrea Maki walked in, singing from the wings. She joined Deb and me in the front as the piano started playing. More voices started singing in the aisles and choir members started moving in behind us, like a flash mob. A few bars in, the pipe organ came in softly, then grew as the choir filled the choir loft. It sounded like everyone in the sanctuary was singing and clapping by the time the final note echoed. Then the applause started, followed by cheers, whistles, and hoots. We took bows, but the applause continued.

I clicked the mouse to stop the video and I took the DVD out of the slot. Brian blew his nose, and I turned in time to see him wiping the tears from his cheeks. He shook his head, searching for words. "Doc, I don't think that old church has ever been more filled with the Holy Spirit than it was last night."

"I don't know about that."

"I've heard ministers preaching fire and brimstone from that pulpit for seventy years, but I've never seen the congregation as moved as it was by your voice and guitar."

"Deb, and the choir were…"

Brian stood and put out his hand. "They needed a catalyst. Thank you."

I realized that he walked away without ever telling me a joke. It was then that I realized the depth of his feelings and how moved he'd been.

I slipped the DVD into the case and put it in my jacket pocket. With a coffee mug in hand, I walked to the dining room. Karla and Mary were selling cookbooks, with only a half dozen left in the pile. Karla looked up at me. "We're going to ask for a second printing of another fifty cookbooks."

"And you weren't sure you'd sell enough to cover the cost of the first printing."

"I suppose I needed a bit more faith." She paused, then turned. "I heard you brought down the Lutheran Church last night."

"I got trapped into singing a couple songs."

Mary looked past Karla. "I asked our pastor if we could have you and Deb perform at the Covenant Church. Expect a call."

I put up my hand. "I think that was a once in a lifetime performance."

Mary got a sly smile. "I play the organ. Would you deny me the opportunity to play 'I'll Fly Away' with you? It's not something you should restrict only to the Lutherans."

A hand gripped my shoulder. "Yes, Peter," Howard Johnson said, "you should be prepared to perform for the Unitarians, the Presbyterians, the Catholics, and the Baptists. They all deserve your talents."

Andy Passavant was passing by and whispered, "And you don't want to show preference for the Norwegian Lutherans over the Swedish Lutherans either."

I tipped my head back and clenched my eyes shut. For a moment, I'd regretted standing up when Deb called me out of the audience, then I remembered Brian's words and calmness swept over me.

When I opened my eyes, Howard Johnson was staring at me. "Are you okay? I heard you and the police chief got banged up last night."

"I'm fine other than some scratches and sore muscles."

Howard steered me toward the coffee urns and filled my mug. "Wendy and Hulda are selling calendars in the back corner," he whispered as he drew himself a mug of coffee.

I looked at the group of people gathered in the corner but couldn't see either Wendy or Hulda through the crowd. "It looks like sales are going well."

Howard nodded toward the entryway, away from the dining room and the breakfast crowd. "I got a glimpse of a few pages, and the pictures are less…" He stopped, unable to come up with an adjective.

"Is there a picture of Wendy?"

Howard smirked. "Did you know she has a heart tattoo right here?" He pointed just above his left buttock."

"I didn't need to know that, nor do I want to see it."

Howard nodded. "There's much more to Wendy than I've seen before."

I put my hand up. "That's already too much information."

"Ah, TMI as my grandchildren say when I start talking about my medical issues."

"Exactly!"

* * *

Wendy stuck her head in my office. "People are lined up for the van ride to the funeral. You're planning to drive, right?"

I reached for my jacket. "Yeah, I'm driving. It slipped my mind."

There was grumbling among the women lined up for the van. Hulda Packer glared at me as I passed. "You could've had the decency to warm up the van for us."

"It'll be fine, Hulda. It warms up quickly."

I pushed the door open but, like always, Hulda got the last word in before it closed. "I hope we don't have to sit in the front row because we're so late."

* * *

Hulda shuffled up the van steps, moving her walker up a step each time she pulled her feet up to the next step. My attempt to assist her was met with a withering glare. "I'm doing just fine."

Closing the van door and buckling my seatbelt, I checked in the mirror to ensure everyone was seated. Hulda's eyes met mine. "I think my butt cracked the cold Naugahyde seat cover when I sat down."

"I don't know what Naugahyde is, Hulda, but that's not what's used to make seat covers. And I'm sure you didn't crack the seat."

Kathy Christensen was seated behind Hulda, and she smiled at me in the mirror. "The cracking was your knees, Hulda."

Hulda leaned forward. "You'd better get rolling, Peter. The service starts in twenty minutes."

I shifted the van into gear. "The Unitarian Church is only five minutes away."

"Yes, but the seats in the back row fill up fast."

Easing the van through the parking lot, I replied, "I thought you liked to sit closer to the front so you could hear."

"I don't need to hear. I didn't even know Reggie, I'm just going for the lunch. I want to be in the back, closer to the dining room. The cookies and bars get picked over before the people in the front get to the buffet line."

"I think they excuse the mourners from the front, with the family first."

Hulda made a dismissive sound. "I don't wait until the family gets out."

Laughter from the rear of the van made me glance in the mirror. "Did you bring your zippered bag so you could load up on cookies, Hulda?"

"I heard the Unitarians serve more bars and cakes. Cookies are more of a Lutheran thing." Hulda paused. "Does anyone know if Unitarians make Jell-O salads? There's nothing better than Lutheran cherry Jell-O filled with canned fruit salad."

I saw a gleam in Kathy Christensen's eyes. "I think Unitarians serve coleslaw."

"Coleslaw!" Hulda barked. "You can't serve coleslaw at a funeral. Old people have false teeth and can't chew coleslaw. Bah, they won't serve coleslaw. Jell-O is more of a crowd pleaser when you've got senior citizens. There's no chewing involved in Jell-O."

I unloaded the van and had to park almost two blocks away due to the heavy turnout for Reggie's funeral. People were still filing into the sanctuary when I arrived. All my riders were already seated and, as expected, Hulda was closest to the aisle in the back row.

The service was long, with several of Reggie's grandchildren speaking. The minister, not to be outdone by the family, spoke for fifteen minutes about Reggie, her life, and her service to the church.

An older woman sitting next to me leaned close. "Reggie coordinated the food at every wedding and funeral. They're probably going to serve store-bought sandwiches and cookies."

The minister was giving his final blessing when scraping sounds came from the rear of the church. Several heads turned as Hulda pushed her walker out of the sanctuary, banging against the doorframe while making a beeline for the dining room.

I waited until the ushers released my row and got in line for the buffet. Pleasant chatter surrounded me, and several people commented about what a nice service it had been. I was nearly to the dining room when I heard Hulda's outdoor voice. "Is this decaf? There's really no point in drinking decaf coffee. You might as well serve dishwater as decaf coffee."

A gray-haired gentleman in a suit accented with a brass name tag, which I assumed meant he was a deacon or church elder, turned to me. "You brought the van from Whistling Pines, right?"

"I did."

He smiled. "It's nice to know that Mrs. Packer hasn't changed."

"You've known Hulda for a long time?"

"She was my third-grade teacher."

"I assume she was a force in the classroom."

He chuckled. "She didn't take lip from anyone. One day she lifted Ronnie Benson by the ear because he was talking during a test. I swear his feet never touched the floor as she dragged him into the hall."

The pleasant gentleman and I chatted about Hulda and my job as we shuffled ahead with the crowd. We were entering the dining room as Hulda blurted out, "Where's Peter? I'm ready to go."

My new friend's eyes sparkled. "I bet you thought you were going to eat."

Hulda pushed her way through the dining room, banging her walker into chairs and rolling over toes. She stopped next to me and glared, just as I picked up a plate. "I told you to sit in the back row. Go fetch the van. The frosting on the brownies in my purse is going to get soft if we hang around here any longer."

The other van passengers were finishing their coffee and picking up their coats. I shook hands with my friend and left the line to get my coat. I heard him introduce himself to Hulda as a former student.

"I don't think you were one of my students. I never taught anyone with gray hair."

The drive back to Whistling Pines was somewhat subdued until Hulda stirred the pot. "What's wrong with those Unitarians? Haven't they heard of cherry Jell-O? I mean, really, who serves lime Jell-O at a funeral? Certainly not the Lutherans. They'll serve orange Jell-O with those canned little oranges in it, but not Lime Jell-O with pears."

I heard laughter in the back of the van, and someone asked, "Hulda, how many brownies fit in your zippered bag?"

Hulda snorted. "I tried to get five in, but the last one mushed all the others. I'll have to eat them with a spoon!"

Kathy Christensen leaned over the back of Hulda's seat. Her grin told me whatever she was going to say would set Hulda off. "I don't think I've ever had brownies with macadamia nuts before." Kathy leaned back and smiled at me in the mirror.

Hulda tried to twist around to see Kathy but was wearing too many layers of sweater and coat. "Macadamia nuts? What the heck is a macadamia nut and who'd put one in a brownie?"

Hulda pulled the plastic bag out of her purse and started prodding at the brownies with her thumb. "These white dots, are they the macadamia nuts? Hey, does anyone know if macadamia nuts get under your dentures? Do they break into little pieces like peanuts? I can't stand peanuts."

She was just finishing her rant as I pulled under the portico and opened the door. I took Hulda's hand as she stepped down, then I handed the walker to her. She hesitated for a second and I thought she was going to thank me. Instead, she pulled the zippered plastic bag out of her purse as people waited behind her. She jammed the bag of smashed brownies into my hand.

"Here, you eat these. I don't want to take a chance on getting those academic nuts under my dentures."

"They're macadamia nuts, not academic nuts."

Hulda waved off my correction and walked inside.

Kathy's red hair was visible behind another passenger. Isabel Trondheim passed before I saw Kathy's smile. She patted my arm as she passed. "Enjoy the brownies, Peter. I think you'll need a spoon."

* * *

I refilled my coffee, ignoring the growing crowd around Wendy and Hulda. Alma Kotter walked past showing another woman a picture inside the calendar.

Spotting me, Alma broke away. "Peter, have you seen my picture in the calendar?"

I turned my head away before she got the calendar open. "I've heard it's very…glamorous."

"Oh, that's such a nice adjective. Yes, it's glamorous."

She walked away, and I turned in the opposite direction to avoid viewing the picture as she showed yet another resident her photo. The nursing office was ahead, so I decided to check on Jenny. The rings under her eyes were dark, almost as if she'd been punched.

I sat down in her guest chair. "Do I look as tired as you?" she asked.

"You might want to put some concealer under your eyes."

She blew out a breath and took a mirror from one of her desk drawers. "Oh geez, I've seen more lifelike cadavers." She pulled out a makeup bag and smeared some flesh-tone cream over the black rings.

"Brian Johnson brought a DVD of last night's performance."

"Good. We'll have to watch it this weekend."

"Mary Gilbert asked if we'd repeat the performance at her Covenant Church."

Pausing her makeup application, Jenny looked at me. "I suppose you have to be ecumenical. Have you mentioned it to Deb?"

I shook my head. "It can be a topic for a different day. I just want to survive the rest of today without having to think or plan."

Jenny put away her makeup bag and stared at me. "That's certainly an interesting approach for the man who's in charge of planning recreation and entertainment."

A shadow passed the door, then backed up. Nancy walked in and put her hand on my shoulder. "Between the cookbook sale, the calendar sale, the ongoing rumors about the cooking show, and your concert performance, Whistling Pines is buzzing."

"How many of those are good things and how many are bad?" I asked.

Nancy shrugged. "I've recovered from my concern over the calendars. They seem to be well received, at least by the residents. Two of the other three are neutral."

"And the fourth?"

"At least a dozen people have asked if you and Wendy will perform, 'I'll Fly Away'."

"Maybe next week. I'll talk to Wendy after she peels herself away from the calendar sales."

Nancy sat on the edge of Jenny's desk, a move I'd never seen before. "I wasn't at the church last night for the carpet fundraiser, but several people who attended have raved about your duet with Deb Stone." Nancy paused, composing her thoughts. "I apologize for not saying this enough, but I really appreciate the two of you. You're both wonderful Whistling Pines ambassadors, both here and in the community. Thank you."

Jenny glanced at me, then looked at Nancy. "I think you should direct those thanks to Peter. He's the one who brought the house down last night."

"Peter's certainly the one who's out front, but Jenny, you enable him. Your quiet confidence and professionalism are incredibly important, too. Thank you both."

Nancy stood up and took a step toward the door, then she paused and closed the door. "Go home. You're both dead tired, and I'm afraid you'll hurt yourselves by falling asleep and tipping out of your chairs. Leave the kids in school and daycare. Go home and take a nap."

Jenny looked at her desktop. "But..."

"Whatever's there will be taken care of by someone else, or it'll be waiting for you Monday. Go home. That's an order."

Nancy left and Jenny looked crushed. "I've got so much to do."

"You'll be more efficient and less likely to make a mistake if you've had more than a couple hours of sleep." I pulled her up from her chair. "Get your coat. I'll meet you at home."

* * *

We didn't even change out of our clothes, just curled up on the bed under the quilt and fell asleep. I awoke when I heard the back door slam, signaling Jeremy's return from school. I was tempted to go back to sleep but got up and closed the bedroom door so Jenny could continue to rest.

I startled Jeremy by coming downstairs as he was smearing peanut butter on bread. "Why are you here, Dad?"

"My boss sent Mom and me home. She said we'd done enough work for this week."

"My teachers never say that. They always give us more homework." He dropped the knife in the sink and bit off a corner of his sandwich. "What's for supper?"

"I think we're having the rest of the tater-tot hotdish."

"Okay," he said, taking his glass of milk and sandwich to the dining room table. He pulled some worksheets out of his backpack and sat down with a pencil. I was amazed and pleased with his diligence and

307

responsibility. I knew Howard and Barbara, my in-laws, had drilled that into him, and I hoped I'd be able to do the same for Amy.

Jenny wandered down a half hour later, wiping sleep from her eyes. "How's homework going, Jeremy?"

"Good."

"Do you have much?"

"Yeah."

"Do you need any help?"

Jeremy never looked up as he issued his one-word answers. "No."

"Did your teacher have green hair today?" I asked.

He looked up and cocked his head. "That'd be stupid. Teachers only have brown or gray hair." He went back to his work.

Jenny grinned at me. "I'll get Amy from daycare if you make supper."

We ate, cleared the table, and Jenny asked me to cue up the DVD Brian had given me. Jenny was in awe. Jeremy was yawning. He was roused from his lethargy by the ringing phone.

Chapter Sixteen

Jeremy beat me to the phone, disappointment spread on his face before handing it to me. "It's Jacob's dad. He wants to talk to you."

"Hi Kerry, what's up?"

"Are you planning to meet me at Pastor Olafson's office tonight?"

I glanced at the clock. "I think I'll pass. Jenny needs help putting the kids to bed and we're still tired."

Sighing, Kerry paused. "I'm not excited about this either, but Deb heard about our meeting and she's virtually pushing me out the door. I don't know him and I'm not going alone."

Jenny was giving me a *"what's up?"* look. I put my hand over the phone. "Pastor Olafson invited Kerry and me over to meet in his office. It's kind of late..."

"Go. You deserve a night out with the boys."

"Um, an evening meeting with the police chief and minister is hardly..."

Jenny smiled. "It's not like you're going out for a wild night of debauchery. You're having coffee with a minister and the police chief. Just go.”

“Jenny told me to get out. I guess I’m meeting you at the church.”

* * *

There were three cars and a pickup truck in the Swedish Lutheran church parking lot, including a police cruiser, probably a replacement for the car we’d crashed. The light afternoon snow still covered the parking lot, but someone had shoveled the sidewalk to the church. I followed the wet footprints on the floor down a tiled hallway to a door leaking light onto the tile. Male voices echoed in the narrow hallway, making me wonder if I’d stumbled into a church deacon’s meeting or something.

Ron Olafson jumped up from his seat at a round meeting table and rushed to shake my hand. “I’m so glad you could make it, Peter.”

Kerry smiled from one of the seats. The other two men looked familiar but weren’t people I’d met.

“Peter, this is August Heinz. He runs the goat farm north of town.”

I shook hands with the burly bald man. He had large, calloused hands, but his grip was gentle. “Please call me Augie.”

“And this is Kevin Jenkins, the game warden.”

Kevin was trim, his gray hair cut short and shaped by his cap. "Nice to meet you, Peter. Although Ron calls me the game warden, my official title is conservation officer."

Ron closed the door and gestured for me to take the fifth chair at the table. He carried white coffee mugs to the table and passed them around. "I made decaf, so we'll all be able to sleep tonight," he said as he carried a carafe from a coffee maker sitting on a credenza.

Augie reached behind himself and dug in the pocket of his coat. "I don't know if any of the rest of you take cream in your coffee but…"

I expected a bottle of goat's milk but was surprised by the pint bottle of Irish crème in Augie's hand. He removed the cap and poured a substantial dollop into his cup, then handed it to me. I hesitated and looked at the others, expecting them to be surprised by the offer of booze in the church office.

Kevin produced a small bottle of Kentucky bourbon. "I'm not a cream man, myself. I prefer something stiffer in my coffee."

Kerry laughed. "You know, Kevin, I'll have to ticket you if you bring a partial bottle home in the cab of your pickup."

Kevin nodded and ceremoniously dropped the cap into the wastebasket. "It's not leaving the church, at least not in the bottle."

Ron leaned forward and put his hands flat on the table. He scanned our faces earnestly. "Augie, Kevin, and I have been meeting every few weeks, mostly to get away from our wives for a few hours, but my secret mission has always been to provide a place where we can relax with others who've shared the horrors of war and be at ease. I invited Peter and he suggested I extend an invitation to Chief Stone as well. Don't worry, this is not a therapy session. However, what's said here doesn't leave this room. Understood?"

Olafson looked at Kerry and me, and we both nodded.

"Good! And, there will be no mention of booze in the pastor's office." Olafson turned and opened a door in the credenza and brought out a deck of cards and a plastic tray of poker chips.

Augie reached for his wallet. "We're pleased you two are here. Poker isn't as much fun with only three guys." He set two one-dollar bills on the table.

Kevin grabbed a stack of white chips and started counting them out. "These are one cent chips. The blue chips are a nickel, and the red chips are a dime. Throw in two bucks for your chips. We ante one white chip, and the maximum bet or raise is a nickel."

Kerry smiled and reached for his wallet. I hesitated. "I'm not much of a gambler. I'll just watch."

Kevin slid stacks of chips to me and smiled. I looked at the pastor for an escape.

"Just so we're clear, this is not gambling," Olafson said as he took out the cards and started shuffling. "You get chips, but the two dollars is a donation to the children's library and stays in the church. If you run out of chips, you can request a refill. In return for more chips, you'll have to attend the next men's club workday."

Augie leaned over to me and whispered, "I'd rather pay another two bucks because giving up a Saturday to clean up around the church is way more painful than donating another couple bucks. I was outvoted during the second poker night."

Shaking his head, Kerry held his wallet with the scarred fingers of his left hand and took out the cash with the fingers of his right hand.

Augie watched, then slid his chair away from the table. "We each carry our scars." He pulled up his right pants leg exposing a prosthesis.

Olafson started dealing cards. "The ante is one white chip."

We spent the next two hours drinking coffee, talking, and laughing. Ron, Augie, and Kevin shared comfortable banter, trust and friendship earned over time. The kidding slowly included Kerry and me as the evening progressed.

Another pot of coffee was brewed, more dollops of Irish crème and bourbon were dispensed. Luck moved around the table with chip piles growing and later disappearing. No one got drunk. There were no winners or losers. Barriers came down as we talked about our lives, our families, our histories, and our plans.

A watch started beeping and I looked at the clock on the pastor's wall. It showed nine o'clock. Olafson shuffled the cards. "Last hand boys. Cowboy stud and all betting limits are off."

"Cowboy stud?" I asked.

Olafson dealt one face-up card to each of us. "You get five cards, dealt one at a time, all face up. High hand bets first."

Augie considered the nine he'd been dealt, which was the highest card on the table. "C'mon pastor. You expect me to bet on a nine?"

Kevin picked up his five and waved it at Augie. "Quit complaining, at least you got a nine. Bet it, or I'll tell them about the wolf you scared to death."

I looked at Augie. "You scared a wolf to death?"

Augie threw a white chip in the pot. "He was chasing my goats."

Kevin tossed a white chip in the pot. "He shot once, then called me. I got there and found a dead wolf in his pasture. I know what a crappy shot Augie is, so I determined the wolf died of fright and hauled it to the landfill."

Olafson threw a white chip in the pot and dealt another card. "Augie, weren't you a Marine sniper?"

Augie looked at the deuce dealt next to the nine. "I shot in the air, to scare him." Then he looked at the other cards and glared at Olafson. "Where'd you learn to deal? My nine is still the high card."

The pastor shrugged. "Either bet or pass to Kerry's eight and four."

Augie rolled his eyes and threw in a blue chip. "I'm sure this is the start of a full house. I'm betting a nickel."

Kevin threw a blue chip into the pot and looked at Kerry. "You should ticket Augie for shooting inside the city limits."

Kerry looked between the two of them and laughed. "Augie's farm is ten miles outside town."

Kevin nodded, his eyes sparkling. "But you could've heard the shot from town."

Kerry laughed and waved off Kevin's kidding as Olafson dealt him another four. "Looks like the price of poker just went up," Kerry declared. "I've got a pair!"

Olafson set the deck down and scanned the table. "Yes, you've got the high hand, a pair of fours. I wouldn't bet the house because Peter and I both have fours. You won't get three of a kind."

I considered the cards I'd been dealt. "I'd fold this hand if I was betting real money."

Augie reached over and spread the four, six, and eight in front of me. He tapped his finger on the gaps. "Oh no, Doc. All you need is a five and seven to fill in this straight. I'd bet the house."

I looked at him. "Only Brian Johnson calls me Doc."

Augie leaned back. "I called the Navy Corpsman who dragged me out of a burning Humvee, Doc. He couldn't save my foot, but he saved my life. Calling you Doc is as much an honorific as calling an officer, sir."

I nodded, touched by what he'd just shared.

Olafson dealt our fourth cards, giving me an ace. "Great, Ron. You've messed up my straight."

Augie slid the new eight he'd been dealt next to the other eight. "Chief, your hope is gone. My eights beat your fours. There's only one card left, and all the fours are on the table." Augie pushed four blue chips into the pot.

We laughed and matched his bet.

Kevin had no hope of winning, so shoved all his chips into the pot with disgust. "I've lost. I'll have to console myself with a piece of sour cream raisin pie at Prince Olav's Café on the way home."

The pastor let the anticipation build, slowly dealing out one last card to each of us. "Ooh, Kevin. That pair of twos just won't do it."

Everyone laughed, but something flashed in my mind as Kerry's last card was revealed. Olafson shook his head. "Kerry, I was sure you'd pair up one of your other cards. Looks like Augie's got you beat."

I put up my hand before my last card was dealt. "I didn't realize Nola had opened Prince Olav's."

"It opened a couple days ago. She told me her whole menu is from Whistling Pines recipes. People are raving about the ethnic recipes like lutefisk, poteka, and rice pudding."

I looked at Kerry. "There isn't a sour cream raisin pie recipe in the cookbook, but there's one missing from Reggie Sandberg's house."

Kerry flipped over his losing hand and signaled for the pastor to deal my last card while he thought.

Olafson looked contrite. "I'm sorry, Peter. I couldn't pair your ace."

Augie's pair of eights was high on the table after his fifth card, and it appeared he'd won.

Olafson looked at his four unmatched cards and shook his head. "The only card that'll help me is if I can pair the king." He flipped the last card and beamed. "Well, look at that! I got a king."

Augie scooped up his cards and flipped them on the pot. "Darn it, Ron. You do that every week. If you weren't a man of the cloth, I'd accuse you of cheating."

Kevin and Augie sorted the chips in matching piles while the pastor gathered the cards. Kerry leaned over to me. "How about a piece of pie?"

"It's kind of late."

Kevin overheard us and dropped the empty bourbon bottle into the wastebasket. "I'll come along, just in case you need backup."

Ron Olafson pulled the bourbon bottle out of the wastebasket. "Kevin, you know I can't leave a booze bottle in the wastebasket. The custodian will empty my trash tomorrow morning and the choir director will call me on the carpet over drinking in my office."

Kevin smiled. "I know."

Augie laughed and handed Olafson the empty Irish crème bottle. "I'll save you the trouble of digging it out of the trash." He pulled on his winter jacket and hesitated. "A slice of pie sounds pretty good right now and the café is on my way home."

Kerry looked at Augie. "I don't know what's going to happen. It might be safer if you went home."

Augie clapped Kerry on the shoulder. "The Marines are always saving the Army's butt. I'll be standing alongside you, no matter what."

Kerry nodded. "We've got this covered, Peter."

"Um, I'm the one who put the pieces out there. I'm coming along to see if they fit."

The four of us were at the office door when Olafson called out. "Hang on. I'm having pie too."

Kerry turned. "I think…"

Olafson put his hand on Kerry's shoulder. "You shouldn't eat pie this time of night without a prayer first."

"This isn't about the pie, Pastor."

Olafson flipped off the office lights and closed the door. "This is about four friends helping out a buddy. Didn't you figure that out while we've been sitting here the past two hours?"

Chapter Seventeen

Ron Olafson spoke up before we sat. "I've heard rave reports about your pies. Do you have a slice of sour cream raisin left?"

Marcie wiped her hands. "I think there are a couple in the cooler. Let me check. What would the rest of you like?"

Not a fan of raisins, and firmly against sour cream and raisins in a pie, I asked. "What other pies are on the menu?"

Marcie glanced at the pass through as though Nola was going to shout the answer. She took an order pad out of her apron and read from the back. "I'm not sure how many of these are left, but earlier we had pumpkin, cherry, blueberry, coconut cream, banana cream, and French silk."

I chose blueberry pie. Kerry and Augie both decided on pumpkin.

Marcie, obviously not a salesperson into upselling, shook her head as she asked, "None of you want your pie ala mode, right?"

The pastor shook his head and smiled. "I'd like to congratulate Nola on her grand opening. Is she in the back?"

Marcie nodded. "I'll get her. I think she's kneading dough for tomorrow's cinnamon rolls."

Kerry had chosen a chair where he could see both the kitchen and front door. I could see that Kevin had clipped on his pistol before leaving his pickup, and Augie shrugged off his coat then clenched and unclenched his fists before sitting down, ready to react to whatever happened. I felt unprepared.

Nola walked out of the back, wiping her hands on a white dish towel. Her apron and arms were dusted with flour. She smiled when she saw us. "Gentlemen, welcome to Prince Olav's."

Olafson stood and smiled. "Congratulations! We heard your ethnic menu is outstanding."

She nodded to me. "I have to thank Peter and the cooks at Whistling Pines. All the recipes are from the Whistling Pines cookbook."

The pastor nodded. "We heard your sour cream raisin pie is to die for."

Nola hesitated for just a second, glancing at Kerry's badge. "It's been a hit."

I let out a deep breath. "There's no sour cream raisin pie recipe in the Whistling Pines cookbook, but there's one missing from Reggie Sandberg's house." Kerry was on his feet before I finished my sentence.

Nola threw the dusty towel in Kerry's face and dashed for the kitchen. Kerry danced around Pastor Olafson and past the neighboring table. I dashed after Nola, feeling like a dog chasing a car—unsure of what would happen if I actually caught her.

I was a half-step behind when she hit the release bar on the back door. I reached out, but only snagged the loop of her apron. The door rebounded into my shoulder, which knocked me off balance and into Kerry who was right behind me. I tripped over my own foot and pitched to the right. My flying feet got tangled in Kerry's legs and he fell forward, catching himself before doing a faceplant into the muddy gravel parking area behind the restaurant.

Rolling onto my hands and knees, I was ready to continue the pursuit when I heard Kevin laughing and Nola cursing. I got up. Kevin had stopped short of the pileup with Kerry and me and was laughing. I looked in the direction he was staring. Nola was kicking and flailing at Augie who had her wrapped from behind in a bear hug with her feet off the ground. Kerry got up, brushed himself off, and pulled out his handcuffs.

With Nola handcuffed, Kerry called for a sheriff's deputy to transport her to the county jail. He looked at Augie, who was grinning. "The Marines to the rescue again."

"How did you catch up to her?" I asked.

"You chose the straight-ahead assault. I went for a flanking maneuver by running around the building."

Ron Olafson strolled up to us, smiling. "Looks like you've caught your murderer."

Nola glared at him. "I didn't kill her."

"Who didn't you kill?" Olafson asked.

"Reggie Sandberg."

"How did you get the sour cream raisin pie recipe?"

"It was on the internet."

Marcie was listening from the back door. I followed her back inside, to make sure she wasn't destroying evidence. She marched over to a three-ring binder and flipped through it. She stopped and held it open for me to see. "All the recipes she got from Whistling Pines are neat copies of recipe cards. The sour cream raisin pie recipe is a note card taped to a sheet of paper. It's handwritten and reads 'Oscar's' on the top. She didn't get this recipe from you."

I carried the binder outside as a brown sheriff's department car rolled into the parking lot. Pulling Kerry aside, I said, "I've got Oscar's recipe. It's taped to a piece of paper, and I assume you'll be able to lift Reggie's fingerprints off the card."

Nola glared at me. "That's private property and you don't have a search warrant."

Pastor Olafson made a tsking sound. "Nola, confession is good for the soul. You should unburden yourself."

She glanced at him, then back to Kerry. "I want a lawyer."

* * *

Jenny was sitting on the couch nursing Amy when I got home. She glanced at me, then at the clock on the television cable box. "Late night with the boys. I hope you had a good time."

I walked in and sat down next to her. "It took a lot longer at the sheriff's office than I'd planned."

"The sheriff's office?" She looked at my clothes and saw the mud from my tumble in the parking lot. "What happened?"

The explanation of the guy's night turning into the closing of the murder investigation took longer than Amy's midnight snack. I followed Jenny upstairs, continuing the story of the restaurant confrontation, the arrest, and the trip to the sheriff's office to give a statement.

With Amy tucked in, we went to the bedroom where I changed out of my dirty clothes and put on flannel pajamas. Jenny leaned back against the pillow and watched. "You're not going to fall asleep."

I pulled back the sheet and blanket, then crawled into bed. "It's been long enough

324

since the adrenaline rush. I think I'll be able to fall asleep."

Jenny turned off the light on the nightstand and snuggled against me. "You know, I'd be okay with you taking a job as Kerry's investigator."

I sat up and turned the light on. "Where did that come from?"

"You and Kerry are like two peas in a pod. He trusts you and you're a sounding board for him. Tell me you didn't get into the thrill of the chase."

"I did NOT get into the thrill of the chase. I was hit in the face with an airbag at the end of the car pursuit and scraped up when I fell in the mud behind the restaurant. None of that was fun." I paused to compose my thoughts. "I really don't want to be a cop. I don't mind bouncing ideas around with Kerry, but I'm much happier working with the residents and playing my guitar."

"You're sure?"

I turned off the light and lay down. "I'm certain."

Chapter Eighteen

Day 8

I made coffee, put bread in the toaster, then peeked at the thermometer. A cold front had moved through, and the temperature had dropped. The thermometer said -2F. I flipped on the outside light and saw a thick coat of frost on the windshield. We weren't even in December and winter was already hitting us with a gut punch. *Where's global warming when you want it?*

Jeremy bounced down the stairs. He gathered his breakfast and was crunching on corn flakes before my toast was buttered. I poured two mugs of coffee and carried them to the table with my plate of toast.

"Is your homework done?"

Engrossed in something on the cereal box, he didn't look up. "It's Saturday, Dad."

I checked email on my cell phone and read the international news. Palestinian rockets had hit Israel and the Israelis were trying to decide how best to retaliate. *I'm so glad we live in the US and not the far east.*

Jenny's voice broke my concentration. "Will you make a piece of toast for me while I feed Amy?"

"Sure," I said, getting up with my plate of crumbs and half cup of coffee.

"What were you engrossed in when I came down?" she asked from the dining room.

I dropped a piece of bread into the toaster. "I was just thinking how lucky we are to live here and not in the Middle East."

"What brought on that thought?"

"Israel had a rocket attack. I was thinking about how fortunate we are to have Canada for a neighbor and not Palestine."

"I remember a class in Minnesota history. The teacher said the US and Canada have the longest undefended border in the world."

Jenny's toast popped up. I spread butter and marmalade on it and brought it to her. "I'm going to start the cars and scrape the windshields."

"It's Saturday. I'm off."

Sighing, I nodded. "Yeah."

"My mother's coming over to watch the kids this afternoon while I go shopping."

I drove through Two Harbors in the dark, meeting a few cars and seeing a few semis going north. The parking lot was empty except for the few frosty cars owned by the residents and the overnight staff. The night receptionist nodded as I walked in, then went back to the book of word puzzles I knew she kept behind the counter.

The table Karla, Mary, and Kathy had been using for cookbook sales had a sign that read, "sold out-more coming." I wondered if Wendy and Hulda had also sold out all the calendars. The only overnight emails were spam I quickly deleted. With my mug in hand, I walked to the dining room and drew coffee from the urn. Wendy was engrossed in a crossword in the back corner.

I sat across from her, breaking her concentration. "It looks like the calendars are a hit."

"Sales are going well, but Nancy talked to me. She thought we should've done something more tasteful." Wendy looked around, then leaned over the table. "I've received orders from two companies that want to put them in their on-line ads. They've already printed their Christmas catalogs, or they would've offered them there. We'll have to take the pictures next July so we can tap into the Christmas sales."

"Do you think there will be a calendar next year?"

"Peter, this is a big thing. The women had a good time, and we're raising hundreds of dollars. If we'd been better prepared for Christmas sales, we could've sold thousands of calendars."

I closed my eyes and sighed. "I heard your picture was a hit. Are you sending calendars to your parents and siblings?"

"Um, they may not be pleased about some of the tattoos that were exposed."

"The tattoos themselves, or the location of the art?"

"I think it's a little of each."

I started to stand up, but Wendy reached out and put her hand on my hand. "I heard your performance at the Norwegian Lutheran Church was a big hit." She paused. "Lucy Hernandez, the drummer from my band, was there. She was moved to tears."

"Do you remember the *moment* at the Buccaneer Days when we sang "I Can't help Falling in Love with You'?"

I didn't need to say more. Wendy nodded, recalling the trio performance she, Jenny, and I sang with her band. "That's only happened to me like three times. The band, the crowd, and I have been somewhere else, somewhere far away. It's rare and close to rapture."

"Think of that with three hundred people, all clapping and singing along. A pipe organ rattling the rafters, and a choir singing behind you, and…"

"And what?"

I felt the tears welling in my eyes. "You know I'm not religious, but wow, when I watched the DVD of the performance, I was moved."

"Three people have asked if we'll perform 'I'll Fly Away' at our next singalong."

"I think we should print out the words and encourage everyone to sing along for the last verse."

Sensing my emotion, she nodded. "I think that'd be great."

My cell phone rang as I walked out of the dining room. "Peter, can you be under the portico in five minutes?"

Kerry's voice was tight and urgent. "Sure, what's wrong?"

"Put your coat on and be out front."

"What..." I was listening to a dial tone.

I trotted to my office, trying to not slop coffee. With coat in hand, I ran back to the front door just as Kerry pulled up in a different Two Harbors police car than the unmarked car we'd crashed. I got in the front seat, and he was driving before I buckled my seatbelt.

"I've got a search warrant in my pocket for Nola Saarvala's restaurant, house, garage, barn, SUV, and pickup."

"Why are you taking me along?"

"You pulled the pieces together. I felt you deserved to be part of the closure."

"What are you looking for?"

"Pink barn boots, bloody gloves, and Reggie Sandberg's recipes."

"You have Reggie's sour cream raisin pie recipe from the restaurant."

"I couldn't take it when we were there because it'd be the legal equivalent of fruit from the poisonous tree. The court could view it as evidence found during an illegal search."

"You must think you'll find more recipes."

"You pointed out that Reggie's recipe box was missing. I hope we'll find the rest of her handwritten recipes and the recipes from Oscar's."

"Nola's still in jail, right?"

"Her lawyer bailed her out this morning, so she's probably at the house."

We raced through town without lights and siren but pushing the speed limit. "Who else is going to be there?"

"We're actually superfluous. The BCA sent the northeast regional team with their mobile crime lab. Our job is to watch but stay out of the way. We may be called as witnesses to the search."

"Oh no. I'm not a cop. I'm not testifying in court."

Reaching into his shirt pocket, Kerry handed me a badge. "Pin this on. You're a reserve officer. Len swore you in."

"I'm not a cop."

Kerry glanced at me. "It's a long walk from Saarvala's place back to Two Harbors. I suppose you could call a cab or an Uber."

I sighed. The absence of cab service, or even Uber drivers, in Two Harbors was a standing joke.

A Winnebago RV with the Minnesota Bureau of Criminal Apprehension logo on the side was sitting in a farmyard. Kerry turned into a driveway marked by a faded sign that read, "Saarvala's Machine Shop."

We walked to the front door where Nola Saarvala, who was out on bail, was yelling at a man dressed in a white Tyvek suit with a badge stenciled on the left side of the chest. Kerry jogged to the door and stepped between them, holding out a piece of paper to Nola.

"Here's the search warrant, signed by Judge Renfroe. It covers every building on your property and your vehicles."

Nola snatched the paper out of Kerry's hand and scanned it. She crumpled it into a wad and threw it into a bare bush next to the front steps. "This is bullshit. What are you looking for?"

The front door opened and a BCA tech with thinning gray hair stuck his head out. "I found these boots." He held up a pair of barn boots with pink uppers and black soles. "The tread is oily and marks on the soles match the shoe prints from the crime scene."

Kerry smiled and looked at Nola. "It looks like you're going to prison."

"Those aren't my boots! I don't know where they came from."

The BCA tech stepped out of the house and held up a pair of leather gloves. "I suppose these gloves, found in your coat pocket, aren't yours either."

Nola was about to say something but closed her mouth. "I want my lawyer here for the search."

The white-clad BCA tech nodded for us to come into the house, then handed us purple gloves. Kerry put the glove on his scarred left hand, but struggled to get the other glove on, using his partially functional scarred left fingers.

The tech put his hand out to me. "I don't think we've met. I'm Jeff Telker, the lead evidence technician." I introduced myself. "My partner, Sonny Carlson, is in the kitchen looking for a recipe box."

"Are you related to Karla Telker?"

Jeff smiled. "She's my sister, the one who's institutionalized."

I was taken aback by his comment. "Karla's a resident at Whistling Pines Senior Residence and she's very bright. Being institutionalized has a different connotation."

Jeff's smile spread and his eyes sparkled. "I know. We just like to tease her. She was the wild middle child. My oldest sister and I have never let her forget her rebellious years."

With both gloves finally on, Kerry looked up. "Don't engage Sonny in a conversation about his Finnish heritage, tractor repair, or..."

Jeff laughed. "Sonny can expand on any topic." He held up the leather gloves he'd found in Nola's coat and pointed to an imperfection on one of the fingers. "I'm sure this will match up with the marks on the murder weapon. We'll probably find blood when we pull the stitches out of the seams, too."

"But will you find enough to match it to the victim?" I asked.

Another tech in white came out of the kitchen carrying a recipe box. He pushed his glasses up with the back of his hand. "As my Great Aunt Stella used to say, I think we've hit the jackpot! Half the recipe cards have Reggie Sandberg's name written on top."

I extended my hand and introduced myself.

"Another new face in the Two Harbors police force?"

"I'm a reserve officer. I'm just riding along with Kerry."

Sonny's eyes sparkled. "Chief Stone, isn't that how you got roped into your job?"

I swore I wasn't going to take a job as a cop, and we laughed. Sonny and Jeff continued to search. Kerry steered me outside, where Nola was yelling into her cell phone.

Kerry started the car and drove out of the driveway. "Can I buy you lunch? It seems like the least I can do after you pulled together the case and identified the murderer."

"I think the VFW is serving pasties today."

We talked over lunch and Kerry told me Deb had been unable to talk about anything but the church concert. "She's had half a dozen calls from churches asking if she'd arrange a similar concert for them."

"I hope she's refusing," I said, swirling a bite of pasty in gravy.

Squirting ketchup on his pasty Kerry said, "You know you're a heathen for pouring gravy on a pasty?"

I waved my fork. "Like I said, I hope Deb's refusing the concert requests."

Kerry set down his fork and looked at me. "That concert was magical. I think you need to share it."

"My experience has been that magical moments only happen once. I don't think we'd have the same reaction if we repeated the exact same concert."

"Deb's already spoken to Brian Johnson and the high school jazz combo about a Christmas concert at the Swedish Lutheran church. They're all willing to perform again. All she needs is you."

"Let me talk to Jenny about it."

"Jenny and Deb are having lunch at Judy's. I suspect your discussion with Jenny will be short."

"That's underhanded."

Laughing, Kerry wiped his mouth. "Deb can be very devious. Don't underestimate her."

"Have you heard if Jonathan's lawyers contacted Hailey?"

"I heard Hailey was offered ten thousand dollars to forget about Jonathan Edwards."

"I hope she's holding out for more."

* * *

I drove a vanload of seniors to Duluth on a shopping trip, which consumed the afternoon.

Jeremy was working on homework when I got home. I left him undisturbed and fried hamburger, then boiled noodles for a pot of goulash.

Jenny fed Amy while Jeremy and I set the table. Jeremy dove into supper and I was about to bring up the concert when Jeremy stopped eating abruptly and set his fork down. "Jacob's family is getting their Christmas tree next weekend. Why don't we have one yet?"

Jenny looked at me and shrugged. "I suppose we could cut a tree next week."

Nodding, Jeremy dug into his goulash. "I'll bring the decorations down from the attic."

"We have to put a stocking up for Amy this year," I said.

Jeremy cocked his head. "Where do you buy Christmas stockings?"

"We already have a stocking for her," Jenny said.

"When did you buy it? Why wasn't I along?"

"An elf dropped it off last Christmas."

Jeremy cocked his head. "Amy wasn't here last Christmas."

Blushing, Jenny took a breath while composing her answer. "Santa knew Amy was coming."

Jeremy stopped eating again and stared at Jenny. "Jacob says his parents are Santa. There aren't elves at the North Pole who make toys."

There it was—the bomb we'd been expecting to drop. Jenny set Amy in the vibrating chair and took a deep breath. "Santa is the spirit of Christmas, not a man who comes down the chimney. It doesn't matter where the gifts come from. We want to keep that spirit alive, so we're not going to tell Amy. We'll let her believe in Santa. Okay?"

"Will Santa still bring me something?"

Jenny touched his hair. "Of course, he will. And he'll put something in your stocking, too."

Jeremy pushed his chair back. "May I be excused? I'll get the Christmas decorations down from the attic, so we're ready when we get our tree."

With Jeremy gone to the attic, I looked at Jenny. "It's still November. I think we're rushing the Christmas season."

"The stores have had their Christmas displays up since Halloween. I think it's okay for us to start decorating since we're past Thanksgiving."

After carrying down the boxes of decorations and hanging the Christmas stockings, we had a quiet night of television and popcorn. Jeremy and Amy both went to bed without a fuss, and I had every hope we'd get a good night's rest. I was under the covers when Jenny turned off the lights and got in bed.

"You're going to do the concert at the Swedish Lutheran Church with Deb."

"Is that a question?"

Jenny snuggled close. "No. Deb says you two should do 'O Holy Night' as a duet instead of George Strait, then wrap up with 'I'll Fly Away'."

I saw no point in arguing, so I closed my eyes.

"I've been expecting the Santa discussion."

So much for going to sleep, I thought. "It was inevitable. You handled it very well."

"Mom and Dad really missed playing Santa last year. Dad used to wait for Jeremy to fall asleep, then he'd sneak out to the

338

trunk of the car where he stashed Santa's gifts. He was like a kid himself."

"We'll cut a tree this weekend and decorate it with your parents. It'll help all of us get into the Christmas spirit."

The hallway light turned on and Jeremy's feet padded toward the bathroom. I kept my eyes closed until I felt him crawl in bed alongside me. "Dad, are you awake?"

"What's the matter, buddy?"

"How much does a baseball glove cost?"

Half asleep, his question caught me off guard. "What?"

"How much does a baseball glove cost?"

"I'm not sure, maybe thirty dollars."

"Will you pay my allowance ahead? I'll do extra chores."

Trying to wake up, I rolled over. "Did you lose your glove?"

"No, I want to buy Amy a baseball glove for Christmas. I'm going to teach her to catch and throw."

"It'll be a couple years before she's big enough to catch a baseball."

Jeremy snuggled against me. "I guess, but I want her to have a glove from me when she's old enough."

"Let's look for a glove when we go Christmas shopping in Duluth next month. I'll loan you the money and you can pay me back later."

Jeremy rolled over and looked at me earnestly. "Am I going to have a brother someday?"

"I don't know."

"When we put up Christmas stockings, you hung up two, one each for Amy and me. Why were there five more in the box?"

Jenny rolled over and put her arm around me. I hoped she was going to field the question, but she snuggled into my back silently.

"Grandpa brought seven stockings last year and left them under the mantle. He was joking with us."

"Larsons have seven kids and seven stockings. Does Santa think I'm going to have six brothers and sisters?"

I felt as much as I heard Jenny laugh. "He was joking with your mom and me when he did that."

Jeremy turned so our noses were almost touching. "Grandpa said I was spoiled, living with them. It was okay, but I like living in this house with you, Mom, and Amy better."

"I think so too."

"Is Amy going to stop pooping in her diapers pretty soon? It's really disgusting."

"It'll be more than a year before she's potty trained."

"If you and mom have five more babies, will they all poop in their pants for years?"

The bed jiggled again as Jenny laughed behind me.

"Infants poop and pee in diapers for a couple years. As for five brothers and sisters, I'm not sure if God will give us more children, or if He's decided that you and Amy are enough."

"God only made Jesus. That's what they said in Sunday school. Jacob's mom said she and Chief Stone made Jacob while they were sleeping. You and mom sleep together every night. Are you making another baby?"

Jenny whispered, "Busted," in my ear.

"Not right now. It's something your mom and I have to think about. Babies are a lot of work and cost a lot of money. We'll talk about it and decide if a bigger family is right for us, or if you and Amy are all the children we need."

Jeremy crawled out of bed and walked to the door. He stood there, silhouetted in the hallway light. "I think you should make a couple more babies. I'd like to have brothers and sisters, like Larsons."

He padded down the hall and the light clicked off. Jenny pulled me close. "Do you want more children?"

"I always felt cheated as an only child. I saw bigger families and wished I had siblings. How do you feel about more kids? You're the one who suffers through morning sickness and the pregnancy."

"There's a lot of room in this old house. Someone who lived here used all seven of the hooks under the mantle. Jeremy's stocking is hanging from a hook in the middle and Amy's is to the left. I think it'd look better if there was a stocking on the third hook. You know, just so they're symmetrical."

I rolled over and hugged her. "I think that's a pretty good plan."

I tried to kiss her, but she pushed me back. "Don't get any ideas tonight, sailor. We're not having another baby until Amy's out of diapers."

I brushed the hair back from her face and cupped her cheek in my hand. "You're going to have a discussion with Jeremy about how babies are made."

"Nope. Dads have that discussion with their sons. I'll talk to Amy about how *not* to make babies, when the time comes." Jenny snuggled into my arms. "A lot has changed in a year. Are you happy being married and a father of two children?"

"I've never been happier."

The End

Also by BWL Publishing Inc.

Whistling Pines cozies

Whistling up a Ghost

Whistling Pirates

Doug Fletcher mysteries

Stolen Past

Washed Away

Dead in the Water

Death in Shifting Sands

Devils Fall

Prairie Menace

Down River

Burnt Evidence

Gator Bait

Grave Survey

Pine County mysteries

Killer Secrets

Deadly Mixture

Fatal Business (Coming the fall of 2022)

Dean Hovey is the award-winning and best-selling author of three mystery series. He uses his scientific background, extensive research, and a number of consultants to add reality and depth to his stories. One reader said his characters are like people he'd like to invite over for a beer and discussion.

Hovey's Fletcher mysteries follow U.S. National Park Service investigators Doug and Jill Fletcher as they solve crimes in a series of parks and monuments, sometimes with a bit of humor and often with their evolving relationship. The Whistling Pines mysteries are humorous cozies set in a northern Minnesota senior residence, following Peter Rogers, the Whistling Pines recreation director, as he stumbles through the investigation of murders in his small town. The Pine County mystery series follows sheriff's deputies as they investigate murders in east-central Minnesota, dealing with crimes, criminals and their own personal dilemmas.

Dean and his wife split their year between northern Minnesota and Arizona.